Also by Diane Les Becquets

The Last Woman in the Forest
Breaking Wild
Season of Ice
Love, Cajun Style
The Stones of Mourning Creek

Where the Water Meets the Sky

Diane Les Becquets

Simon & Schuster
New York Amsterdam/Antwerp London
Toronto Sydney/Melbourne New Delhi

Simon & Schuster
1230 Avenue of the Americas
New York, NY 10020

First Simon & Schuster hardcover edition May 2026

Interior design by Milly McKinnish

Manufactured in the United States of America

1 3 5 7 9 10 8 6 4 2

Library of Congress Control Number: 2025945405

ISBN 978-1-6682-2189-1
ISBN 978-1-6682-2191-4 (ebook)

For my dad, John "Jack" Francis, with love

—the eviscerating heat, the forgiving water—I see the horizons of my life. My desire to arrive, to cover this distance is so acute I whimper like a colt when I breathe.

—BARRY LOPEZ, "WITHIN BIRDS' HEARING"

Prologue

January 1986

Garden Peninsula
The Upper Peninsula of Michigan

THE AIR WAS QUIET THAT night, the moon bright, almost full. For more than two hours, Gale, a name chosen by her parents because it meant a strong wind, had been walking through the timber, her mind lulled by the sounds of her footfall as the snow compacted tightly beneath her boots. Mostly, she stayed on deer trails, subtle threads through dense woods of white cedar and pine that abutted farmland.

Though the winter had been mild so far, that afternoon a storm had moved through leaving almost a foot of snow, and the temperatures had dropped into the seasonal low teens. Gale had left the house at midnight, dressed in layers of fleece and a camouflage jacket. In her right hand she carried a pair of night-vision binoculars, and clipped to a strap she wore across her body were her monopod and camera, with its six-hundred-millimeter telephoto lens, the shooting pole hanging down the side of her back, the body of the camera resting on her shoulder.

She'd stop about every fifty feet or so and scan the lower trunks of the trees for whitewash, the chalky white excrement of owls that appeared as either cascading stains down the bark or splashes near a tree's base, and look for pellets of undigested fur and bones on the ground, which were easier to notice on a blanket of snow. Sometimes she'd collect the pellets. She liked to bring them into school for her students to try and assemble and identify.

At this particular hour, Gale was hoping to spot at least one of the great horned owls she'd heard duetting when she was up reading the night before. The great horned owl's song was distinct, typically a five-syllable *whoo* refrain—"*Who is awake? Me too*," with the male's voice slightly lower in pitch. She'd gone farther than she intended, without any sign, when she heard the call of what she determined to be the female owl. She left the trail and moved in a southeastward direction.

It was the bill clapping, much like the noise a woodpecker makes, mixed in with the owl's *wac wac* cry, announcing an intruder, that let her know she was close. Gale raised her binoculars. It was then that she saw the owl's bright-yellow eyes staring back at her. In a seventy-foot northern pine, the two-foot-tall owl, with its pointed, feather tufts resembling horns, was perched in the tree's upswept branches.

As smoothly as she could, she hung her binoculars over her left shoulder and went for her camera. She held the shooting stick to the ground and steadied the lens. The owl turned its head. Something else caught its attention. Gale waited to press the shutter. The owl took off from its perch, its wings powerful and quiet as it swooped over the treetops.

That's when she smelled the smoke, faint at first, like someone's woodstove. Then she heard the snap of a branch up ahead and the clinking of something metal. She returned her camera over her shoulder and reached for her binoculars. More branches snapped, accompanied by the rapid pounding of footsteps in the snow. In the gray light of the night-vision lenses, Gale caught a person's eyes, like miniature headlights glancing her way, and the shape of a young child's face with round cheeks, and long hair that shone brightly and floated upon the child's shoulders.

She lowered the binoculars to her side. "Hey! Is everything okay?" she yelled.

From the moonlight's reflection off the snow, she was able to see the image with her naked eye as it appeared and disappeared between the trees. The body was moving parallel in front of her, close enough that Gale could hear the high frequency of the child's heavy breathing.

"Are you okay?" Gale tried once more, yelling louder this time.

But the child kept running, moving farther away until the sight of her was lost in the woods, and the sound of her footfall was no longer heard.

The smell of smoke grew stronger. Gale saw the opening of a field up ahead. She ran forward, ducking every so often to avoid knocking clumps of snow from the low-hanging branches. The smoke continued to thicken, appearing like black, raging storm clouds over the treetops. And then there was the sudden breaking of glass and the loud crackling of timber.

She pushed through a shelterbelt of pines and into the snow-laden field where, less than a football field away, she saw the forty-foot blaze erupting from a small farmhouse. She ran toward the structure, holding one hand on her camera to keep it secured above her shoulder and pumping her other arm. The camera stick knocked against her back, her heels kicked up bursts of powder, and despite her efforts, her movements were clumsy and slowed down by the snow, which was deeper in the open space.

Within two hundred feet she felt the heat. A hundred feet more and she saw the roof collapse, heard the deafening roar of the flames. She moved past an open barn, and then past an old, metal swing set and a gray pickup truck, and a Christmas tree, lying on its side, with silver tinsel icicles tangled in its branches. At the front of the house, now fully inflamed, she tried to gauge her bearings and determine who might be the closest neighbor. She took off for the road, the air in and out of her lungs drowning her thoughts: *It's too late. It's too late.*

Ten Years Later

Loon

1

ABBY DROVE OUT THE MICHIGAN highway that early June morning and across the UP to begin her summer. Mostly she headed east, among fields and farms and summer places, and stretches of state forest, past children on bicycles, boats on trailers, pickup trucks and gun racks, bunches of houses and then hardly anything at all.

June can still feel like spring on the Upper Peninsula of Michigan. The maples are covered in purple and red buds, like an impressionistic painting; the tips of the jack pine and white pine are as bright as the flesh of a kiwi; the birch trees with their silver-white trunks shimmer with new leaves.

In the community of Vans Harbor, nine miles down the western side of the Garden Peninsula, a young man, already eighteen, carries a handling tray of whitefish on ice—maybe a hundred pounds, he thinks—and brings it over to the forklift, T-shirt sleeves blowing in the wind, oiler draped over his chest and thighs, tall rubber boots. He sets the tray down on the pallet, then turns to retrieve another tray from one of the local fishermen. Banter passes back and forth between them—the conditions of the water and wind, the nets pulled up south of Round Island and Burnt Bluff, the size of their catch. Noon sun bakes down from a milky, blue sky; gulls swoop and squawk and light on nearby pilings. There's the waft of gasoline from the boats, the glistening of fish scales like confetti spread over the concrete dock, the feathers of gulls and piping plovers and mallards and cormorants floating among driftwood and limestone cobble on the shore.

Abby parks beside a flatbed truck and gets out, walks into the tall grass and around the side of the fish house. She stands beside a cluster of birch trees and looks beyond the trees, past the brambles and beach grass and pallets stacked six feet tall, through sunlight reflecting off the water and the metal siding of the building. She brushes hair away from her face, tucks flyaway strands over her ears, a smile lifting her cheeks, her eyes soft.

Brew's back is angled toward her, hands now in his pockets, a ball cap pulled low over his forehead, arms already golden brown. She hears his laugh. The fish trays have been rinsed. Two fishermen are loading them onto a large boat made of steel. Brew turns to open the back door of the fish house and steps inside.

Abby calls his name, but the fishermen have started their engine. The boat is pulling away. Brew doesn't hear her.

She turns from the trees and extends her stride back through the tall grass, burrs sticking to her jeans, moves once more around the corner of the building, her body mostly hidden behind her car and the flatbed truck. She sees Brew leave out the front door, that pause and roll of his shoulders, and beyond Brew a young woman leaning against a blue pickup truck, legs crossed in front of her, smile on her face, hair braided off to the side. Brew stands in front of the woman now, their hands reaching for one another. He walks around the woman's truck to the passenger side and gets in, windows down, voices from inside the cab. The truck backs out and they pull away.

• • • • • • • • •

The Garden Peninsula is a twenty-two-mile-long finger of land, sandwiched between Big Bay de Noc to its west and Lake Michigan to its east, and off those waters, more bays and tributaries and wetlands, and migratory birds, and minks and martens, and black bears and deer, and approximately forty thousand acres of heavy forest, and nearly twenty thousand acres of farmland, and rolling bales of hay, and fishing ports, and wolves and coyotes and bobcats. The people work the land and waters—fishing and logging, and some work in the village of Garden, while others make long commutes to jobs in construction or manufacturing or various trades. Sprinkled about are summer cottages and camps and communities. There are two townships—Garden and Fairport. Brew lives in Vans Harbor, a fishing community in the township of Garden. Abby once lived there too. Now she visits—holidays mostly, a weekend here or there—until winter turned into spring, and spring turned into June, and now she is here for the summer.

She remembers a day in January, less than five months before. Dull sky through the windows, chicken thighs thawing on the counter, TV playing in the background—sports or news or Sunday afternoon talk hosts, Abby on the sofa, legs tucked underneath her, book on her lap, her father in his recliner, reading the newspaper. The light through the window was changing. The sun was going down. Abby switched on the lamp. She continued reading. The house was drafty. She pulled a blanket over her. Words stared back at her on the page, as if they were looking right at her, as if they could truly see inside her soul—*Abby, look, don't you see?* This is what the words said to her, and when they spoke, she felt she understood a little more than she had a moment before, understood a sliver of something. She placed a hand on the page, glanced at her father, his feet in suede slippers, calloused hands holding the newspaper. She looked out the window at the darkening sky.

Because every January was the same—the air felt heavy and she found it harder and harder to breathe. Her chest ached, her legs felt leaden.

Sometimes in the winter when the lakes froze over, there she'd be standing on the shoreline, looking out at the fishing shanties and hearing the revving of snowmobiles racing across the ice. She'd imagine herself out there with the others, the ice breaking and her falling through, her swimming in the dark water, arms growing numb as she tried to get out, as she ran out of breath.

That past Christmas, she and her dad visited Garden. A bonfire was built by the lake. The family was gathered around—snow parkas and hats and gloves and hot beverages. Everyone taking turns on the machines, racing them across the bay in front of Nonna's house.

Brew pulled up alongside Abby, a warm grin on his face. "Hop on," he said. And then, "I promise, we'll stay off the ice." So she straddled the machine, sitting behind him, and wrapped her arms around his torso.

Always, Abby looked beyond the trappings of her heart and saw beauty out there. She caught images and memorized their details. The wingspan of an osprey floating overhead, the pink shadows in a gray morning cloud, the metallic taste of the cold air on her tongue. And there was Brew—copper eyelashes catching the sun, russet hair in messy waves, that smile of his that broadened as he looked away, taking in a moment that he'd think over, respond to thoughtfully, blue eyes making contact again, plumbing something deep in his friendly way—he had his ways. She'd meditate on this beauty, collect an image in her mind, tuck it into bed with her at night. But still she wondered how to live fully, how to live beyond the pain of a world that could not love her.

I love you, the words would say back to her. *I love you,* said the sky and wind and osprey.

Then whose love am I looking for?

But she knew. She always had. She was looking for her mother. She was looking for a different past.

She rose from the sofa and moved to the kitchen. She put the chicken thighs in the refrigerator.

"I'm going for a walk," she told her dad.

He looked up from the paper. "You want me to preheat the oven?"

"No, I won't be long."

Abby stepped outside that Sunday afternoon into the dusk, into the cold air—the glow of lights from the smattering of houses, lawns covered in white, a thin layer of crunchy snow over ice on the sidewalk, and then no sidewalk at all, just the hard-packed road, the frozen landscape, the windswept path to the beach, the sky becoming darker still.

She walked the beach, the clack of icy stones underfoot, the subtle sinking of footsteps in the snowy sand, wave song in her ears, evening sky between her gloved fingers and in her long tresses of hair that hung beneath her cap. Darkness spread around her, that strange stillness of the earth, the lake like an ocean, big and vast and mysterious. And this is what she felt—powerless. But the darkness didn't feel so dark anymore. Somewhere in that darkness was light—an invisible light. She felt the invisible light like gentle snowflakes catching in her hair, on her clothes, melting against her skin.

She was more than the girl whose mom died in a fire, the child who ran through the woods on a cold night in January ten years ago. "An angel was with you," someone said to her—a nurse, a doctor, a neighbor. And, "Can you tell us what happened?" others wanted to know. But Abby couldn't tell them anything. The only thing she remembered was the backseat of a car—cold vinyl, the smell of exhaust, heat blowing full-blast, cold fingers, cold toes, a prickly sensation in her fingertips, a matchbook in her left hand.

Or did she remember the matchbook because that is what people told her?

These were the trappings of her heart, and on the other side of those trappings was the invisible light. *You are more, Abby. Your life is waiting for you.*

She was more than her past. There was more to her life—there was *more.* That was what she hungered for.

2

BEFORE THERE WAS A FIRE and a girl, there was a young woman, a mother to be, whose true love jumped to his death in a foolish accident. He was just a kid, only sixteen, and the mother to be just two years older. The week after his funeral, the woman took her family's truck and headed north on Highway 41.

Over two hours later, she missed the left-hand fork of the highway, and ended up in L'Anse next to the L'Anse Indian Reservation, where she found herself traveling on a two-track, sand road up the Abbaye Peninsula, pronounced Abby.

She went as far as the road would take her, with only the sound of her thoughts, and the calling of birds, and the crashing of waves off Lake Superior. Then she got out of the truck and kept moving forward along a footpath. When she finally reached the end, she stepped onto a large shelf of sandstone and looked out at the hazy outline of the archipelago in front of her, and the iron ridge of the Keweenaw Peninsula far off to her left, and the Huron Mountains across the bay to her right.

Just as she felt the first flutter in her abdomen, she saw a faint flicker of light, like a star on the horizon, from a lighthouse on one of the Huron islands. It was then that she knew in the deepest way of knowing things that she was carrying a girl, and she was going to name her Abby.

Abby lives with her adoptive father now, on the Keweenaw Peninsula, in the small town of Eagle River on Lake Superior's southern shore. They've lived there going on five years, the longest they've lived anywhere. There's not much of anything in Eagle River, other than pine trees and junipers and sand dunes, and the rosy shades of beach cobble—reds, and pinks, and purples—and the fifty or so people, like Abby and her father, commuting to jobs and battening down their houses and lives for the winters. By winter, the migratory birds have long traveled south, the tourists have returned home, and something deep and quiet settles in. Abby and her dad cook together and do the dishes and watch something on TV. He turns in early, and Abby turns in to read, and each year there are more books that have collected in stacks beside her bed, or on the pine bookshelves her dad built for her, or beside the sofa.

Until that summer, Abby worked at a bookstore in Copper Harbor, a half-hour drive northeast along the shore from her home in Eagle River. She loved listening to the stories of the patrons—local artists and naturalists and historians, and of the tourists who visited in the warmer months. Some would arrive from Canada, others from as far west as Oregon. She loved seeing the books they purchased about the area's local flora and fauna and history, or the novels they chose to read to pass the three-and-a-half-hour ferry ride to Isle Royale, a chain of islands that form a national park.

She visited the islands once, with her uncle, her mom's younger brother. She remembers the ferry ride to the main island, her uncle lying on a bench with his cap over his face, windbreaker flapping against his chest, and Abby on the bench beside him, twelve years old then, reading a book, oversized sunglasses, feet propped up on her backpack in front of her.

Abby and her uncle slept in a screened shelter that night—down sleeping bags, thermal layers. Beside Abby's head, she left a pair of flip-flops in case she needed to get up to relieve herself. But when she woke in the morning, her flip-flops were gone. She unzipped her sleeping bag and walked barefoot across the floor and past her uncle who was still sleeping. She opened the door, noticing the wide hole in the screen, then stepped onto the chilly ground and walked away from the shelter and into the conifer cover. She didn't find her shoes, but she found other things—a forest floor covered in morning light and needle duff from spruce and balsam fir, and miniature pine cones and miniature flowers, some purple, some white, petals as small as ladybug wings.

She pulled down her thermal underwear and squatted to the ground. And then she heard the sounds, like a horse chewing on hay, or a cow chewing her cud, and the heavy breaths of a large animal sniffing the air. She pulled up her thermals and stepped around the boughs of a spruce, and there they stood, a mother moose and her calf, about forty feet away. They were beautiful, Abby thought, this mother and her calf, munching on young saplings and wildflowers, and warming themselves in the sun. Abby should feel afraid, she knew she should. She should back up slowly, but she wasn't afraid, and when the mother and the calf lifted their heads and moved in the opposite direction, Abby waited a few seconds and then followed. She hid behind the trunk of one tree and the boughs of another, until she heard the crashing sound of the two animals making their way over limbs and slash and other debris down the steep embankment to the cove.

Abby stood at the edge of the rise, one arm hooked around a large aspen, morning sun rising, white orbs over the water. She heard splashing and watched the mother moose's body lumber from side to side as she waded into the cove up to her chest. The moose looked back over her shoulder. Her calf stepped into the water, swam out to her mother, and eventually all Abby could make out were their two heads moving farther away and around the edge of the cove's rugged shoreline.

This is what Abby saw—in her mind, in her imaginings—her own mother looking back, extending a hand, and Abby stepping toward her.

Years would pass before a similar incident would occur—maybe not so similar, but meaningful in a similar way. Abby driving home from somewhere, a winter night, wind blowing. She pulled into a gas station, and there in the other lane beside her was a gray pickup truck, and beside the truck, a woman filling the truck's tank—just this, a woman, in a thick, canvas coat with a corduroy collar, shoulder-length brown hair, smooth and wavy, jeans tucked into snow boots with synthetic fur over the tops. The woman returned the nozzle to the gas pump, walked around the front of her truck to the convenience store. She stood at the entrance, hand on the door, looked over her shoulder—at what?—her vehicle? Had she left something behind—a purse, a wallet? Abby thought she saw the woman say something, but there was no one in the woman's truck whom she could be speaking to.

Completely struck by the woman's appearance, Abby left her car and entered the store, if only to glimpse her mother—this woman who looked like her mother—one more time.

The highway was mostly empty that night. The store was quiet. Abby walked the aisles and looked around and passed a sign for the restrooms. A rack displayed mixed nuts, fruit snacks, bags of potato chips. Abby picked up a small bag of pretzels, then opened a door to a cooler and retrieved a beverage. There were no other customers. She paid for the pretzels and beverage and twenty dollars of gas, and stepped back into the cold.

The pickup truck was gone. The highway was quiet. Abby stood beneath the lights of the canopy, wondering how she'd missed the woman leaving the store.

Through the glow of the canopy light Abby saw snow. She filled her tank, climbed into her car, and pulled away, sharp, tiny snowflakes falling like hard rain, lighting up the sky around her.

She went on, cheerfully enough, the intermittent swiping of her wipers, heat and defrost both blowing, the sound of the wind somewhere out there. Abby had seen her mother—the woman who looked like her mother, and she thought about water and rain and snow that reflect light when a sky is dark.

She brushed against something mysterious that night, as she had that morning on Isle Royale—touched upon it, and then it was gone. But not completely gone. She felt the largesse of the earth and sky and water and ether, and all the elements of what she experienced—each element and particle a part of her also, bones and flesh expanding, her world becoming bigger.

And because of all the things written in her heart—moose and coves and osprey and morning clouds and snow clouds and storm clouds and light in the dark and a woman who looked like her mother—when her uncle was given a grant to study the trees and forests of his childhood and asked Abby to assist him over the summer, she felt something lift, like the sash of a window, saw herself straddling the window frame and crawling through.

3

ABBY HELD A PIECE OF notebook paper over the steering wheel of her little, blue car. Written in her neat script were the directions to the camp her uncle rented on the eastern side of the peninsula.

She took the third left, the second right, another left, down dirt and gravel roads, everything at once familiar and unfamiliar. She had a couple more miles to get to the camp. And then she knew—she was coming up on the driveway that led to the burn site, nothing more than an overgrown tractor trail now.

She'd not been back to the burn site before. She and her dad moved from Garden after the fire—at first to a couple towns over, and then another, never too far away, until eventually they ended up in Eagle River. But they visited plenty of times—birthdays and celebrations, other times on a whim—a bright day in summer because her dad said it was a good day for fishing, or a cold day in winter because he said the ice fishing was just right. A two-hour drive or so on the UP was nothing to the people who lived there. They were used to covering large distances in a single day—two hours for a doctor's appointment, an hour for groceries.

Abby understood, in different ways, these visits to her mother's family. For her, they were a chance to see Brew, to spend time with her grandmother, to encamp herself with all that was familiar. And perhaps it was the familiar that called her father back as well. Her dad and Uncle Buckley and Uncle Ronnie in the small living room in Uncle Buckley's house, a football game on the television, wind blowing outside, conversation and cheers and storytelling, and her dad's laughter over something or other—laughter, that is what Abby heard, that is what she saw on her dad's face. Then after a quiet ride home, and winter or summer blowing outside, her dad would make coffee and drink his coffee from his recliner, and this is what Abby saw also: the evaporation of a bit of happiness.

Yet, in all the trips they made, they never returned to where their house once stood. Still, Abby remembered, as sunlight ricocheted off her windshield, and golden rays fell over the overgrown tractor trail. Yes, she was sure.

She slowed her car. *I had a mother. She died here. I had a mother. She smelled like black cherries and fresh air and woodsmoke. She painted my fingernails the color of lilacs.*

There were no flowers, no crosses, just weeds and brambles and detritus.

Farther down the road was an old cattle farm, and from there, rolling hayfields, and scrub saplings growing along ditches, and stone walls, and more woods. She checked her directions. Another mile and she made the left-hand turn. About a hundred feet ahead was the camp, a weathered gray structure surrounded by woods. A sign above the door read *Bear Slide*, and beside the front steps was Uncle Dennis's green Subaru with its *STOP CLIMATE CHANGE!* bumper sticker. Abby parked beside his car. She unloaded her duffel bag and backpack.

"Hello!" she called out.

She opened the screen door to the camp. Uncle Dennis wasn't there.

Aside from a small bathroom, their quarters consisted of a single room with a bunk bed in the corner. Papers were strewn across the eating table. More papers lay in stacks on the coffee table in front of the couch. Abby picked up one of the articles—"Ecoscience: The boreal forest biome."

There was beer in the fridge, a can of coffee on the counter, a glass jar full of teabags. Cans of soup. Cans of pears.

Uncle Dennis had set up his laptop on the small eating table pushed up against a window. On top of the laptop were stickers—*Wildly Free*; *There is no Planet B*; the Alaska state flag. Abby picked up a sheet of paper scribbled with grocery items. At the bottom of the list was her name with a question mark. She laid the paper aside and picked up a framed photo of her uncle kneeling in the snow, arms around a black Lab, the two of them smiling, her uncle looking at the camera or the person behind the camera, and his dog looking at Uncle Dennis, lids slightly closed. She set the photo back on the table. The only sound was the rising and falling of Abby's breathing.

From the window, Abby saw a small clearing—a charcoal grill, two wooden folding chairs tinged green with algae, a circle of large stones creating a fire pit, and beyond the small clearing, a tangle of young forest growth. Abby retrieved a book from her backpack. She left out the back door and pulled up one of the chairs by the fire pit.

For a couple of hours Abby was by herself. She read from the large book on her lap—*The Grapes of Wrath*. She liked the way Steinbeck described the different landscapes as the Joads made their way from Oklahoma to California. Mostly, though, she was compelled by the story of the migrant workers, especially that of Tom Joad, who'd been wrongly imprisoned, and though he remained obliged to his family, there always burned in him the desire to live as a free man.

Abby closed the book and looked at the bare sky dipping into the crowns of the trees. The temperature was dropping, that familiar chill that came toward the end of day. Amid the stillness, she heard the barking of geese. She searched for their formation. Eventually she saw them moving farther north. The peninsula was a stop along the way, a waypoint, and she wondered about the place they were returning to—somewhere in Canada, maybe Thunder Bay, or Lake Nipigon, or Polar Bear Provincial Park.

Then she heard another sound, farther off in the woods, an intermittent hammering. Abby set her book on the ground. She rose from her chair and walked across the clearing until she was thick in the trees—maple, pine, hemlock, balsam fir, a blue spruce that looked like a Christmas tree standing by itself. Her uncle called these woods the snow forest—another name for boreal. In Russia, they called the boreal forest the taiga. Abby was stepping in the southernmost part of the boreal transition ecoregion. Everything around her was part of the world's taiga biome, the largest land biome in the world. The lower temperatures slowed down decomposition, allowing the forests to build up stores of carbon in the soil over hundreds of thousands of years, which was one of the greatest assets to slowing down climate change. This was why Abby and her uncle were here—to study the effects of climate change on these woods.

Abby ran her hands through low-hanging branches. She smelled pine resin. She stepped over deadfall and low-growing shrubs and blueberry bushes with their pale green berries and white flowers. She'd picked blueberries in these woods. She'd helped her mom bake a blueberry pie.

She remembered the two of them sitting on a screened-in porch, listening to the barred owls. Her mom mimicked their call: *Who cooks for you? Who cooks for you all?* Back and forth it went between her mom and the owls, each time the owls sounding closer and Abby trying to contain her laughter. These were the things they were up to—summer nights on a porch, Abby awake past bedtime, a blanket made out of scratchy yarn and blotted with drips of chocolate ice cream, Abby's feet bare and grass-stained, owls and fireflies, bats and swallows.

She thought of her drive earlier that day, the familiar passage onto the peninsula, the summer cottages and hunting camps and large swaths of state forest, the water and sandy beaches, the school buildings on her left, and beside them the New Garden Cemetery.

She didn't stop that morning, though other times she had, especially when she was with her father. They'd walk leisurely through the cemetery grounds. Sometimes he pointed out grave markers that belonged to other members of Abby's family. They'd sit in the shade of a pine tree in front of the headstone for Abby's mom—*Beloved wife, mother, daughter, sister, friend. Loved by all.* There would be background noises—cars driving by on the road behind them, children playing on the playground at the elementary school. Before leaving, her dad would walk over to the headstone, bend down, and kiss the smooth marble.

Though Abby didn't attend the funeral, this is what she knew—her mother's body wasn't buried at the cemetery. Her mother's body was never found—consumed in the fire, is what people told her. In lieu of a coffin, the family buried a box with mementos—rosary beads from her mother's baptism, a grade-school photograph, a purple scarf her mom knitted for an aunt, a jar of sand, plastic farm animals her mom played with as a child, a gold wedding band—the only thing her father had.

As Abby walked in the woods, she envisioned her father taking off his ring, twisting it until it slid from his finger. She could feel the heavy weight of his shoulders. Maybe someone held the box out to him, or maybe he knelt beside the box on the ground. He would have made the sign of the cross, she thought, before placing the ring in the box, before stepping away from the box and letting the ring go.

Her father, the gentle mechanic who'd adopted her when she was two. He'd wanted to be a farmer and milk cows alongside her mom and raise chickens, and grow hay and alfalfa and bale silage. He and Abby's mom worked on many farms between the Garden Peninsula and Eagle River. Each time they packed up their belongings and unpacked them in a different township, they tried to save a little money and make a little more, with dreams of buying their own farm one day, which Abby's dad said felt like digging a hole with a bent spoon.

Abby had few memories of living on those farms, and the older she got, the fewer memories she seemed to have. But every once in a while, something would come to mind, like the image she had of herself in a swimming pool, squinting her eyes toward the sun. The water was very blue. Around the pool were poolside chairs and redwood decking. Beyond the decking was a cedar fence. More than once, Abby asked her dad if they ever lived on a farm with a swimming pool, and he said that they did not, and when she told him about this memory, he said he didn't recall it.

In the end, her parents never did purchase their own farm. Her dad settled into a maintenance job with an electrical manufacturing company that made printed circuit boards. Instead of thinking about farms, Abby often found him staring wistfully at boats in magazines and newspaper advertisements. Other times they'd pull into a boat lot. He'd park his truck and let out a high whistle and say, "Would you get a look at that."

• • • • • • • • •

Abby no longer heard the hammering, but instead the incessant squawking of a bird, a large bird from the sound of it, and when she strained her eyes, she saw its broad wingspan. It flew closer and lit upon the skeleton of a dead tree and perched itself erect. A pileated woodpecker, getting a good look at Abby. There were books back at the camp that she'd brought from home—mostly novels, but also a reference guide to the different birds' symbolism. A Canada goose represented nature, community, and changing seasons. A pileated woodpecker brought the message of persistence, focus, and evolution.

The hammering started up again, this time much closer. Abby slowed her footsteps and approached quietly, then stood maybe fifty feet away, and observed her uncle through the trees, his body knelt over the ground, a hammer in his hand. He set the hammer aside, picked up another tool, then stood and stretched out a tape measure, and stepped away from the stake he'd set.

He looked like a boy who'd been left outside to play for a really long time—jeans that were dirt-stained and faded at the knees, a loose T-shirt, a ball cap pushed so far back on his head it seemed to defeat the purpose of wearing one at all, his unruly blond hair sticking out from underneath.

The mosquitos weren't too bad, maybe because of the breeze that remained constant, but the blackflies were annoying. Abby slapped at one on her neck. Uncle Dennis turned around just as she was stepping away from the tree and the pesky insect.

"Abby! How long have you been standing there?"

"Not long."

He pulled her into a hug.

"You smell like bug spray," she said.

"Don't knock it. Deet will become your best friend."

"I can't wait."

He picked up a spray can from his supplies on the ground and tossed it to her. She sprayed the hem of her jeans, sprayed her arms and the back of her neck.

She hadn't had any trouble finding the camp—they talked about these sorts of things—Abby's drive that morning, the directions Uncle Dennis had given her. The camp was close to Portage Bay, Uncle Dennis said. Abby said she thought it was. The woods reminded her of the Ninga Aki Pathway, a trail that abutted the bay. The trail meant *Mother Earth* in Ojibwe. Abby and her uncle explored it when she was young, taking their time as he identified the trees and mushrooms and flowers, and taught her words like *woodrush, mooseberry*, *cobble shore*, and *forage*.

Abby asked Uncle Dennis what he was doing with the stakes.

On the ground was a clipboard, and tucked into the clipboard was a map. He showed Abby the map covered with random dots. The dots represented the plot locations they'd be establishing over the summer, parcels of forest, twenty meters long by fifty meters wide. They had fifty-four plots to map over the next ten weeks, and would begin by hiking into those closest to the camp.

He told her about the inventory they'd be recording in any given plot—the number of overstory trees, the number of saplings, the different tree species and their diameter and growth factor—which would give them an estimate of the trees' age.

Abby helped her uncle with the plot markers. She held a ball of string while he tied the end to a flagged stake. Then she walked the ball of string to the next stake. As they worked, they mused about things—the summers on a farm in Wisconsin when Uncle Dennis and Abby's mom and aunts were young, the quilts on the beds that smelled of cedar and lavender soap, and the great-grandparents Abby had met only once.

"Probably why the idea of farming got stuck in your mom's head," Uncle Dennis said. "I think it got passed down through her DNA."

"What about your DNA?" Abby asked.

He talked about their ancestors who were fur traders, others who were Anishinaabe. "We weren't always fisher people," he said.

Abby knew something about this, on her grandfather's side of the family.

They finished setting the plot. Uncle Dennis sat back on the ground. Abby sat beside him.

"When I was young, I came across a book called *The Red Book: Wildlife in Danger*. It talked about mammals and birds, plants and trees—the Persian fallow deer, the giant sable antelope, the rusty numbat, the rufous-headed robin. It talked about sycamores and redwoods. I'd walk these woods and I'd see things differently—I saw the birds, I saw the trees, I saw all of it in danger. Once you know about something, you can't look the other way. You can't separate yourself from something you know. It'll make a shell out of you."

Abby thought about the things she knew—the whales were moving north, Greenland was shrinking, half the arctic sea melted in one year.

Uncle Dennis worried that the boreal forests were shrinking and that if the temperatures continued to rise, these woods would lose the white cedar and balsam fir and hemlock and blue spruce, and the paper birch and aspens. And when the trees were gone, the birds would be gone too—the owls and eagles and falcons, and about three hundred other kinds of bird species.

"You ever hear the saying, when a leaf falls from its tree, it always goes back to its roots? I think my roots are in these woods," Uncle Dennis said.

"Is that why you came back?" Abby asked.

"That's part of it. That's a big part of it actually. The rest is something I'm still trying to figure out."

Abby's mind turned to her own DNA and the biological father she never knew. His family didn't live on the peninsula anymore. His name was Jimmy. Uncle Dennis and he had been friends. Over the years she gathered bits of information about him. He liked to fish, he wanted to own a horse one day, he was an average student at best, but none of these things resonated with her.

Uncle Dennis wanted to finish up some of his notes. Abby said she was going to head back. She still needed to unpack, and she and Brew were supposed to get together later.

She left her uncle and began retracing her steps through the woods, moving in what she believed was a northwestward direction.

As she stepped on needle duff and smelled cedar and white pine, she imagined all the places her uncle had been—the Tanana River valley in Alaska, the rainforest in British Columbia, the Pacific Rim National Park Reserve. He'd even come face to face with a grizzly when backpacking on glaciers with friends in Alberta. Instead of staying on at the family's fish house, he earned a master's degree in forest science and was now finishing his doctoral degree in forest ecology.

With these thoughts came other thoughts, more of a feeling really, that her life was trapped by her vulnerability, that she was afraid. And yet there were moments when she'd look into the eyes of another and see their vulnerability too—each person connected by this great big thing called mortality. All she had to do was look the person in the eyes, really see the person, as if taking a photograph on portrait setting. She'd become filled then with such tenderness, such gentleness, such love—filled to the hurting point. It was all too much sometimes.

Yes, these were her thoughts, until she realized she had no idea where she was—or rather she had a vague sense of where she was, but no idea exactly. She moved in one direction and then another, and at once became irritated and winded. The breeze blew through the trees. She thought she smelled water, which would mean she'd traveled east instead of west. She could call out for her uncle, but he might not hear her.

She stood still then and slowed the beating of her heart. She closed her eyes. Her thoughts recalled the place, allowed it to rise up in her. She imagined seeing the trees and flowers, as when seeing a person—the life within her looking into the life of everything around her. And then she felt the trees, the flowers, the sky, the moon, the pileated woodpecker that had perched on a tree—this great big world of nature returning her gaze, beholding her. Was this what God was? Looking into her eyes and filled to the hurting point? She held her arms out wide and began to dance with the trees, her body swaying in the breeze, as if all these years, these woods had lain silent within her. She wasn't afraid. She knew where she was, and when she opened her eyes, she spotted the small spruce that looked like a Christmas tree, and a little farther ahead the low-growing blueberry bushes.

4

ABBY SAT ON A LOG by a fire, sand and rocks and weeds underfoot. Brew wasn't there yet, but he would be soon.

About fifty feet away, the lake lapped against the shore. It was still light out. The sun didn't set until almost ten this time of year.

Abby listened to the noises around her—clusters of voices, the popping metal of a beer can opening, a car here and there, a truck engine running, doors closing, the gritty clacking of footsteps over rocks. Someone added more wood to the fire. Sparks shot up in the air.

She rose and walked toward the vehicles that were parked off the road and looked for Brew's jeep. A person's hands covered her eyes from behind. Abby swung around startled. There was Brew. They leaned into one another and bantered back and forth and laughed about nothing in particular.

A couple of guys approached. "You remember my cousin Abby," Brew said. Abby knew who they were, from gatherings on the beach when she'd visited in the summers, and parties at one or another's house, and from a day riding all-terrain vehicles up the sand dunes.

A blue truck pulled up alongside them, windows down, music

playing. Tracy leaned her head out the window. She brought the food, she said.

Brew lowered the tailgate and climbed into the bed to get the cooler that had shifted toward the cab. Tracy set up the propane grill.

Tracy was from a large family. She worked at the restaurant in Nahma, a small town west of the peninsula, about twenty minutes away. She was a strong brunette with a strong personality and strong arms, and wore a sleeveless tank even though the air was chilly. Abby knew her in the same way she knew Brew's other friends.

Alex was one of those friends. He stood with Abby, the two of them making conversation—how had her year been, and she asked him how was graduation, because Brew and Alex graduated the week before.

"Your cousin's a good guy," Alex said. "He's going to do well at Northern."

When they ran out of things to say, Abby stepped away from the group and wandered past the fire and down to the water.

She hadn't seen Brew approach, but there he was.

"Hey," he said. "Where are you going?"

"I thought I'd go for a walk."

He said they'd be grilling soon, that there would be food to eat.

"I'll be back," she told him.

"Don't go too far. You just got here."

She watched him turn away, watched him join the others. Then she, too, walked away, moving along the water's edge, stepping over waterlogged stumps and pieces of driftwood, and large rocks that had been hauled in as breakers, until she was at *the graveyard*. From early on, that's what she and Brew called it. It wasn't a real graveyard, per se, but rather a big, empty lot along the water, about a hundred yards from the family's fish house. And yet the lot wasn't actually empty at all. It held many things—driftwood, pilings, fishnets, floaters, and the wreckage of an old fishing boat.

The air was full of the lake wind and the sound of the water. The sky was less blue, almost a metallic color with the clouds that had moved in.

Abby stepped toward the bow of the boat, her eyes searching the gray steel, until she saw the etchings, dulled over the years. She stood beside the boat, looking at her name and Brew's name beside hers.

How many times had the two of them been here, in this same spot?—she and Brew only five years old the day they met.

She'd been staying at Nonna's, and sat with her parents that morning in the kitchen, windows open, a breeze blowing off the bay, breakfast dishes pushed aside. There was a boy about Abby's age, Nonna said, and wouldn't it be nice if the two of them could play together. Abby remembered the way her mom was holding a brown mug of coffee beneath her chin, as if she'd lifted the cup to take a drink, but then stopped long enough to smile.

Nonna took Abby's hand. She opened the storm door and led her across the patio and the small driveway, and then down the road to the fish house. Aunt Reese was there, wearing an oiler and big rubber boots, and was hosing down the floor. Nonna asked her daughter, "Reese, you wouldn't happen to know where Ronnie's boy is?" Aunt Reese told her she'd seen him in front of Uncle Buckley's house.

Nonna was still holding Abby's hand. They walked a short distance down the road to the lot across the street from Uncle Buckley's. A little boy, wearing a funny hat shaped like a dome, was on his knees, digging in the sand.

The boy smiled and waved and ran up to see them. "Hi, Nonna."

"Can Abby play with you?" Nonna asked.

The boy nodded and ran back to where he was digging. Then he looked over his shoulder and yelled, "You can help me find treasure!"

Abby ran over to the boy and knelt beside him, the two of them convinced they'd find treasure. Brew *did* find a transistor radio that no longer worked, and Abby found an old bottle that she brought back to the house and put flowers in. And there were fishing lures and bobbers and fishing line that had washed ashore.

A year later, Brew's dad married Abby's aunt Reese, the youngest of the Treadwell sisters, on a hot day in July, in front of the cabins. Abby tossed rose petals, some landing in the water and floating against the shore. Daisies and baby's breath were woven in her hair. Brew wore a tuxedo and carried the rings. There was fried fish and smoked fish, casseroles and cornbread, music and dancing.

Brew and Abby wandered past the cabins and down to the graveyard, where they looked for smooth rocks and bright-colored fishing lures, and scratched their names in the side of the boat wreckage.

That night it rained, and people kept dancing, bare feet sliding in the mud, while Abby and Brew fell asleep in the boat's cockpit, backs slumped against the helm of the old gillnetter, heads leaning against one another.

They were six then, and then seven, and then eight, and then nine. Even after the fire, even after Abby moved away and would come back to visit, they still came down to the graveyard and scavenged for things—driftwood and rocks and pieces of polished glass—and climbed into the boat and pretended they were out at sea.

On one of those occasions, when Brew was standing at the helm, and Abby was standing on the shore trying to untangle a fishing net, Brew shouted, "I see something!" Just like that, he leapt over the side of the boat and ran a few paces. He knelt to the ground and began pushing rocks aside.

"What is it?" Abby asked.

"I think there might be a body."

Abby screamed and dropped the net.

"What are you screaming for?"

"I don't know," she said.

He picked up a large, flat stone, and holding it with both hands, began clearing a circumference around whatever it was he'd discovered. As his arms moved, Abby saw a flash of something whitish like the color of bone and turned away.

"Is it a dead person?" she asked.

"Probably just a deer or something."

She was curious and said, "In that case," and began walking toward him.

Brew quickly stood and rushed over to her. He grabbed both her arms and led her away. "You don't want to see this, Abby. It's not good."

She must have understood something, because she didn't resist. She let him lead her away until there was enough distance between where they stood and where he'd been digging that she couldn't see what it was he discovered. Only then did she pull her arms free and demand to know what he found.

Brew stood there looking at her with a puzzled, serious face. Then he shook his head and said, "Sorry, Abby. I can't let you see it."

In a rage, she turned from him and strode away.

• • • • • • • • •

Abby could hear the party going on behind her. She continued along the beach, past the graveyard and the gillnetter, and on to the fish house. She walked down the concrete dock, passing her grandfather's commercial fishing boat the *Daline*, named after his mother, that Uncle Buckley still took out. The wind blew stronger, and she tucked her hands in the pockets of her jacket. The jacket didn't belong to her. It had been Grandpa Pete's. Uncle Dennis gave it to Abby when he dropped her off, saying she might need it.

Abby was fourteen when her grandfather died, either from a heart attack that caused him to fall out of the boat and into the cold water, or else he fell into the cold water from his boat and the cold water gave him the heart attack. The jacket still smelled of him—diesel fuel, cigars. In the right pocket, Abby discovered a stub of paper, like a numbered ticket from a machine at a deli counter. On the back of the pink stub was the name *Pelletier* and a telephone number written in her grandfather's small script. She wondered how long it had been there. That was all there was to her thinking, other than perhaps a fleeting image of her grandfather leaning over the small table in the kitchen by the phone, a pen in his hand, grabbing the first thing he could find to write on.

Abby was supposed to get a ride with Brew after the party, and she was hungry. She turned to head back. At the point where the dock met the shore, among the rocks, she spotted a feather—shiny black, with two dabs of white side by side at the tip, like neatly painted brushstrokes. A loon feather, she knew. She climbed down to the water's edge and retrieved the feather, ran her fingers over the downy tuft at the bottom of the shaft, then tucked the feather behind her ear.

• • • • • • • • •

Back at the party there was music playing and the smell of food. It was dusk by now—a muted dusk, the sky thick with gray. Someone handed Abby a paper plate with a hamburger. On the ground beside a log was a bag of chips. She poured some onto her plate, then sat on the log and ate the dry hamburger and watched the group around her. Some people were dancing. She looked for Brew but didn't see him or Tracy or Alex, and soon the sky was too dark for her to recognize any of the vehicles.

She finished her food, walked up to the fire, and tucked her plate into the embers. Then she stood back, away from the others, pine smoke in her hair, music and voices pulsing around her. The music changed. Her body began to move from side to side in time with the beat.

That was the first time Abby noticed her, dancing alone among the others. Her eyes were closed and her head was rocking to the thrum of the electric guitar. She then drew her right foot along her left calf and raised her arms high, as if in a yoga pose, floating effortlessly with the music, as if she were completely unaware of anyone else around her.

Ever so subtly, the girl's head began to rock once more. Her hair swept over her face, and all at once her limbs and hips started moving again. She opened her eyes and was smiling and nodding her head, as if saying to Abby, *"Yeah, you got this. We got this. Let's keep dancing."*

Abby stepped closer. The two of them began dancing together, hips swaying, hair tossing from side to side.

The music changed into something slow. Abby was about to recede from the group when the girl touched her arm. At first Abby paused, until the girl's fingertips brushed the side of her face and the curve of her ear. She removed the loon feather from Abby's hair, traced Abby's jawline with the tips of the vane, then ran the feather down the neckline of Abby's flannel shirt.

"Dance with me," the girl said. Abby hesitated, only for a second, then gave a small nod. The girl asked if Abby wanted to be the girl or the boy. Because Abby wanted to know what a woman's body felt like beneath the hands of a man, what Brew's hands felt on a female's waist and hips and shoulders, she told her she'd be the boy.

The girl pulled her hair up off her neck into a knot and secured the knot with the feather. Abby then positioned a hand on each of the girl's shoulders. The girl only smiled and tilted her head to the side and slid Abby's hands down to her waist. "You're the boy, and I'm *the girl*, remember?"

So that's how they danced, how they moved, as easily as a silhouette. Abby felt relaxed, her muscles strong, her body graceful. She twirled the girl around, who smiled in surprise. Then Abby returned her hands to the girl's waist.

The song ended and another began. The tempo was fast and the guitar loud. Raindrops began to fall, slow at first, hissing in the flames. Voices picked up around them. The rain fell harder.

The girl pulled away, carefree and easy, and with a skip to her step, joined up with a group of others who were laughing as they ran for their cars. She slowed and turned around, taking steps backward. Then she was off again, disappearing into muffled voices and car doors slamming and engines starting.

5

ABBY LIFTED HER JACKET UP over her head and raced through the rain to find Brew. She saw Tracy's truck, but she couldn't find Brew or Tracy or his jeep anywhere.

"I think he went to get more food," someone shouted.

The rain fell harder. A car drove up beside her. "Abby, get in."

It was Alex. She opened the back passenger door and slid in, and was surprised to find the girl in the backseat with her.

Another boy was riding up front. Abby didn't know his name. The air-conditioning was blowing, to keep the windows from fogging, Alex said.

By now Abby was soaking wet and cold, and could swear the car had a subwoofer directly behind her head.

The passenger boy lit a cigarette. With the air-conditioning blowing, the smoke quickly filled up the backseat. The girl told the boy to roll down his window.

"It's pouring outside," he said.

Then Alex said, "Dude, just put the cigarette out."

Abby wanted to be done with it all—the percussion, the cigarette fumes, the rain. She'd ask Alex to drive her back to the camp. But just as she was getting ready to say something, the girl said she had an idea and told Alex to pull the car over.

Alex slowed the car and pulled off to the side of the road. The girl rolled her window all the way down, then hoisted herself through the opening until she was sitting on the edge of the door. The music was blaring and the rain was pouring, and everyone was talking at once, while the girl climbed on top of the car. She lay across the roof and leaned her head over the windshield, her face upside-down as she laughed through the rapid *thwomp, thwomp, thwomp* swiping of the wipers.

Alex lowered his window a few inches and was yelling for her to get back in the car. The passenger window was still partway down from the boy who'd tossed his cigarette. The girl had now extended her arms and was gripping the car frame through the two openings on each side, while her feet dangled over the rear window. She wanted Alex to pull back onto the road.

"Are you crazy?" he yelled.

"Come on, Alex!" the girl yelled.

The boy in the passenger seat said, "This really isn't safe."

Then Alex edged the car forward and drove back onto the road.

"You better hold on!" Alex yelled. The girl let out a whoop. The car slowly accelerated. Alex revved the RPMs, shifted from third to fourth, and cruised evenly for about a hundred yards. The girl's fingers gripped the car tighter. She let out a high-pitched scream, like something wild and crazy, and she *was* crazy, Abby thought. Alex shifted to fifth. That's when Abby yelled, "Slow down!"

Alex let up on the gas and downshifted. Eyes glinted yellow ahead and to their right. *No, please wait, don't move. Please stay right where you are*, Abby said to herself.

Alex braked just in time as a fawn leapt in front of them. There was the squealing sound of the girl's wet clothes and skin as she skidded across the roof, and Alex's headlights and the deer's eyes staring back at one another. The fawn's body appeared frozen in front of them. The girl's body was slumped over the windshield. She'd spread her hands out in front of her to catch her fall. Abby didn't see how the girl wasn't thrown from the car.

The fawn looked over her shoulder in the direction from where she came, and in one sweeping leap, turned around and bound back toward the trees.

Everyone was now out of the car making sure the girl was all right. The girl began to laugh. "I felt like I was flying," she said.

"That was insane," Alex told her.

The other boy just lit a cigarette, shaking his head.

The girl climbed off the car, her clothes and face dripping, and somehow there was Abby's feather still tucked in her hair.

Abby had had enough and slipped away from the others.

"Hey, where are you going?" the passenger boy said.

"I'd rather walk," Abby said.

"We'll give you a ride," Alex said. "Hold on."

"I'm fine," Abby yelled back.

Car doors slammed behind her. She heard Alex accelerate. His headlights beamed brighter. He pulled up beside her and turned down the music. "How will we know you got home all right?"

"Because I will," she said.

"Come on, Abby. Just get in the car," Alex told her.

But she ignored him and kept walking. Alex drove on. The passenger boy held his arm out the window and waved. The taillights grew dimmer until she could no longer see them at all, and eventually the sound of the car disappeared as well.

6

THE RAIN HAD MOSTLY STOPPED. The clouds had thinned, revealing a silver glow from the moon. Abby recognized a farm coming up on her right. She remembered the farm because of the fieldstones that had been gathered into two columns and wrapped in chicken wire.

She still had a ways to go to get to the camp, but there was now a hayfield to her left and another field to her right so that the light appeared brighter. She listened to the chirps and trills of crickets in the grass and her footsteps against the gritty road. Moisture collected on her face. Her clothes clung to her skin. Eventually, there was the sound of water like that of a spring emptying into a ditch.

Despite how different everything appeared at night, she knew that the overgrown path coming up on her right, nothing but a tractor trail now, led to the burn site. The house had been white with green trim. Sheer curtains hung in the windows.

She continued a few more paces, and then she heard the music, as faint as a murmur at first, so faint she wasn't sure she'd heard it at all. Abby stood as still as she could, and yes, she was sure, it was music that was playing, the solitary bass notes of a cello seeping through the trees from beyond the field. The music, though still faint, began to intensify. She thought she recognized the song. She tried hard to recall it. And while she stood there, still and quiet, she inhaled slowly, as if bringing the music deep into her lungs, as if breath and air and sound were all interwoven. The night felt warmer now that the rain had stopped—warm and cool, like Nonna's kitchen—morning air through a window, steam rising from a mug of coffee, hot toast on a plate being scraped with butter.

A dog began to bark from somewhere off in the distance. The music stopped. The dog's bark had a husky tone to it reminding Abby of Rudy, the dog she had as a child. Rudy was a cattle dog mix with a brown, spotted coat and may have had some hound dog in his lineage, because he could howl, which was what this dog was doing now.

Without much thought to it, Abby cupped her hands around her mouth and howled in the dog's direction. She dropped her hands and listened. The dog didn't howl in return.

A little farther, and a car approached her from behind. She pivoted, shielding her eyes from the glare of its headlights. The vehicle slowed, and Brew's voice called out. Abby walked up to the side of his jeep where his window was rolled down. Tracy wasn't with him.

"What are you doing?" he asked.

Abby said, "I could ask you the same."

"I was looking for you. Come on, Abby. Get in. You're soaked."

She walked around to the other side of his jeep.

When she climbed in, Brew said, "I ran into Alex. He told me about what happened. About the car surfing and them almost hitting the deer. He said he should have made sure you got home all right."

"It wasn't his fault. I was really set on walking."

Then she told Brew the camp wasn't much farther, and she gave him directions.

When they got there, he shut off the engine and lights and slouched back in his seat.

"Hey," he said, and turned toward Abby. "I'm sorry I wasn't there. We ran out of propane. I went to get another canister. When I got back, you'd already left.

"Hey," he said again. "You had me worried."

Already Abby had slipped out of her sandals and was leaning back with her feet on the dashboard.

Brew shifted in his seat so that his body was facing her. "We didn't get a chance to talk much. How have you been?"

The windshield had fogged up. Abby pressed a big toe against the glass. She drew a face—two eyes, a nose—her foot halted a couple of seconds before drawing the mouth. She made the line, barely a smile, but it was there. "I'm okay." She thought for a moment. "Let me rephrase that. I'm okay now."

She was glad Brew pulled up. She was glad they were talking.

Then Abby said, "I drove by the burn site earlier today, on my way to the camp. I passed by it again tonight while I was walking."

Brew's head was down. "I drove by it too, when I was looking for you."

"Have you been by there before?" Abby asked.

"No, have you?"

"No."

Abby told Brew about the strange cello music followed by the dog barking, and how the dog sounded like Rudy. "I still miss him."

"I know you do."

Then Brew said, "I saw you dancing, before I left. You seemed like you were having a good time."

"I was," Abby said. "I met someone."

"Who?"

"Honestly, I couldn't even tell you her name."

Abby pressed her head into the upholstery of the seat. She breathed deeply. "Can I ask you something?"

"Go on," Brew said.

"Are you leaving me behind?"

"What are you talking about?"

"College, Tracy—"

"I'm not leaving you."

Abby exhaled, rocked her head from side to side. "Maybe it's just life, leaving me in the dust. It's like I want to run and grab it and say, 'Wait up, take me with you,' but it keeps moving farther ahead, and I can't catch up."

"I don't get it, Abby. You've got as much life ahead of you as the rest of us. You're the one who graduated early."

"I'm a hamster."

Brew laughed. "You're not a hamster."

"Sure I am. I'm like a hamster on one of those exercise wheels."

Brew was quiet.

"I should get inside," she said. She dropped her feet from the dashboard and reached for the door.

Brew said, "Do you remember anything? About the fire?"

She sat back in her seat. "No. But I want to."

"Do you think that's a good idea?"

"I think it's important."

"The matches—" Brew said knowingly.

"Yeah. Why was I carrying them?" She looked straight at Brew.

"When I passed the farm tonight, or what used to be the farm, I remembered a sunny day and me running down the driveway," she said. "I think I was chasing something. I could see myself. I was smiling. My hair was past my shoulders. I was wearing a green-and-cream-colored blouse and cutoff shorts. I loved that shirt. I could see it so clearly. I wore it all the time. And I missed it. Does that sound weird? I really missed it. I wanted it back. I completely forgot about it until tonight."

"I remember that girl, the one running down the driveway."

Their eyes stared back at one another. She felt as if she were that girl all over again, wearing cutoff shorts and her favorite blouse.

And then Abby started to laugh. "I totally forgot," she said.

"I have no idea what you're talking about, you know."

"It's just something Uncle Dennis said, when we were in the woods. He was talking about wolves. He said that when wolves want to find their people, meaning their pack, they howl. When I heard the dog, I started howling back at him, and then you showed up."

"You're crazy, you know that?" Brew was smiling and laughing a little.

"But it's funny, right? I mean, here you are."

"It's funny that you were standing in a field howling back at some dog in the middle of the night. What time is it anyway?" The clock on his dashboard was broken, and neither he nor Abby was wearing a watch.

"It's late," she said. Her face turned serious and she looked at Brew. "I'm glad you showed up."

"I'm just glad I found you."

• • • • • • • • •

When Abby entered the camp, Uncle Dennis was asleep, lying on the sofa with an open book facedown upon his chest. Even after Abby set the book on the coffee table and turned off the lamp, he didn't stir. She moved about quietly getting ready for bed, then climbed onto the bunk with her backpack and turned on the reading lamp on the wall above her head.

The window to her right was open. She could hear the rainwater dripping from the trees. She opened her pack and took out a book titled *Call of the Loon* that she bought Brew for his graduation. The book was written in the format of questions and asked whether loons returned to their mates. She'd been sad to learn that instead of remaining faithful to each other, the loons remained faithful to their territory.

A memory was so close, Abby could touch its details—the orbs of light over the water, the can of nightcrawlers beside her, Brew's reddish-brown mop of waves and soft blue eyes. She and Brew were in Grandpa Pete's aluminum fishing boat that they'd christened the *Little Daline*. Water lapped against the sides of the hull. They were eleven, long and lanky. They'd been fishing all morning when Brew said he wanted to show her something.

He steered them toward the wide-mouth opening of a cove along the southern end of the bay. Then he killed the motor and reached for one of the oars. The cove was clear and shallow, four to five feet deep, and surrounded by cattails and reeds. A school of chub minnows glided and darted around them like liquid silver.

Quietly, Brew slid the oar back underneath their seats. "This is close enough," he said. And just as quietly, he dropped the anchor.

He was standing partway, carefully balancing himself. He took a couple of small steps and reached for Abby's seat. "Scoot over," he said. The two of them sat side by side facing the cove, their knees and shoulders touching. Brew leaned forward, supporting himself with his arms on his legs.

"Why are we here?" Abby asked.

He held his finger to his mouth. "Shh, just listen," he said.

Abby turned her attention to the chorus of frogs and marsh wrens and warblers, to the hollowed-out sound the aluminum hull made every time the water moved beneath them. And then the eerily beautiful, lonely, two-note vocalization from a larger bird along the shore. A similar mournful wail sounded from farther away, somewhere outside the cove.

"Loons," Brew said. "A pair of them." He pointed toward the tall grasses about sixty yards to the right. "They're nesting," he said. "The one on the shore is saying, 'I'm here, where are you?' And the other one is calling back to her, 'I'm over here.'"

"That's sweet," Abby said.

"Yeah. He's never too far away."

The next summer, the loons returned. And the summer after that, they returned once more. But after the third summer, Brew and Abby didn't see them again.

• • • • • • • • •

Abby turned out the light and lay on her back. There was a cool breeze from the camp window, a sweet, earthy scent, and with it, the thought of Brew. He was her people, her pack. And yet she had a fleeting sensation that she needed to do *this*—whatever it was—alone. And what was *this*, she wondered, that lay out there, that made her blood run, that made her feel something as big as fear? She closed her eyes and thought about the night—the girl on top of the car, the walk back to the camp, the music, the dog. She thrummed her fingers against the comforter on her bed, trying to imitate the rhythm of the cello. She couldn't recall it exactly. She kept trying. Was it possible that the cello she heard was only the sound of the wind and the rain?

A car slowed and came to a stop outside the camp. The engine remained running. Doors opened and closed. Abby slid off the bunk. Uncle Dennis was still asleep. Before she made it to the front steps, the vehicle drove away.

She walked across the hard-packed driveway toward the road. Somewhere a barred owl called, and farther off another, and there was the sound of katydids and peepers, a whole cacophony around her. She wondered if she'd locked her car. When she opened the driver's side door and the light came on, she felt a quickened beat in her chest. On the seat lay the loon feather she'd found on the beach and that the girl had taken and worn in her hair.

7

"RISE AND SHINE," UNCLE DENNIS said.

"What time is it?" Abby asked from beneath the comforter.

It was almost five. He'd been up since four.

She groaned and lowered the covers from her face, lamplight reflecting in the dark windows, her uncle's quick activity about the place. She thought of her dad's sluggish movements in the mornings when he was getting ready for work, and how smoothly the two of them transitioned into their days, hardly saying a word to each other.

Abby climbed down from the bunk and joined Uncle Dennis at the table. He slid a plate of toast in front of her, a cup of steaming coffee, and a bowl of instant oatmeal. While she ate, he laid out the map covered with random dots. He pointed out the forest plots they would be marking that day. As he'd mentioned earlier, they'd start with the plots closest to the camp. He brought out the GPS device and began showing her how to use it to locate the plot locations.

They packed lunches and snacks and water, and their necessary equipment: measuring tapes and flagging, rebar stakes and hammers, clipboards with data sheets and graph paper.

Abby dressed in what would become her usual attire—a tank top and the overalls she liked, a pair of hiking boots, and a field shirt with pockets. They left camp with barely enough light to see in front of them. Gnats and blackflies flitted about their faces. Larvae where water had pooled were developing into mosquitos by what seemed like the thousands. Abby's clothes, already saturated with bug spray, quickly became wet with dew.

The bugs didn't seem to bother Uncle Dennis. He loved mornings like this. He showed Abby how to follow the plot's coordinates. They walked about a mile to the first location. Then they established the plot's corners by marking them with flagged rebar in vegetation so dense they could hardly see their stakes, and connected the stakes with string. They further divided the rectangle into ten different squares, ten by ten meters each.

Once they established the plot, they tagged and mapped the overstory trees, both living and dead. Afterward, they identified and counted the saplings. These same plots would be observed over the next ten years, Uncle Dennis said.

By midmorning Abby was famished and soaked with dew and perspiration. She worried every dark speck on her clothing was a tick. There were scratches on her hands and bug bites swelling on her skin, despite the repellent and head netting.

They came to a pond where deer drank—the impressions of their hooves all around them—and sat on a log to eat lunch. Abby thought she heard the whinnying of a horse not too far off, which made her think of her biological father because he wanted to own a horse one day. But what she heard was a screech owl, her uncle told her.

Abby wanted to feel different—less bothered and encumbered. She wanted to capture the magnitude of everything she experienced the night before—the unknown, the sense of something out there waiting for her, beckoning her attention. She searched for it as they worked—as Uncle Dennis pounded a stake into the ground and she looked off into the trees, as she stretched the measuring tape across a grid, and as they walked, determining their steps by the GPS device. But instead, all she felt were the tangibles—the science, the data, the discomforts.

Over the rest of the week Abby grew more confident in her ability to mark the plots, and with the resource sheets Uncle Dennis provided, was trusting herself when it came to identifying the different tree species. Though they worked together in the mornings, Uncle Dennis began giving her separate assignments in the afternoons, an individual plot here and there. He'd catch up with her later, he said, and check her work.

Only once had she seen Brew since the night of the party. She was driving to the corner market to buy bread and orange juice. Brew was approaching from the other direction and pulled his jeep alongside her. They talked to each other through their rolled-down windows. Brew was telling her a story about a man he used to work with at the fish house—Wayne Emerson. Did she know him? He had a couple of young kids. He died the other day, during that storm on Wednesday. Abby remembered the rainstorm that swept over the peninsula—the thunderclouds and wind. Wayne was cutting down trees, Brew said. A limb fell on him. There's going to be a funeral sometime next week. They're waiting for family to get into town. Brew was thinking he should go. He wanted to know if Abby would go with him.

She'd go to the funeral, she told him. He just needed to let her know when.

A car pulled up behind Abby. Brew said they'd talk soon, and the two of them drove on.

But there were other things Abby wanted to talk to Brew about. She wanted to explain her thoughts to him—this longing for that feeling she couldn't grasp. She even drove her car to the burn site one night, hoping to hear the cello again, but nothing came to her.

• • • • • • • • •

At the end of her second week, Abby woke to the sound of a can of whipped cream being shaken and the smell of slightly burnt French toast. Although Uncle Dennis didn't have birthday candles, he lit a citronella candle and told Abby to make a wish.

They sat in the wooden folding chairs outside and ate and watched the sunrise. There would be an early dinner at Nonna's house, but Uncle Dennis said he couldn't make it. He had somewhere he had to be in Escanaba.

This was their first day off after working eleven days straight.

"Got any other plans for the day?" he asked her.

"I don't think so. Brew's probably working." She was still wearing the clothes she slept in—pajama shorts and a T-shirt. Her feet were bare. The blister on her big toe had turned into a callous. There were multiple bug bites on her arms and a blackfly welt on the back of her neck.

"Don't worry. Things will get easier," Uncle Dennis said.

"How so?"

"Moving forward, we'll work Tuesday through Friday. You'll have Saturday through Monday off. You'll be working entirely on your own," he added. "We can cover more ground that way."

• • • • • • • • •

Abby drove to the fish house later that morning, if only to glimpse Brew's jeep, if only to see him standing on the dock unloading pallets from one of the boats or watch him drive the forklift. She'd park her car and climb into the forklift and work the levers and gears, sitting on the edge of the seat with Brew sitting behind her, his legs on either side of her. He'd laugh at her mistakes and hold his hand over hers on a lever as he showed her how to get it right.

When she saw he wasn't there, she drove to the corner market and bought a bottle of orange pop and packaged donuts coated in white powder. She sat on a bench outside the market finishing the donuts and licking her fingers.

The sun reflected off car hoods. Sweat trickled down her scalp. Abby left the market and drove to Portage Bay, and despite her earlier vow to steer clear of the woods, she walked the path that led to the water. All around her were dabs of white—Canada mayflowers with their delicate cones of minuscule buds, and northern starflowers, brilliant atop their dark-green leaves. She surprised herself, knowing the names of the flowers—information she'd gathered from sourcebooks Uncle Dennis kept at the camp, or else from the knowledge he passed on to her.

She picked blue violets and the tiny, yellow cinquefoils that grew low to the ground like wild strawberries, and dropped them into the empty pop bottle like confetti. The tiny flowers reminded Abby of the tiara Aunt Jo-Jo wore in her hair when she married Uncle Brian—an army corporal now stationed in Bosnia. The reception was held in a giant barn at a beautiful farm. Abby and Brew stood outside the barn holding plates with wedding cake, the two of them sliding forkfuls of sweet icing into their mouths and looking out at a rolling, green meadow under a dusky summer sky. The moment spoke to Abby of a peace so full, so rich, so perfect, as if the world were a perfect place.

Back at the camp, Abby took her time getting ready for dinner, blow-drying her hair and putting on a summer dress. Then she gathered her dirty clothes in her duffel bag so that she could do her laundry at Nonna's house.

As Abby drove to her grandmother's, different images from the week came to mind—specific images—like the shell of a wild turkey egg lying exposed in a field of clover, at first appearing as a large, sun-bleached seashell, and the blanket of trillium beneath a canopy of maple and hemlock. She thought of the day earlier that week, when she lowered herself to the ground and looked at the steel-gray thunderclouds moving in and felt the weight of the wind pass over her, the same wind that shook the limb that fell on Wayne Emerson. She wondered when the funeral would be. She'd ask Brew when she saw him.

But when she walked through the door at Nonna's, Aunt Jo-Jo said, "Brew isn't coming. He and Reese are up in Marquette for his freshman orientation."

Aunt Jo-Jo finished laying the silverware, then walked around the table and gave Abby a hug.

Nonna gave Abby a hug as well. "You've gotten a lot of color on your face. Doesn't she look good? You look good, Abby."

"She looks like Cathy," Aunt Jo-Jo said.

Nonna thought so too. "You look like your mother." She took Abby's duffel bag and said she'd get a load of wash started. Abby tried to convince herself that Brew's absence wasn't a big deal.

They feasted on perch and trout panfried in butter and cornmeal, potato salad and deviled eggs, green beans cooked with bacon and garlic, fresh strawberries.

Aunt Jo-Jo's girls, Catherine and Gracie, ages seven and five, helped Abby blow out the candles on a chocolate cake. Abby thought of Brew as she made a wish. She was curious when he'd be getting back.

Aunt Jo-Jo and the girls gave Abby a necklace made out of glass beads that looked like emeralds. Catherine said the beads reminded her of trees. Aunt Reese gave her a pair of matching earrings. Then Aunt Jo-Jo and Nonna talked about the gallery in town, because the jewelry was made by a local artist.

The last gift was from Abby's dad—a poetry anthology about wildflowers and butterflies and all things of the natural world. In his card was a hundred dollars and a note saying he couldn't take credit for the gift. He'd gotten Ian at the bookstore to help him pick it out.

Once the dishes were put away, the family gathered on the back porch overlooking the water. Aunt Jo-Jo brought out her guitar and was strumming tunes by Kate Wolf and Arlo Guthrie and Joan Baez. Nonna reached over and held Abby's hand.

"How's your dad doing?" she asked.

"He's good," Abby told her. Abby called him the week before from a pay phone at the market, just to say hi. He'd finished roto-tilling the soil in the garden and was getting ready to plant tomatoes and lettuce and cucumbers. "I'm turning the yard into a salad." His comment made Abby laugh.

The evening had grown cooler. The sky appeared like blue copper ore and the stars were out. So were the bats, swooping and darting like swallows.

Nonna said she was going to go inside to get a sweater.

Aunt Jo-Jo said she needed to get the girls to bed. Abby kissed her cousins good night. Catherine's hair smelled of fresh air and salty skin, and Gracie said, "I love you, Abby." She had a slight speech impediment and drew out the second syllable, pronouncing it with a long *a*.

Abby stayed outside awhile longer. She slid down in her chair and watched the stars flickering against the rich, night blue. She thought of the northern starflowers and how they appeared as stars on the forest floor, their petals refracting the sunlight. But mostly Abby was thinking of her father and a particular evening in late March.

She'd spent the day helping Ian at the bookstore. When she returned home, the sky was fading into this same rich blue and the stars were out. She stood in the driveway before going in. Through the front window she could see the lamp glow next to her dad's recliner and the blue lights from the TV.

Inside, there were dirty dishes in the kitchen sink. Abby stood in the wide doorway that adjoined the living room.

Her dad glanced at her quickly. "Don't bother," he said. "The dishwasher has to be emptied. I'll get to it in a minute." Then he stared back at the TV. "Oh, Jesus, would you look at that."

One of the news stations was playing footage of a ten-car pileup in Buffalo.

"What did you have?" Abby asked.

"What's that?"

"What did you have for dinner?"

"The chicken we had the other night."

Abby nodded and turned back to the kitchen and began unloading the dishwasher.

"What are you doing?" her dad yelled.

"It's okay, I got it." She finished unloading the dishes, then rinsed the dirty ones and set them in the lower rack.

"Did you get something to eat?" her dad asked.

"Yeah, Ian picked up something for us."

"Did he order you something from the Mariner?"

"Yeah."

Her dad's laugh was a deep nasal *ho-ho* from the back of his throat that blended right into the next word he was saying. He gave Abby one of those laughs—"*Ho-ho* you lucky dog. What'd you have? Did you get the walleye?"

"I had a grilled cheese."

"Grilled cheese? A guy treats you to dinner and you order a sandwich?"

"It was the ultimate grilled cheese, Dad. It was good."

"Yeah, I bet it was good."

Abby finished the dishes. She walked into the living room and sat on the sofa. Her dad's eyes were still on the TV. Advertisements from the newspaper were in his lap. His feet, in their tan, suede slippers, were propped up on the footrest.

"You want some ice cream?" Abby asked him.

"No, I'm good."

"I think I'm going to get some."

"It's ten degrees outside and you're wanting ice cream. Get me some too, will you?"

She was in the kitchen rummaging through the freezer when she heard the voice of Alex Trebek. Her dad had switched the channel to

Jeopardy. "You better get in here," he yelled. "Books in German for Six Hundred."

"I don't speak German," she yelled back at him.

"You better get in here, Abby. You know this stuff."

"I'm getting your ice cream. I don't know German."

"There's a book about a man who woke up one morning and turned into an insect."

Abby was scooping fudge-swirl ice cream into two bowls. "*Metamorphosis*," she said.

"How did you know that?"

"A lucky guess." She carried their bowls of ice cream into the living room.

"You didn't get your brains from me, I can tell you that."

Their spoons clinked against their bowls. She took a bite of ice cream and said, "*The Sorrows of Young Werther*," answering another clue.

Her dad looked at her and shook his head.

"Don't be so impressed. We read that one in school."

Though Abby was looking forward to spending the summer with her uncle, as she sat on the sofa eating ice cream and watching *Jeopardy* with her dad, she became aware of another feeling—something deep and sad. She didn't want to leave her father alone.

"Dad, are you going to be okay?" What she meant to say was, *Are you going to be okay without me?*

He set his bowl in his lap and looked at her. "Why do you ask that?"

"Just wondering."

And she wondered this because of all of the little things that existed between them—dinners and *Jeopardy* and slow-morning starts, and because of the day they were eating hamburgers in his truck, with greasy wrappers in their laps. He told her that a whale's heart weighed four hundred pounds. He said this because he was thinking of a story he read about a whale that was beached somewhere in Maine. He felt sad for the beached whale. "That's a terrible thing," he said.

He was staring straight ahead, looking through the windshield, and Abby thought, *I must remember this—this is what a broken heart looks like—this is the heart of a broken man.*

That night as they were watching *Jeopardy*, her father stood up from his recliner and walked over to Abby. He reached for her bowl and carried the bowls to the kitchen. Abby listened to the faucet run, heard her dad open the dishwasher and load the bowls onto the rack.

He returned to the living room.

"Are *you* going to be okay?" he asked. "Because that's all I want, Abby, is for you to be okay."

She knew if she looked at him her eyes would get teary. She nodded. "I know," she said.

Then he nodded too and walked back to his recliner.

8

ABBY REMEMBERED UNCLE DENNIS ASKING her to check the attic space under the eaves in his old bedroom, saying there might be some supplies they could use. In a box of yearbooks, report cards, and textbooks, she found a large hooded sweatshirt, soft and faded red. She'd left Grandpa Pete's jacket back at the camp and slipped the sweatshirt over her head. In another box was a cookstove, a pocket saw, a couple of ponchos. Abby dragged the last box out of the attic and carried it down the stairs.

Nonna had just come up from the basement and was holding the duffel bag with clean laundry. She walked with Abby out to the driveway. Then she set the bag down. "Here," she said, handing Abby the keys to Grandpa Pete's pickup. "I want you to take it for the summer. It'll be safer for you on the back roads."

The truck was older than Abby but ran smoothly. Her mom drove this same truck north after Jimmy Pruitt died. She'd stood at the tip of the Abbaye Peninsula. The story was one people liked to tell. They talked about it wistfully, recalling all the details, as if they, too, had stood there with Abby's mom that day.

Abby hugged her grandmother and said thank you for dinner and the keys to the truck and for giving her such a nice birthday.

Then Abby left her little blue car in Nonna's driveway and climbed into her grandfather's truck. It wasn't such a strange thing sitting up high in the pickup. She'd driven her dad's truck plenty of times, and she and Brew had taken Grandpa Pete's truck out before, Brew behind the wheel, and Abby riding shotgun with her feet on the dashboard and her arm draped over the open window. They drove to Escanaba—a small city with all of life's amenities, a little over an hour away—because the truck needed new tires and mechanical adjustments. On their way back they took a detour along the Escanaba River, for no other reason than they liked to explore places.

They pulled off at a portage and walked along the river's edge. Brew said he'd like to fly-fish there sometime, and Abby said he could bring her with him and teach her how to cast a fly rod. They stopped walking and stood along the river's edge, caddis flies jumping, mosquitos buzzing. Brew stepped behind Abby and reached for her wrist. He raised her arm to her side and rocked her elbow back and forth. "Like this," he said, and then extended her arm and brought her hand forward.

The whole thing went smoothly, until the moment became awkward, until they stopped saying anything, and Brew stepped aside, and they began talking about meaningless matters—the rumble the new tires on the truck made because of the hard tread. "They just need some more miles to break in," Brew said. Then Abby heard a white-throated sparrow, yes, she was sure—"*Oh, sweet Canada, Canada, Canada,*" Abby said, mimicking their call, and Brew's and her words didn't seem so meaningless anymore.

• • • • • • • • •

The route back to Bear Slide took Abby through town, past a Catholic church on one side, a Protestant church on the other, a small restaurant that served fish, the post office, the art gallery, and Jake's—the only bar in town. There were cars parked in front of the bar, including Uncle Dennis's green Subaru.

Abby pulled off to the side of the parking lot thinking she'd go in and say hi. But when she climbed out of the truck, she was caught off guard by someone shouting. A man had come out of the bar. Maybe he was in his early twenties. His dark beard was shaved into a goatee. The rest of his face looked gaunt. His jeans hung low on his hips. The girl Abby danced with at the party and who rode on top of the car was yelling and charging toward him.

"What are you doing here? Are you following me?" the girl demanded.

He yelled back, "What did you do with my money?"

"Are you seriously accusing me?" The girl swore up and down that she didn't take anything that belonged to him. "You shouldn't have come all this way. You're wasting your time."

"Where is it?" he yelled.

He wasn't a large man, but he was tall and no doubt strong, and was taking steps toward her.

"You're fucked up, Piper," the girl said.

He smiled then, and there was something mocking to it. "No more fucked up than you."

The girl lunged forward, shoving him in the chest.

"Hey!" someone shouted from across the street.

Abby turned to look. There was Brew, standing next to Tracy. His jeep was parked behind him with the engine idling. Abby knew he must have just gotten back from Marquette and wondered if Tracy had gone with him.

The girl's attention was now on Brew. "What are you looking at? You think I can't take care of myself?"

"Go home, bro," the man said. He was still smiling, like all of this was way too funny.

Tracy stepped in front of Brew and placed a palm across his

chest. She was saying something to him. Abby imagined her telling him to let it go.

A middle-aged couple came out of the bar, drunk and loud. The man stumbled toward the girl. "Is there a problem?" he said.

"No problem," the girl said.

The man called Piper looked at the girl. He stepped closer. "Come on, what are you doing here, anyway?" He placed a hand on her shoulder, but she flung his arm away.

"Get away from me, Piper!"

Abby watched the whole thing play out—Piper pivoting from the girl, that moment of hesitation, hands now on his hips. "You know what, keep the money. I'm out of here," he said.

He walked to his car and climbed in. With a bursting rev of his engine, he pulled onto the road.

Abby looked across the street at Brew, who was shaking his head. He and Tracy got back in his jeep. His top was down. Country music played from his speakers. They drove on. Abby turned once more to the bar, her eyes swimming in the floodlights. The girl was gone. Abby called out to her, but all she heard were the loud voices of the drunk couple climbing into their pickup.

She was relieved when Uncle Dennis emerged from the bar. He took his keys from his pocket and walked to his car. Abby jogged over to him.

"Hey," he said, his voice surprised and his eyes glassed over.

"How was your birthday?" he asked.

Abby's mind was elsewhere—on the girl, on Piper, on Brew. She said her birthday went well. "How was Escanaba?" she asked.

"It was—" He looked away.

"I probably shouldn't drive," he told her.

"You don't have to. I got you."

He walked alongside Abby but then stopped when he saw the truck.

"Nonna gave it to me for the summer," Abby said.

"Too many potholes for the Smurfmobile to handle?"

"Something like that."

After they pulled onto the road, Uncle Dennis reached over and tugged on the sweatshirt. "Hey, where'd you get this?"

"It was in the attic." Abby told him about the box of supplies in the back of the truck.

"Oh, yeah? What'd you find?"

She ran through the list of items.

He said the ponchos would come in handy.

Then he looked at Abby again. "I forgot I had that." A handful of seconds passed. "It belonged to your dad," he said.

She gave Uncle Dennis an inquisitive look.

"It belonged to J.P." He reached for the hood of the sweatshirt and pulled it over her head. "Little Red Riding Hood. It looks good on you."

"Are you serious? This belonged to my dad?"

"Yeah, it's crazy, isn't it, that you found it? After all these years."

"And on my birthday," Abby said.

"Yeah, I know."

Abby pushed the hood back down because she was trying to see the road. "Do you believe in that sort of thing?" she asked. "I mean, some things seem too random to be a coincidence, right?"

"I wish I did, but I don't know."

They continued down the empty road in silence. She thought of the events around her biological dad's death—swimming in the lake, his foolish jump off a ledge. Maybe he hit a rock. Maybe the water was too shallow. Biological was how she thought of him, because she had a father. He was in Eagle River. On the weekends he worked in his garage. He repaired neighbors' lawnmowers. He tinkered with engine parts. Sometimes he sat at his workbench and drank a diet cola and got quiet. He woke early most mornings, and at night often fell asleep in his recliner with the TV on.

"You okay?" Uncle Dennis asked her.

"Yeah, I'm okay."

"Birthdays are hard. I should have been there."

"No, really. It wasn't hard. It was nice."

"Hey, I got something for you." And then, "Oh, shit, it's back at the car."

They were too tired to turn around.

"I'll get it for you in the morning," he said.

They rode in silence for a while after that, until Uncle Dennis said, "Sometimes what's done has to be done over and over."

"Does this have to do with the sweatshirt or your trip to Escanaba?"

He reached in his back pocket and pulled out his wallet. Then he removed a picture and handed it to her.

Abby held the photo over the steering wheel and glanced at the woman's face several times before handing it back to him. "I didn't know men did that, carried pictures of girlfriends in their wallets." She looked at him just long enough to see him study the image before returning the photo to the plastic sleeve.

He didn't talk about her right away. Instead he talked about the white caps of the Alaska Range and a two-hundred-mile river that wound through bogs and floodplains and uplands. "We explored all of it together, the natural changes in the ecosystem structure, the young stands of paper birch and white spruce. Most of the older trees had been wiped out by fires in the highlands and erosion in the floodplains."

He continued, "Her name was Tawny. We had this thing we'd do whenever we'd come upon a tree that had made it over two hundred years. We'd open a bottle of some kind of spirit to celebrate all the years the tree had survived. It was Tawny's idea, and she'd make a toast and wish the tree well." His tone softened. "That's really beautiful, right? That she would do that?"

"Maybe kind of weird and beautiful," Abby told him.

"Anyway, you know that thing where you're talking, and the other person is paying attention, really looking at you," he said, "and they respond in kind with a similar story or a similar thought, and the conversation just keeps going. I guess you could say the conversation stopped going. So I tried harder. It's rather pathetic when I think about it, how much I wanted her approval.

"One night we were in Fairbanks, and I'd had too much to drink, which you should never do, by the way."

"Point taken," Abby said.

"Yeah, so I'd had too much to drink, and I said some things I shouldn't have said. She did this thing where she squinted into her drink, and then she told me, 'I think that's enough. I think I've had enough.' She complained about her space like she was talking about legroom on an airplane. And that was it. We broke up. I decided to apply for this grant. But then my Lab, Monty, got sick. Tawny heard about him and reached out. She asked if she could see him before I had to put him down."

"So what happened?" Abby asked.

"Tawny came to see Monty. She was being really kind like she used to be. The next day after Monty was gone, she called to see how I was doing. We stayed on the phone a long time. I thought something might still be there between us, so I kept her picture."

He went on to tell Abby about his meeting up with Tawny earlier that night.

"She emailed me last week. Said she was in town visiting family. She wanted to know if she could see me." There wasn't a phone line at Bear Slide, but a friend of his in the village had dial-up Internet.

"You got your hopes up," Abby said.

"Yeah, what can I say, I got my hopes up. It's funny how that can happen. How a person can give something more meaning than is actually there."

After a long pause, he said, "I shouldn't be telling you all of this. It must be the alcohol."

"I don't mind."

He stopped talking, and Abby thought about how quiet the inside of a car or a truck is at night and wondered why that was. She looked over at Uncle Dennis to see if maybe he'd fallen asleep, but he wasn't asleep. His eyes were wide open, and he was just looking around at all that night outside the window.

"I don't think you're pathetic," she said. "I think you're gallant."

He laughed, full-throated. "Well, now that's a word I've never been called before. *Gallant*." Then he became serious again. "Have you ever been in love, Abby?"

"I thought I was," she said.

"What happened?"

"I guess he doesn't feel the same way."

"Well, that makes two of us."

Abby felt sad for Uncle Dennis losing his dog and his girlfriend, and told him so.

"I kid you not," he said, "losing Monty is a whole lot worse."

There was just the hard-packed grit of the road and their thoughts and the shadows of the trees, and Abby said, "That's because he never stopped loving you."

9

A WEEK AFTER ABBY'S BIRTHDAY, she saw the girl again. It was Saturday morning. Abby had stopped at the market to pick up miscellaneous items—peanut butter and bread and apples, and canned ravioli, which she'd been craving. Uncle Dennis said to grab some cans of mandarin oranges while she was at it. Then she drove to the post office to mail a postcard to her dad. That's when Abby saw the funeral notice taped to the post office door—*Services for Wayne Emerson, 10 am, St. John the Baptist Catholic Church*.

She drove up the hill where cars were parking alongside the street and filling up the church parking lot. Abby wasn't dressed for a funeral. She wore a sleeveless, floral shirt and jeans and sandals—but she could sit in the back and wait for Brew, and the peninsula was never a formal place.

She walked up to the church behind a group of others, to where a man wearing a dark suit greeted them at the door. There was a guestbook in the narthex, and a basket with funeral cards on the vestibule table. Abby picked up a funeral card, then entered the nave and slid in a pew at the back. She looked at Wayne's image on the laminated card—sandy hair, smiling face, a sky behind him. He looked young, and he was—only thirty-three.

The rest of the pew filled up from the other end, and there was the girl from the party on the beach now sitting with Abby.

They acknowledged each other and introduced themselves because neither had done so at the party. The girl's name was Seda.

Abby looked around as more people entered the church. "I thought Brew would be here."

"I think he had to work," Seda told her.

There were bodies shuffling in the pews, and the stuffy sweetness of flowers and old wood and old varnish.

The opening hymn was announced, pages were turned, and soon the room filled with the sounds of the organ. Abby sat next to the aisle and watched the pallbearers wheel the casket with Wayne's body to the front of the church. Behind them were Wayne's wife and children and parents, moving to the front rows.

All of it came back to Abby—her grandfather's funeral—her family sitting in the same pews as Wayne's family, Brew sitting beside her, and on the other side of her was her dad.

A baby cried. One of Wayne's nephews sang the prayer of St. Francis. The church felt warmer than it had, sunlight through the south-facing windows, different people fanning themselves with the funeral program.

Father Bruce stood and relayed the words of the Twenty-Third Psalm and talked about how it was written by David who had been a farm boy. Wayne Emerson had been a farm boy. His two sons were growing up on a farm now.

These were Abby's thoughts—the itchy feel of hay on her skin, the earthy smell of a barn—pine shavings and fermented silage and the subtle waft of ammonia—the clucking of chickens, the flapping of pigeons, the sound of the tractor starting—and there was the light—golden and subdued and dusty. She was five when her parents moved back to Garden and rented the white farmhouse with the big, red barn, and filled the barn with chickens, a tractor, a spreader, a baler, and that next spring, planted hay and alfalfa in the south meadows.

• • • • • • • • •

Father Bruce had stopped speaking. Long silences followed. Abby's face felt flushed. The sun beat stronger. Then the simple movement of air from the narthex, a subtle breeze from an open door, clean and clear—lake air, Abby thought.

The Agnes Dei began—*Lamb of God, who takes away the sins of the world, have mercy on us. Lamb of God, who takes away the sins of the world, have mercy on us. Lamb of God, who takes away the sins of the world, grant us peace.*

A woman and a man led the Eucharistic hymn. Abby stepped into the aisle behind the others to receive Communion, the music picking up around her. Her heartbeat quickened, her chest and lungs so full she was sure she couldn't breathe. This was what was happening to her and she couldn't stop it. She turned away and receded to the back of the church, walked through the vestibule and out the heavy doors.

She didn't know that Seda had followed her, that Seda was with her now, until Seda placed a hand on Abby's arm. The two of them stood there on the sidewalk in front of the church, sunlight in their eyes, minutes passing by. Then Seda said they should get out of there, because that would be the best thing, just to leave and go somewhere else.

Abby's truck was parked across the street. A place came to Abby's mind, where she'd once parked her car and looked out at the Summer Islands, patches of emerald on the lake. Was she sixteen then?—she thought so—the sky cast with an amber hue like the color of a deer. She could almost feel that sky now, gentle and amber, even though the sky before them was blue.

So Seda and Abby walked across the street and climbed into the truck. Abby turned the truck around and drove south through town and onto the county road.

10

ABBY CONTINUED SOUTH, PAST DEVILS Corner and Snake Island and Fayette Park, past Sand Bay and Sac Bay. At some point Seda said she had a headache. There was aspirin in the glove compartment and a bottle of water in the cupholder in front of the seat. Seda swallowed a couple of tablets. When she returned the container, she found a piece of construction paper.

She unfolded the paper and was looking at a drawing of a boat and a stick figure with a fishing pole. At the bottom of the picture was the name *Kee Kee*, the nickname for Abby's mom.

Abby reached for the drawing and held it against the steering wheel. She'd never seen it before. "My mom drew this."

Abby folded the paper, and Seda returned it to the glove compartment.

They were both quiet then, windows down, Seda's head against the headrest, Abby's arm on the door. Seda turned up the dial on the radio. A station was playing soft rock—Bryan Adams, Elton John, Robson and Jerome.

Abby drove through the township of Fairport to Anderson Point, where the pavement ended at Peterson Brothers Fairport Fishery and boat launch. She pulled up to the water and looked out at the fishing boats and the Little and Big Summer Islands. Water lapped against the shore and against the boats that were tied to mooring posts along the jetty. Gulls squawked at one another.

Abby watched the movement of a man and a woman walking back from the wooden dock that extended off the jetty. A boxy-shaped dog was trotting around them. As they came closer, she recognized Tanner—one of the tribal fishermen who supplied her family's fish house. She'd known him since he was a boy, delivering catch with his father.

The woman bent over and stroked the dog's head, then turned and began walking away. The man started jogging toward her. "Hey, Gale," he called out. He had something for her in his right hand. After she'd taken the small package from him and they'd exchanged a few more words, she continued across the parking area, eventually walking by the truck. Abby noticed the way the woman was dressed—overalls, much like the ones Abby wore in the field, a tank top and brimmed cap.

The breeze was nice through the windows. Sunlight sparkled on the windshield.

Seda said, "Have you ever been to the islands?"

Abby didn't think she had. Maybe when she was small, but she couldn't remember.

"We should go sometime," Seda said.

Abby leaned her head out the driver's side window and looked up at the sky. A plane was flying above them.

"Have you ever been on a plane?" Abby asked.

"No, have you?"

"No. Brew and I used to talk about going to California. He wanted to see the redwoods."

"He has a girlfriend," Seda said.

"I know."

"And he's your cousin."

"Not by blood or anything." Then Abby said, "We're friends, that's all."

Seda asked, "Why do they call him Brew?"

"It's short for Brewster. It was his grandfather's name, on his mother's side of the family."

"It sounds like something you'd name your dog. *Brew*, sit. *Brew*, lie down. *Brewster*, come!"

"You're making fun of him."

"I'm not making fun of him."

"Seriously. Why are you smiling?" Abby said.

Abby thought about the night at the bar, and Brew getting out of his jeep and Tracy standing beside him.

"I saw you at Jake's the other night," Abby said.

"With Piper?"

"Yeah."

"It's not what you think. We're not a couple. We just hang out sometimes."

"He said you took something of his."

Seda was quiet. She was looking at the sky—mostly blue, with tufts of white. "What do the clouds remind you of?" she asked.

"They're cumulus clouds. They remind me of summer."

"I see a snowy hillside."

A large bird soon appeared, soaring as high as the clouds. "What do you think it is?" Seda asked.

"It looks like a waterbird, with its wingspan and long body. Maybe a blue heron," Abby said.

They fell silent after that, Seda now looking straight ahead, eyes that were burnt brown with caramel flecks along the edges. Then she said, "I took Piper's money, almost four hundred dollars. I'd gone to the kitchen to get a glass of water. Piper was asleep. There was a knife on top of a couple of dirty plates in the sink. I picked up the knife and held it over my wrist."

Abby gasped.

"I didn't do anything, but that's how I felt," Seda said. "Then I saw Piper's wallet lying on the counter. I thought maybe I'd just take a twenty. I didn't know there would be that much."

"Does anyone else know?" Abby asked.

"Who would I tell? I'm on my own, Abby. I'm so fucking alone."

You think of things later. Always you think of things later, things you wish you'd said, but Abby's mind was drifting. When she was fifteen, she'd ended up at a party with some people she barely knew from school. She found herself in a trailer filled with smoke and beer and noise and a tweed sofa that made her bare legs and the palms of her hands itch. Someone handed her a beer. She accepted it because she wanted to be invisible, but she didn't drink the beer. The can was moist, and everyone around her was talking in loud voices, including the people who'd brought her there and then left her on this couch and were now slowly fading into a backdrop of smoke from weed and cigarettes. Abby stood from the sofa and walked outside into a yard with patchy grass and a bench swing hanging from a rusty metal frame. She poured out the beer. It splattered onto her feet and sandals and legs, as if a drunk boy had been standing next to her relieving himself. She dropped the can and walked over to the swing. She swung for a while and, every so often, would lift up her thighs and peel off pieces of white paint.

Seda stared out the passenger window. Abby wanted to believe that Piper would forget about the money, that Seda would be all right.

The smell of gasoline wafted in from the boats, and there was the smell of decaying plant matter and the fresh mineral tang of lake water. Abby smelled sweet things too—ripe clover and milkweed that was growing in bunches among pallets stacked near the shore, and the suntan lotion she'd applied earlier that morning.

Seda was wearing dreamcatcher earrings, large, dangly things the color of turquoise. "Hold still," Abby said. She removed one of the earrings and held it up to the diamond sunlight on the windshield.

Seda laughed. "What are you doing?"

"I'm protecting you," Abby said. "I'm keeping all the bad omens at bay."

Seda pulled her legs onto the seat and crossed her ankles. She wore her hair in loose braids. Long wisps hung around her face.

Abby brushed the strands aside with her fingertips and slid the earring back in place. Then she rolled the rubber band off the ends of the left braid and combed through Seda's hair, carefully working out the knots. She separated the hair again and re-braided it. Seda turned her head slowly, offering the other side. Taking her time, Abby re-braided the right section as well.

Seda told Abby she wished she had her own place. "Where there aren't coffee stains in the cups I drink from, or when I go to brush my teeth, Piper's whiskers aren't scattered all over the sink."

Abby was confused. "You live with him?"

"No, but I stay over at his apartment sometimes. Then we start fighting. Things aren't any better at home."

Seda continued, "There's a story Piper told me. He'd gone hunting with a couple of friends. He couldn't get a buck, so he shot a doe. Nobody wants the doe, he said. Everybody wants the trophy. But the doe didn't die. And when he found her, he had to shoot her a second time. He said she was looking right at him when he pulled the trigger. I don't want to be the deer anymore. I want to be the falcon that gets away."

Then Seda asked Abby if butterflies die, because one just lit upon the windshield. "I mean, do they die when the summer is over and the flowers are gone? Don't they need the nectar in the flowers to survive?"

"They migrate," Abby told her.

Seda was registering what Abby said. "But they're so small."

Abby told her how the monarchs could migrate all the way from Canada to Mexico, and about the billions of songbirds, some weighing less than half an ounce, that traveled each year across deserts and oceans and back again. Abby learned this information from a customer at the bookstore, an older man who spent his summers bird-watching. She told Seda how the forests and green spaces gave the birds waypoints. "They need places to rest, to refuel," Abby said. "And the vegetation helps keep them safe from predators."

"That's cool, the way you know this stuff," Seda said.

The butterfly flitted off, its amber wings catching the sunlight.

"They call that one the Eastern comma, or sometimes the comma anglewing," Abby told her. "I used to catch them. I'd study them and draw pictures, and then I'd let them go. They don't migrate like the other butterflies. They hibernate in hollow trees and logs." Abby went on to describe other things about the Eastern comma, how they made their homes in wooded areas and that when they closed their wings, they blended into the bark of the trees, and that instead of nectar, they fed on sap and decaying fruit. She told Seda of the work she was doing that summer with Uncle Dennis and how the anglewings would light upon her arms and shoulders. "They like the minerals in the dirt and sweat on my skin," she said.

"I like their name," Seda said.

"Anglewings?" Abby asked.

"No, *comma*. It's an interesting name for a butterfly."

"There's a silver marking on the underside of their wings. It's shaped just like a comma."

"*Comma*," Seda said. "That's what my life needs. A comma, a pause."

Abby was struck by an idea, and when it came to her, she knew it was something she had to see through, as if all of it were part of a larger plan.

Falcon

11

ABBY'S PLAN CAME ABOUT NATURALLY. Over the past week, she and Uncle Dennis had worked apart from each other, expanding their territory deeper into the forest. They'd pack their supplies for the day, and then drive separately, navigating their way as close as they could get to their respective plots before parking and hiking the rest of the way in.

On one of the afternoons when Abby finished collecting data for plot VSG221, and Uncle Dennis was at a different location at least several miles away, she explored her way back to her truck, taking a different path as she often did. The sun still shone above the tree canopy, and up ahead light pooled in open recesses, like stepping stones toward a larger clearing.

Columbines, with their long, slender stems and red, tubular spurs, flourished in the opening as if long ago someone had planted them there, and beyond them stood a real log cabin, like that a homesteader might have built. She walked through the field of columbines and up to the front porch that creaked and sagged with her weight. Pressing her face against a cloudy window, she looked into a kitchen. There was a black iron stove with a kettle, and open cupboards full of trinkets. She then walked around the cabin to a section of land encompassed by a fieldstone wall that appeared to have once been gardens or a small, tilled field but was now overgrown with weeds. Leaning against the back of the house was a wooden ladder that led to the roof. As with everything else, the ladder looked as if it had been undisturbed for a long time.

Abby checked the coordinates on her GPS. She was still on forestland, which included nearly twenty-two thousand acres spread out over the peninsula, almost all of it tax reverted, and she understood the cabin must have belonged to a property owner who'd fallen behind on their taxes.

And so that afternoon in the truck, as she listened to Seda talk about needing a place of her own, Abby thought of the cabin and told Seda she had a place in mind, not much farther from where they were parked at Anderson Point.

Abby drove as far as they could down an old logging road. To their right, in a field of yellow grass, were sand cranes the color of hot chocolate. It was Seda who saw them first, who pointed them out and asked what they were. Abby told her she had a good eye, as the birds blended almost seamlessly into the landscape.

Abby changed into her hiking boots and grabbed her pack, where she'd already transferred some of the grocery items—one of the two loaves of bread, the jar of peanut butter, a couple of the apples—things she didn't think Uncle Dennis would miss.

She and Seda followed a well-worn deer trail that led them alongside a bog and through a fern meadow, and then into an old cedar and pine forest. The trees were larger there, the space between them more expansive. The ground became a cushion of mulch from the tree duff. Up ahead their path widened into an emerald opening of velvety moss.

"It's so peaceful here," Seda said.

"We're getting closer to the water," Abby told her. "We're almost at the tip of the peninsula." The southernmost part of the peninsula, called Point Detour, was less than a half mile wide. Pretty soon, beyond a short stretch of woods, Lake Michigan would surround them on three sides.

The topography changed once more. They crisscrossed their way through a tumble field of windthrow the color of driftwood, and there was the copse of saplings and brambles ahead, and from there the columbines and the little cabin. Upon entering the clearing, Seda took off running. Then, out of breath, she stopped just before the cabin. She doubled over, hot and sweaty and smiling, and planted her hands above her knees.

They stood on the porch in front of the door and removed their shoes, wet with mud, and their wet socks, which they laid out to dry. Abby turned the iron doorknob, and just like that, they were inside. The floorboards felt like cool earth beneath their feet and the air smelled musty.

Seda was whispering half a hundred things at once, and though Abby was happy to have brought her here and was glad to witness her enthusiasm, she began to experience a little trepidation, as if they'd entered a museum and were forbidden to touch any of the relics. But then Seda touched them anyway and picked things up: a glass Coca-Cola bottle filled with dried stems, in the center of a trestle table. She brought the bottle toward her face and pretended she could smell the flowers. Tiny, dry petals were scattered across the tabletop. Seda swept them into her hand, stirring up the dust particles, and said, "Make a wish," and blew dust and petals into the air like confetti. There was a china teacup in a saucer on the counter. She raised the cup to her lips and pretended to take a sip. In another second she flitted over to a black-and-white photo behind filmy glass in a frame on an end table. Abby said, "Maybe you shouldn't," but Seda was already holding the picture of a young man with dark eyes and dark hair and said, "So handsome, don't you think?" They both thought he looked like an old-time Hollywood movie star.

There were paintings on the walls and books on shelves; a red velvet sofa; a small wooden chair beneath the southwest window; ceramic and copper planters with hard, dried stalks and stubbles; a trunk with a leather case on top and next to it a stack of records in paper sleeves. There was a stone fireplace built into the east-facing wall, with a mantel painted white. On top of the mantel were birds' nests and feathers and rocks.

The cabin was a three-room structure, with a front room across the south-facing porch side that included a sitting area and dining area. Off the dining area, through a wide opening, was a small kitchen in the northwest corner of the house. Along the back wall of the sitting area was a door that Abby assumed led to a bedroom at the northeast corner of the cabin. The door was cracked open. A sliver of gray light cast a long shadow across the floor.

Seda had continued moving from one thing to another and was now focused on the mostly closed door. Abby cautioned her not to open it, because she'd been considering everything—the dead plants; the coffee grinds in the bottom of the teacup; the stack of books on the floor beside the sofa, like those a person might have been intending to read; the unfinished needlepoint in an embroidery hoop that someone had left on top of an ottoman—and she feared Seda might find the remains of a person in the room. But Abby was like the air out of Canada, moving in Seda's wake. Seda flung the door open. Her feet were light, and she leapt onto the bed made of iron and painted white, its mattress covered with gold-printed sheets and colorful quilts. She lay on her back and swept her arms and legs open like a child making snow angels.

On the side table next to the bed was a book turned over, a pair of reading glasses, an empty water glass, a vase filled with dried hydrangeas. There was a wicker chair in one corner of the room and a wardrobe in the other. Hanging from a hook on the wardrobe was a large cardigan sweater.

Seda puckered her lips together. “Oohh,” she said. “Look at that.” She climbed off the bed and reached for the sweater and put it on. It hung from her shoulders and she wrapped its gaping sides over herself as if it were a blanket. Then she opened the doors of the wardrobe where inside floral blouses and bibbed overalls hung on hangers. On the top shelf was a flannel nightgown and a wide-brimmed hat made of straw. At the bottom of the wardrobe were tall rubber boots. All around was evidence of a life once lived, and Abby couldn’t help but wonder whose history Seda was replacing.

Seda removed the straw hat from the shelf and pulled it down over her head. Abby loved her in that moment, for this and for all the little particularities that made her something different, and because Abby understood that with every object Seda picked up and held and cradled and claimed in a way that was all her own, she was unraveling something else from another existence.

They returned to the porch and slipped on their damp socks and shoes. Then they followed the property around the house where there once had been gardens and discovered a well pump. The lever worked, and after a workout, the water spurted forth. Once it was clear, they cupped their hands and drank.

That was when Seda saw the ladder. After testing the rungs, she and Abby climbed to the roof, which didn’t appear as old as the house, nor did it look to be in need of repair. From the top of the roof, they could see Lake Michigan. They sat together, and Seda said how cool it would be if there were a deck on top of the roof, just big enough for the two of them.

The air was gentle, the clouds were soft—tiny tufts of white that looked like a honeycomb. Abby knew it was getting late and that they would need to hike back to the truck.

As if Seda could read her mind, she said, “I’m staying.”

Abby was beginning to doubt her plan. She was curious about who owned the cabin and wondered if someone might be coming back, or else why wouldn't the place be in more disrepair?

"I thought you were going to find a body," Abby said. "When you opened the door to the bedroom. You could still find a body somewhere." Abby said this because the house and everything in it, and the untended gardens, and the well pump felt like a ballad that had either stopped abruptly or been interrupted, as if Abby could hear the woman saying, "Hang on a minute, I'll be right back. I just have to make a phone call, or run an errand, or pick some juneberries or raspberries or strawberries. But I'll return, and I'll wash the dishes then. I'll rinse out my glass. I'll finish the books I was reading and the needlepoint."

But Seda said, "Not if her body is in the lake. Maybe she went down to the water for a swim. Maybe she got a cramp, or the water was too cold and her heart stopped, and the waves carried her away."

"But why are all of her things still here? Why didn't someone come for her belongings?"

"Maybe everyone she ever loved died before her."

Seda then pointed out a large piece of driftwood about twenty yards from the cabin. Abby said it looked like a bear sitting on its haunches. Seda said it looked like a Buddha, and she called it her Bear Buddha.

Abby said they should give the place a name, and after thinking about that, Seda came up with the Falcon's Nest, and Abby said the name was perfect.

The light was changing. The birds were starting to make noise. Abby didn't want to leave, but she knew she should get going. "I have the next couple of days off. I can bring more food and supplies," she said.

The breeze carried the sweet, tangy smell of the trees. Seda removed the hat and placed it on Abby's head. Then she tilted her head back and gazed at the sky. "The stars are coming out. It's not even dark, but you can see them."

"Maybe they're satellites," Abby said.

"No, they're stars."

Seda continued to stare at the sky.

Abby said, "So you'll be okay?"

"I'll be okay. As long as you bring me food."

"Whatever you need."

"Something sweet."

"Okay."

"I don't want anyone to know I'm here," Seda said.

"I won't tell anyone."

"What about Brew?"

"He won't know."

They sat perfectly still.

"It feels weird when someone leaves," Seda said. "There's a shift. Like all of a sudden I'm afraid, but then after a while I'm not afraid anymore."

"Do you want me to stay?" Abby asked her.

"No. You need to go."

"I'll see you tomorrow?"

"I'm not going anywhere."

12

WHEN ABBY RETURNED TO THE camp, Uncle Dennis was standing outside in front of the headlights of a Delta County Sheriff cruiser. The car was backing out of the dirt drive. Abby waited with her blinker on until the deputy pulled away.

"Who was that?" Abby asked.

"A guy I went to school with."

She followed Uncle Dennis into the camp. He told her there had been some break-ins in the area—antiques, fishing gear, cash were stolen. The officer wanted to know if they'd seen anything suspicious, and Uncle Dennis said no, nothing at all.

Uncle Dennis emptied the bag of groceries, not paying attention to what Abby had or had not purchased, just as she'd predicted.

She walked over to the table to return his change to his wallet. When she opened the wallet, there were the photos he kept in their plastic sleeves—school pictures of her and Catherine and Brew; an old church photo of the family when Uncle Dennis and her mom were young; a photo of Uncle Dennis and J.P., Abby's biological dad, shirtless and in jeans, posing with their fishing rods. But the picture of the Tanana Valley girl was gone.

Uncle Dennis said he'd grill steaks. He went outside to light the charcoal while Abby went to take a shower. She dressed in jeans and the red sweatshirt, then joined Uncle Dennis in the small clearing behind the camp.

He'd already put the steaks on the grill and was standing watch over them. His right hand was wrapped around a bottle of beer. "There's another one in the fridge," he said. Abby was surprised. He'd never offered her alcohol before.

They stood side by side drinking their beers. Fat drizzled and popped and hissed on the charcoal, and among the glowing coals were shards of a glossy photo curling at the edges and turning black. Abby knew it was the picture of Tawny.

"It feels kind of like a funeral," Abby said.

"I guess it is," Uncle Dennis said. "Sometimes you just need to put something in the past or else you can get really stuck. Besides, I know what Tawny looks like. I don't need the photo to remind me." He tapped his head a couple of times with the index finger of his left hand. "Got everything stored up here. Those were good times," he said. "I'm not going to forget them, but it's time to move on."

"I think that works nicely as a eulogy."

Uncle Dennis laughed. "I think you're right."

They clinked their beers together.

"How was your day?" he asked.

"I went to another funeral," Abby said. "A real one."

"Oh, yeah?"

"Wayne Emerson. Did you know him?"

"Heard of him."

"He wasn't very old," Abby said,

"Make you think of your mom?"

"A little."

"Wasn't aware you knew Wayne."

"I didn't. I was supposed to go with Brew. But he got called into work."

Uncle Dennis told her about his trip to Escanaba to pick up supplies but said he spent most of the day compiling data and building maps.

Then their conversation moved on to other things, like glaciolacustrine deposits and dolomite fractures, because Uncle Dennis had become fascinated with the underworld of the trees. "It's like their roots are the most powerful jackhammer in the world. They can penetrate through anything."

At some point when they were back inside eating their steaks and potato salad, Abby noticed a couple of books, including one with a bright-colored cover about the hidden world of fungi, and another about mosses and lichens.

For her birthday Uncle Dennis had given her a forest-green hat made out of Merino wool and a card to the public library in Escanaba, their closest book resource. He had his own card and while he was there had checked out some books for himself. Abby picked up the book about mosses and lichens and flipped it over to read the copy on the back.

"I was thinking," Uncle Dennis said. "Maybe we should include all the different lichens in our inventory."

Abby laughed at first. How could they do that? The lichens were everywhere. But then again, so were the trees, and she reminded herself that they were only conducting inventories of small-sized, random plots.

Uncle Dennis told her how important the lichens were and how they absorbed carbon, heavy metals, and other pollutants. Scientists were able to extract those toxins from the lichens to determine the levels present in the atmosphere.

He went on to explain the complex life form of the lichen as a symbiotic partnership between a fungus and an alga, with the fungus being the dominant partner. The fungi provided protection and the algae provided food. And though Abby wasn't one to gravitate toward scientific topics, she found herself identifying with the conversation and giving it special meaning. She thought of Seda and the cabin, as if Abby and Seda had their own sort of symbiotic partnership.

Uncle Dennis opened the book Abby was holding, to show her pictures of different lichen species. She pointed to all the ones she recognized and learned their names: foliose, crustose, fruticose. There were the reindeer lichen, the color of sage, a type of fruticose species, that grew in small bunches. She'd crouched to the ground and run her hands over their small, shrub-like branches, and thought to herself that she'd like to grow them in pots, because she loved their texture and muted color.

And then Uncle Dennis began talking about the woodland caribou because the lichens were the caribou's primary sustenance. Nighttime had fallen by now. They were still sitting at the table, talking beneath the glow of the small fixture that hung from the ceiling. Uncle Dennis told Abby that the last caribou on the Upper Peninsula's mainland was killed in 1912, and on Isle Royale in 1928. "They used to dominate these woods," he said. "From Hudson's Bay all the way to Mackinac Island." The old-growth forests had diminished. Everything was shifting north. That was why he and Abby were here. Uncle Dennis called the caribou *forest wraiths*. "Their spirits are all around us."

A picture formed in Abby's mind—an image of a caribou, ghost-like in the woods—a large, beautiful creature, and the caribou's breath was warm, like vapor, like a warm cloud moving through the trees.

13

IN THE MORNING, ABBY TALKED to Uncle Dennis about bringing the *Little Daline* down to Fairport and mooring her at the marina. She told him the boat would give her easier access to the survey plots at the southern tip of the peninsula, which was true, but it would also make her trip to the cabin and the transport of provisions easier. Her idea made perfect sense to him. She asked if he thought Nonna would mind, and no, he didn't think she would.

Uncle Dennis had his own agenda that day and left the camp before Abby, which allowed her to collect some items she knew he wouldn't miss—the camping stove and cookware she'd found in the attic at Nonna's, a flashlight and batteries, a lantern and a couple of canisters of white propane.

Then there was the business of purchasing supplies at the corner market—would Seda prefer peach preserves or raspberry jam? And what flavors of canned soup did she like?

As Abby was paying for the items, she noticed a woman standing at the community bulletin board—the same woman she'd seen with Tanner the day before, red cap pulled over her head, sunglasses slid over the brim. She was jotting down a number on the brown paper bag she was carrying.

Abby stopped at the bulletin board on her way out—a quilt raffle at the gallery, a barbecue dinner at the township fire department, free calico kittens, a flier for Wilson Pelletier Boat Rentals with a number to call. Abby knew she'd seen the name before, but it wasn't until arriving at Nonna's that she remembered the piece of paper in the pocket of her grandfather's jacket.

Nonna thought Abby having the boat was a good idea. After they lifted the trailer onto the hitch, Abby asked her, "Who are the Pelletiers?"

"They're a family in town. Do you remember them?"

"No, should I?"

"It was Don Pelletier and his wife who found you the night of the fire. They brought you back here."

Abby tried to remember. "I was on the road," she said, because this is what people had told her.

"That's right," Nonna said. "That's where they found you."

Nonna knelt on the ground to put the hitch pin in place. Abby told her about the piece of paper in Grandpa Pete's jacket.

Nonna was surprised. She thought she'd checked all his pockets.

Then Nonna said, "I think you used to play with one of their granddaughters."

Abby was about to leave. She turned to look at her grandmother. She could see herself younger—small body, summer skin, golden hair, like apples—the smell of chlorine, blue water, a green blow-up float. "They had a swimming pool," Abby said.

"I'm not sure."

"There were a bunch of girls."

"I think so."

Abby remembered paneling inside a house; a silk-flower wreath; tall, plastic tumblers. "I only played there once. But I think I remember this. There were teenage girls. I was playing with the younger sister.

“Was her name Nan?” Abby asked.

“I don’t remember. The girls are mostly grown now.”

Abby shook her head. “Why was I there? It was the summertime. We would have already moved.” And then she knew. The summer after the fire. Her mother’s memorial.

She was young, her family told her. She’d already been through enough. Abby thought of Wayne Emerson’s service—the toddlers and babies and young children. She thought of her grandfather’s funeral. Catherine and Gracie were there.

The day before, at St. John’s, she’d felt a strong need to be in the church again. And yet, in the same strange way, not there, with so many people and the community of voices all around her, so that when she stepped into the aisle, it was all too much. The funeral was too much. Yes, that is what her family knew, that is what they understood. That is why on the day of her mother’s memorial, she was at the Pelletiers’.

• • • • • • • • •

The Sunday was cool and cloudy and interspersed with light rain. At the boat launch at Peterson’s, a fisherman straddled a four-wheeler and drove up the hill. He pulled alongside Abby’s truck, rain hood over his head, then motioned with his hand for her to roll down her window.

That’s when Abby saw the man was Tanner, grown up now, but the same smiling eyes.

“I saw your grandfather’s truck,” he said. “Wanted to see who was behind the wheel.”

And this is what Abby remembered—a younger Tanner and his father approaching her grandfather’s fish house in their boat, Tanner at the bow, ready to leap over the bow rail, line in hand, brown hair streaked with golden highlights from the sun, a smile on his face. Or this—little Tanner on the fish house dock, five-gallon pail held with both hands out in front of him, water sloshing from side to side, boy arm muscles stretched taught, body leaning backward.

Light rain fell. The ATV idled beside her.

"I hear you're back for the summer," Tanner said, because this was the peninsula, and word traveled fast.

"Got your grandfather's little boat, too, I see. Haven't seen her in a while."

"You been on the water today?" Abby asked.

"Just coming in."

"How are the conditions?"

"Misty and wet, but the water's smooth."

Abby told Tanner her plans to take the *Little Daline* around the point. He said he'd help her get the boat in the water.

He parked his ATV off to the side, then climbed in next to the outboard. After Abby backed the trailer down the ramp, Tanner started the engine and put the boat in reverse.

The boat was now rigged with a twenty-five-horsepower outboard with an electric start, instead of the fifteen-horsepower motor Abby and Brew used when they were young. Even so, Abby knew she'd have to stay close to the shore.

Abby pulled away from the water and parked the truck, then carried her provisions down to the jetty. Tanner had already tied the boat to a mooring post and left the engine idling. He pointed to a house on the hill, a little farther from where Abby left the truck. "Live there with my dad's younger brother now," he told her.

Abby remembered Tanner having an uncle.

"What about your dad?" Abby asked.

"Thought you would have heard."

Tanner looked around, past the boats and the buoys. "Got caught laundering fish. He's over in Escanaba. Gets out in a year."

"I'm sorry. I hadn't heard."

Abby knew of this sort of thing—a tribal fisher with a commercial license buying subsistence fish from other tribal fishermen, then selling the fish to wholesalers. Tanner's family held both subsistence and commercial licenses, and the commercial licenses were getting harder to come by.

Tanner was back on his ATV, and Abby said thank you for his help.

She sat at the stern, one hand on the throttle, images of Tanner and his father coming to mind, his father passing talk back and forth with the men at the fish house. She remembered the truck he drove—a flatbed, painted light blue. Hadn't she and Brew and Tanner played in the back of the truck once? She remembered the three of them—Tanner and Brew and herself—climbing the side rails and laughing.

Abby skirted as close to the shore as she could, and after passing a few private parcels of land, all to her left was a thick forest of evergreens. The cloud cover had thinned and the sun broke through, water droplets glistening like diamonds, clusters of seagulls swooping and gliding overhead. The closer she got to the tip of the peninsula, the shallower the water became. She was approaching the brown, rocky reef that jutted almost a quarter mile out into Lake Michigan, preventing the passage of larger motorboats, and not far past the reef was Big Summer Island. The shoreline was dotted with cylindrical rock masses resembling oversized cow pies. She killed the motor, lifted it out of the water, and reached for the oars. Just ahead was a smooth cove, its beach littered with millions of mussel shells, weathered and churned and ground to a coarse sand, and beyond the beach, a broad hedge of cedar trees. She jumped onto shore and dragged the hull over the beach, then tied the line around the trunk of a cedar.

Her path to the cabin wasn't even a hundred yards. Her backpack was weighed down with supplies, and she carried a bag of groceries in each of her arms. As she approached the clearing, she saw the trumpets of columbines and the wild roses the color of flamingo pink. She called out to Seda as she approached. The cabin was quiet.

Abby set her backpack and groceries on the damp plank boards of the porch. She opened the door. "Seda, are you here?" She continued to call for her, then stepped outside again and began walking around to the back of the cabin.

Seda's voice startled her. "You finally made it!"

Abby had been about to climb the ladder to get a bird's-eye view, and exhaled with relief. "I didn't think you were here."

"I told you I wasn't going anywhere," Seda said.

It was already late in the afternoon. They filled a bucket at the cistern and brought water inside. The sun shone strongly through the west window. Every surface of the Falcon's Nest was clean, including the floors.

"You've been busy," Abby said.

Seda was glad about the boat and wanted to go for a ride. They'd put the groceries away, and then Abby would take Seda out on the lake.

They filled the cupboards with food—soups and jellies and crackers, instant coffee and boxes of teabags—and filled a bowl on the counter with the apples and oranges and grapes. Though there wasn't a cooler or a refrigerator, there was a cellar, Seda said, where some of the produce Abby purchased—salad greens, tomatoes, and cucumbers—would stay cool.

They ate sandwiches for supper, and fruit salad and potato chips. When they were finished, they filled a thermos with hot chocolate they made from packets Abby brought, and stored the thermos in Abby's backpack, along with cheese and crackers and chocolate bars. Then they dressed in layers, and with the pack over Abby's shoulders, made their way down to the cove.

Gentle ripples sloshed and lapped against the hull as Abby coaxed them away from the shore before starting the engine. They stayed close to the shoreline, the motor at a low speed, and pointed out things to each other: an exposed rock where cormorants gathered and groomed and dried their wings; a hawk that screeched like a feral cat.

A second hawk appeared. Seda asked if the two hawks were courting or playing or teasing one another, and honestly, Abby had no idea. But she wanted to know; she wanted to know about so many things: the hawks and the pipers and the lichens and the caribou; the great blue heron that stretched its mighty wings and perched on a branch just ahead of the boat, only to take off once more and light on another branch again and again. And with these thoughts, Abby feared the twenty-one-inch circumference of her head could never contain all the knowledge she yearned for.

They pulled into a small inlet and anchored the boat. As they were sharing a chocolate bar, Abby said, "When you were telling me about staying at Piper's, you said things weren't any better at home."

"It's true," Seda told her.

"But why?" Abby asked.

Seda brushed tiny flakes of chocolate from her lap and wadded up the wrapper. "It's my dad I don't get along with. We fight a lot," Seda said. "We yell. He slams doors and I storm off, and sometimes he chases me into the driveway where we yell some more, and then I leave."

"Has it always been like that?"

"For as long as I can remember."

Abby thought of her dad working on her car or flipping pancakes. She thought of his laugh that was so infectious, and the other times when his brow would furrow with concern.

"I hate the TV, I really do," Seda said. "It's always on. He likes cars. He likes to watch them race. It doesn't matter what time of day or night. There's this constant sound, like swarms of bees, round and round and round. You can't get away from it. 'Turn the fucking

TV down!' I'll yell at him. But I still hear it. It's like every kind of insect buzzing in my ears.

"I smashed his TV once," Seda said. "I grabbed the lamp from my bedside table, ripping the cord from the wall, and charged into the living room. He was just sitting there, on the couch with his feet on the coffee table. I turned around and swung the lamp as if it were a baseball bat, and slammed it into the TV.

"I thought he'd jump up and grab me, that we'd finally have it out, that things would get physical. That's what I wanted. The lamp got stuck in all the wires. I was trying to wrestle it out of the TV. There was all this glass on the floor and I was barefoot. By that time, he was sitting forward with his arms on his knees. He said, 'Here, don't move, let me help you,' or something like that. But his face had changed, as if he was sorry, or afraid of me, as if he didn't know what to do with me anymore. So I left, like I always do. In the end it plays out the same."

Seda closed her eyes. "It's times like that night, Abby, when I just want everything, all of it, to shut up and leave me alone."

Abby tried and failed to come up with the right thing to say. Maybe just being there was enough—I'm here, so are you, I'm not going anywhere. Maybe that was all Seda needed.

"The night I broke the TV, I stormed out of the house," Seda said. "I slammed doors. I ran down the sidewalk and down the road. There was something in my left foot. I think it was a piece of glass. It started to hurt and I'm sure it was bleeding. And you know what the weird thing is? I liked the pain, so I kept on running. I ran till the road became dark and there were no more houses. I swear, sometimes I feel like this stray dog out on the streets. You know, something really mangy that nobody wants.

"Anyway, that's pretty much how I met Piper. He was at the general store where I ended up. We struck up a conversation. He had his own place. He had a real job. He worked at a manufacturing plant.

And while we were talking, he and this other guy made eye contact and did that little head jerk thing that guys do when they see each other. The guy said, 'Hey, Boss,' and Piper said, 'Hey, man, how's it going.'

"I walked with Piper out to his car. I said I wanted to drive around. He said he would take me anywhere I wanted to go. I remember liking the way he drove, with his left arm hanging over the steering wheel and his right arm on the console between us. He played his music loud and was tapping his fingers in the air to the beat. At the end of a highway, we came to a dead end. I mean there was a sign, and Piper's headlights were shining on it. Kind of funny now, when I think about it, the dead-end sign. I never believed in omens before, but maybe I should."

Abby watched Seda's reflection on the water, all of her anger and all of her sadness holding the same space. Abby said the first thing that came to her, not meaning to be funny. "I have a thing for stray dogs."

Seda laughed. "I could tell you to be more careful."

"You don't have to. We'll be fine."

The light was softening as it does before dusk. Seda hugged her ribs. "The night I broke the TV, Dad wasn't out looking for me. He was at a bar," she said. "I saw his truck when Piper drove me back to his place. Dad hardly drinks anymore, but he used to. He'd go into his room and shut the door. And if I had a bad dream and cried in the night, he'd be too drunk to hear me."

Seda stopped talking and rubbed her hands together. Abby realized how chilly the air had become. "Are you cold?" Abby asked her.

"It's okay."

Abby thought of the cartons of Diet Coke her dad kept stacked beside the refrigerator, and his empty pop cans she'd turn in for ten cents apiece at the grocery store—her weekly allowance when she was young. She thought of the times she saw him decline a beer at Uncle Buckley's when all the others were drinking.

Abby said, "I'm sorry about your dad." She wanted to say more. She wanted to say the right thing. Seda was beautiful. Seda was damaged. And Abby was just this: the girl named after a peninsula, the girl whose mom died in a fire. She had the image of an orange being squeezed and squeezed, pulp dehydrated, and there was Abby, mouth wide open, waiting for a drop of sweetness.

Seda made fists and raised them to her mouth. She blew on one and then the other. She was wearing a corduroy jacket, some outdated modish thing with wide lapels that she found in the wardrobe. She pushed her hands inside the front pockets. Then she tilted her face upward. "God, look at the sky," she said. "It's as if someone added food coloring."

The sunset was almost over, like a grand finale of brilliant colors. Soon it would be dark. "We should probably head back," Abby said.

Seda didn't answer. She was still gazing at the sky.

"When I was sixteen, I took a job at a grocery store," she said. "It was the middle of winter, and I had to get up early. I'd meet a delivery truck and unload boxes. That was when I started drinking coffee. Dad and I would both be in the kitchen. We'd stand at the counter, side by side, waiting for the coffee to stop brewing, neither of us saying a word, just watching the coffee drip. He'd pour his cup and sit down at the table. I'd pour my cup and sit down across from him. It was nice, just sitting there like that. He'd have already gotten the paper and it would be lying on the table. I'd lean back in my chair, holding my mug with both hands. He'd start flipping open the pages of the newspaper with one hand while he held his mug with the other. He liked seeing what the weather was doing around the country.

"One morning while he was checking the forecasts, he said I was like the weather, that's what he'd been thinking, and wouldn't it be a good thing if I had my own forecast. I set my mug down and reached across the table. I took the pen he kept tucked in the front pocket of his work shirt. According to the paper, it was raining in Cincinnati.

I clicked the button on top of the pen with my thumb and circled the forecast for Cincinnati. My dad had that weary look on his face. It's easy to hurt him. He put his mug down and moved the paper aside. 'Is there anything I can do? Let me help you,' he said. I swallowed more coffee and told him, 'There's nothing you can do.'"

The water was flawless. The boat barely moved. "Thanks for talking to me," Abby said. "I'm sorry for everything you're going through. I can't imagine. I really can't."

14

SEDA AND ABBY WOKE BEFORE sunrise the next morning. Abby lit a fire in the woodstove in the kitchen and made instant coffee, then poured the coffee into the thermos and brought it outside. Seda joined her, wearing a flannel nightgown and the tall rubber boots from the wardrobe. The sky had barely changed from shades of velvety gray to a bluish light, and everything around them was little more than shadows.

They walked around the cabin and navigated their way up the ladder. From the top of the roof, the sky appeared brighter, starlight against cobalt blue. To the east a film of gold and peach had begun to appear over the horizon. All around them was birdsong—mourning doves and robins and pine warblers, and from closer to the water, the call of seagulls.

Then Abby said, "You know about the fire—"

Seda said, "The night your mom died."

Abby hugged her legs against her chest, the mug still in one hand, the remaining coffee lukewarm. "I was walking along a road when they found me," she told Seda. "I was seven years old. My niece Catherine is seven years old now. She's so small and innocent. I don't want anything bad to ever happen to her. Her dad's in Bosnia. What if he never comes home? Gracie is only five. It wouldn't affect her the same way. But Catherine—

"The other night I was watching the girls play. It was dark outside and they were running around chasing each other and catching fireflies. There was this moment when Catherine ran toward the house and the floodlight captured her face. She looked so happy. I wanted to say stay just as you are. Don't ever change. But she'll change, like we all do, and things will happen to her.

"I can't imagine Catherine walking by herself on a dark road in the middle of the night, in the middle of winter, no parents around, all her toys and clothes and favorite things gone, then getting in the car with some strangers. And I can't imagine because I can't remember. I just know what everyone has told me."

"You don't remember anything?" Seda asked.

Abby shook her head slowly. *Did* she remember anything? Were there images from that night, pieces of something—the smell of synthetic fur against her face, an open box of saltines? The mystery of that night moved through Abby's life like thin shadows. On a night in January, Abby's mom died in a fire. Abby survived. That's all Abby knew. She looked for clues but saw nothing. She grasped for details.

"What if we went somewhere," Seda said. "You have the day off. Let's go out and get lunch. I could really go for a cheeseburger and fries."

Abby could already smell the grilled patty and taste the salty cheese and pickle.

Back inside, the two of them rummaged through the wardrobe and held up different blouses. Upon first exploring the cabin, the idea of wearing another person's clothing felt strange to Abby, but that morning she went along with Seda's mood and chose a bright floral print filled with purples and oranges and yellows. If she left the top two buttons undone, the soft cotton lay open like lapels, revealing the beaded necklace that Aunt Jo-Jo and the girls had given her.

"Ooooh, I never noticed this before," Seda said. She reached for the necklace and gently lifted the beads so that she could see them more closely. The beads caught the stream of light through the window, and Seda said, "Ah, look at that. They change colors." Abby told her what Catherine said about the beads reminding her of trees. "She's right," Seda said. "In the light, the beads turn all different shades of green."

They walked through the woods to the cove, and when they went to push the boat out, Seda shrieked because the water was so cold and she'd gotten her shoes wet. Abby told her to climb into the hull and when she did and the boat almost tipped over, she shrieked again, and they both broke out laughing.

The sky was clear blue and the water calm, and both of them were smiling, hair tossing about, sun-shot on their faces. They moored the boat at the jetty, then gathered their things and strode past old fishing boats and enormous anchors and chains, and a flatbed piled high with fishing nets. Abby didn't see Tanner or the boxy-shaped dog, or any of the other fishermen, and knew they must be on the water.

She and Seda climbed in the truck and rolled down the windows and turned up the radio. The air smelled fresh as they drove. Abby loved that smell, the sweet scent of lawns and flowering bushes and warm sunlight on everything.

They headed north and then west toward Escanaba, about an hour-and-fifteen-minute drive from Fairport.

When they got to the drive-in, the restaurant was just opening.

They pulled into one of the drive-in lanes under the canopy and placed their order over an intercom. They talked about their plans for the day. Abby wanted to go to the library and use the card Uncle Dennis gave her. Seda wanted to go by the park at the harbor.

A teenage girl brought their food out on a tray and handed them cardboard containers with cheeseburgers and french fries, and tall paper cups with root beers. When they finished eating, they placed another order for soft-serve ice cream cones.

After the server brought them their cones, a loud truck pulled into the parking lot beside the drive-in lanes. The man who climbed out was large. He walked a few paces, then turned around. "Get out of the truck," he yelled.

The passenger door opened. A small body appeared. Using both hands, the child pushed the truck door shut.

The man cursed and yelled at the girl. Then he disappeared inside the restaurant, letting the door close behind him.

The girl quickened her steps, her brown hair bouncing over her shoulders. She was wearing yellow shorts and a pink tank top. Her feet were bare. She reached for the door and leaned back using her weight to open it, then squeezed her body inside.

Abby and Seda sat in the truck. They'd watched the man and the girl and were quiet now. They licked ice cream from their cones. Then Seda got out of the truck, vanilla ice cream melting onto her hand. She took long strides toward the man's pickup. She looked over her shoulder once, at the restaurant. Then she stepped onto the truck fender, and hoisted herself onto the hood. She pressed the ice cream against the man's windshield and wrote the word *douche* in large, dripping letters.

Abby had followed Seda to the vehicle. Through the restaurant window she could see the man at the counter and the small girl standing beside him.

The man made a ninety-degree turn and walked a few paces. He was picking up napkins and condiments.

"Hurry," Abby said to Seda.

Seda finished. She chucked the rest of her cone across the parking lot. Then her eyes spotted something inside the man's vehicle.

"Hold on," she said.

"Seda, they're coming out. Hurry!"

Seda reached inside the rolled-down window on the driver's side and swiped something off the top of the dashboard. Then she slid off the hood. "Go!" she yelled to Abby, and they took off sprinting toward Grandpa Pete's truck.

Seda looked behind her. "Shit!" she said. "Go! Go! Go!"

The man had stepped out of the restaurant. He carried a bag of food in one hand, a large cup in the other. His head was bent over the cup while he drank from a straw. The girl stepped out behind him and was licking an ice cream cone.

Abby drove out from under the canopy and accelerated toward the highway. She looked in the rearview mirror. The girl was skipping ahead of the man toward the truck. The man had just looked up. Abby slammed her foot on the gas pedal.

Seda was laughing.

"What if he chases us?" Abby said.

"He never even saw us," Seda told her.

Seda was wearing a pair of aviator sunglasses.

"You stole those?" Abby said.

Seda turned up the dial on the radio. She leaned back in her seat. It would be a hot day across most of the peninsula the announcer said, with clear skies for the remainder of the week and light winds from the south off Lake Michigan.

15

SEDA WAS STILL WEARING THE aviator glasses when they entered the library.

"How can you see to read the titles?" Abby asked.

"I'm not the one checking out books," Seda said.

As much as Abby missed Brew, she felt herself falling greedily into a relationship with Seda, like Icarus who flew too close to the sun.

She looked for the fiction section and began perusing books, trying to think of ones she and Seda could read together. In the end, she chose *Jane Eyre* and *Little Women*. Then she picked out a couple of books for herself.

They drove on to the park at the harbor and held sweating bottles of cold drinks and sat on a blanket they'd brought from the cabin. Abby had also packed apples and chocolate bars. Seda suggested they slice the apples and dip the slices in the melted chocolate. The sun gleamed brightly. Seagulls squawked overhead. All around them was the tatter of human voices, the metal dinging of the sailboats' lines swinging against the masts, the riffle of water, the slapping of a jogger's shoes along the asphalt path.

Abby said, "I still can't believe you wrote on that guy's windshield."

"I can't believe the way he was talking to his daughter," Seda said.

Abby leaned back on the blanket and closed her eyes. Then she told Seda, "When we were at the library, I came across a book I'd read before. It was about a soldier who'd gone missing. Everyone thought he was dead. They'd even had a funeral for him. But it was all just a mishap. He'd gotten disoriented during one of the battles and wandered away from his battalion. Then one day he wandered back into everyone's lives.

"They never found my mom's body," Abby went on. "Nothing but mementos are buried at the gravesite."

"Your mom's not coming back, Abby."

"I know she's not coming back. But that would be something, right?

"When we were at the drive-in, I remembered my mom and me riding bikes. She was ahead of me, and I was trying to catch up to her. Her bike was light blue, and it had a basket on the front. She looked back at me. She was saying something to me and smiling, and her hair was blowing around her face. We were on our way to get ice cream. I remember that now. But mostly, I see her face looking back at me."

"What was she saying?" Seda asked.

Abby's eyes were still closed. She was picturing the moment. She tried to recall everything. "I'm not sure.

"There were flowers in the basket on her bike. Flowers she bought to plant at the house. Now my dad plants flowers every spring, and at the same time every evening, stands outside and waters them. My mom used to water them every night after supper. I thought of that today. I would follow her outside summer evenings. It would be really hot and she'd spray me with the hose. But now my dad's out there, carrying on this thing she did."

"He's remembering her," Seda said.

"Seda?"

"Yeah?"

"I need to tell you something else. The restaurant where we went today—I remember going there with my mom. Whenever we went to Escanaba, we'd stop there for lunch. At the checkout counter they had toothpicks and mints and a basket with matchbooks with the restaurant logo. I would always pick up toothpicks to play with and a peppermint."

"Why are you telling me this?" Seda asked.

"The night of the fire, I was holding a matchbook when they found me. What if it was from the restaurant?"

Then Seda said, "So what if you picked up the matches. That doesn't mean anything."

"But it does, don't you see? What if the fire was my fault? What if I started it?" These were the questions Abby always carried.

Seda was quiet, until she wasn't quiet, until she said, "I wonder how many matches were left in the matchbook. If there weren't any matches missing, then you didn't start the fire."

Could it be that simple? Abby thought. Seda's words gave Abby hope. But as Abby made the drive back to Fairport, as she and Seda climbed into the boat and navigated their way to the cove at Point Detour, and then walked the path back to the Falcon's Nest, the hope Abby clung to slowly diminished. What if a match *was* missing—one single match that started the fire? What if her family knew this all along?

Abby and Seda ate an easy dinner of canned peaches, salami on rolls, cucumbers and celery. Abby brought the books from the library over to the sofa. She propped herself against a large needlepoint pillow and opened the one about the life of Marie Curie.

Seda joined her and said, "What are you reading?"

Abby showed her.

After a few paragraphs in, Abby said, "Maybe someone still has the matchbook. Maybe I could find out if any matches are missing."

"Maybe," Seda said.

Abby tried once more to read, but after another paragraph, she set the book aside and leaned her head against the pillow.

A knitted afghan of many colors was folded over the back of the sofa. Seda pulled it down and draped it around Abby. Then she stood and walked over to the east-facing window. Beneath the window was the leather trunk. They'd not opened the trunk, nor had they explored the smaller wooden box on top of it with the metal lever and carrying handle.

Seda lifted the lid and discovered the box was a portable gramophone.

"Abby, check this out," Seda said.

Seda picked up a record from the adjacent stack, removed it from its paper sleeve, and laid it on the gramophone's turntable. Then she cranked the handle and positioned the needle over the vinyl. The room filled with a scratchy, crackling sound as the record went round, as violin and cello and piano played, and Gene Austin sang "My Blue Heaven."

"Whippoorwills call, evenin' is nigh . . ."

Seda moved back across the room, her feet sinking into the old woven rug. She lifted the afghan and curled onto the sofa with Abby. The hurricane light flickered. Outside the evening light had softened, and the air from the open windows brought in the sweet scent of pine and honeysuckle.

16

IT WAS THURSDAY, THE FOURTH of July. Abby and Uncle Dennis had almost completed another week of work, which proved to be a difficult one, as the entire state was under a heat wave advisory. They ate little for dinner—leftover pasta salad, slices of tomato—the heat having zapped most of their appetite. Uncle Dennis said it was too hot to sit around camp and suggested they go into town to see the fireworks.

"Let's take the truck. We'll watch the fireworks from the back," he told her.

Abby drove them to the Garden village and parked at the top of a hill among other cars. People were sitting in chairs in small clusters on nearby lawns. She and Uncle Dennis climbed into the truck bed and leaned their backs against the cab, surrounded by chatter and car radios and the squeals of children, and bare feet running across lawns.

Abby was wearing shorts and a stretchy cotton camisole, the coolest items of clothing she owned. She slapped at a mosquito that had just landed on her arm.

"Can't get away from them," Uncle Dennis said. He was sitting with his legs pulled up, in a pair of faded jeans.

Abby asked, "Do you ever wear shorts?"

"I don't even think I own a pair."

She was sure she could find scissors, and Uncle Dennis laughed at that.

"I bet Nonna and the girls are here somewhere," he said.

And then, "Hey, there's Brew," and he raised his arm and pointed.

Abby saw him too—sitting with Tracy a couple of houses from where the truck was parked. Pretty soon, Alex's car pulled up alongside them, and he and another guy climbed out.

"I don't mind if you want to join them," Uncle Dennis told her.

"That's all right."

"You and Brew doing okay?"

"We're doing okay."

It was then that Abby brought up the topic that had been on her mind all week. "I've been wanting to ask you something," she said. "There was an investigation into the fire, right?"

"I remember an inspector from Escanaba coming out. They thought the fire started upstairs, but there was so much damage, no one could say for sure."

Abby continued, "I was carrying matches when they found me."

"That's right."

"Do you know what happened to the matchbook?"

Uncle Dennis shook his head slowly, like he was thinking, like he was musing over the whole thing. "I wouldn't know. I wasn't there. Nonna might have an idea."

The sky was deepening. Stars were appearing.

"Why all the questions?" Uncle Dennis asked.

There they were, the two of them, having this conversation while kids ran around the truck lapping up dripping ice cream from cones, and car doors opened and slammed shut.

"It's something I've always worried about," Abby said. "Do you think I had something to do with it?"

Uncle Dennis gave Abby a quick glance before looking back over the town and the people. Abby thought his face held surprise, and maybe a hint of relief, too, that the topic had finally come up, as if saying, "Now that you mention it, we should talk about this, we should get it all out in the open."

"There was some talk of that, sure," he said. "Maybe you'd been playing with matches. But I don't know, Abby. You were just a kid. Does a child that age even know how to strike a match?"

"But people were thinking it, and maybe they're still thinking it now."

"People move on, Abby. At least they try to."

Abby continued, "I was talking to a friend and she said if there weren't any matches missing, then I didn't start the fire."

"Like I said, I wasn't there. I really don't know."

Only one other time had Abby asked the question—in some sort of variation—"Did I start the fire? Could I have started the fire? Do you think I had anything to do with it?"

And Brew had answered her sincerely, "No, I don't think you did."

"But have you ever thought that? Did the possibility ever cross your mind?" she'd asked him.

"No, Abby, it never has," Brew said.

He went on to talk about the day they were playing in the barn—"What were we, six or seven? You know, the day we found the mouse nest." They'd moved the green wheelbarrow, and behind the wheelbarrow and beneath a shelf was a mouse nest full of furless babies. "That's what started the fire," he proposed. "Mice got into the walls and chewed on the wires."

He'd given her a new aspect of the story she'd never considered before.

"What ever happened to the mice?" she asked him.

"Snakes got them."

"Are you telling the truth, Brew?" Because she always wondered if he killed the baby mice—stepped on them or, more likely, drowned them in a bucket of water. Mice weren't good, her father told them. They infested the grain and ate up the seeds he planted.

"I'm telling the truth," Brew said.

• • • • • • • • •

Abby and Uncle Dennis sat quiet, looking off at the town, watching the people, letting the seconds pass.

Uncle Dennis said, "How much longer till the fireworks?"

"There's still some light in the sky," Abby said.

He tilted his head back and looked up at the stars and the night blue. "Wonder how hot it is—what do you think, ninety degrees with the heat index?"

"Probably in the eighties. Feels hotter in jeans."

"You want some ice cream?" he asked her.

"Ice cream would be good," Abby said.

Uncle Dennis scooted off the truck bed and started walking down the hill. Lucinda Williams was playing from someone's car stereo. Abby closed her eyes. She listened to the music and leaned her head against the truck's back window. She sat so still. The air felt nice, not as hot anymore, just a summer night.

Abby didn't hear Brew approach, and when he hoisted himself onto the tailgate, her eyes remained closed, because she thought the shift of the truck's weight was from Uncle Dennis.

And then Brew was sitting beside Abby, and he didn't say anything at all until Abby opened her eyes, and Brew said, "Hey."

"Hey," Abby said, surprised. "I thought you were here with Tracy."

"I am."

He leaned his head back next to Abby's. "Saw you sitting up here alone."

"I'm not alone. Uncle Dennis is with me."

"I know. I saw him too."

They fell quiet then, the two of them sitting beside one another, until Brew said, "It was crazy seeing you the other night."

"At Jake's?"

"Yeah. Who was that guy anyway?"

Abby rocked her head from side to side. "I don't know," but there was something dismissive in the way she said it.

"I wanted to punch him in the face," Brew said.

"Probably a good thing you didn't. He was twice your size."

"I could have taken him on."

Abby didn't think Brew could take Piper but said okay.

Once more they were quiet, until Abby said, "That was my birthday."

"I know. I stopped by Nonna's, but she said I just missed you."

Brew had remembered her birthday. But still—

She let it pass.

"I have something for you," he told her. "It's back at the house. I'll give it to you next time."

Abby nodded. "Okay."

She closed her eyes again, because the music was nice, and this was nice, sitting with Brew. She no longer wanted to talk about her birthday, or the night at Jake's. She didn't want to talk about Seda and Piper.

In a quiet voice she said, "She never got to be very old—"

She looked at Brew and finished her thought, "Did we watch the fireworks with her? Do I remember that?"

"Yeah, we did, Abby."

"I think it was snowing. I think one year it snowed, little snowflakes in the air."

"I don't think so. I think that was New Year's."

"Oh—I guess you're right."

Then Abby asked, "Did we watch the fireworks from the water—on the Fourth of July?"

"Yeah."

"In a big boat. It was nice."

"Yeah, it was."

Someone was shouting for Brew, when suddenly the night erupted with sounds and lights. Abby and Brew leaned forward and stared up at the display. He said he should get back, but he didn't leave right away. Uncle Dennis was still somewhere down the hill getting ice cream. Abby hoped he was with the people he knew and watching the colors fill up the sky.

17

TWO NIGHTS AFTER THE FOURTH of July fireworks, Abby sat with Seda on the floor listening to Jelly Roll Morton sing "Michigan Water Blues" and drank blueberry wine from a ceramic mug.

They sat cross-legged, facing the gramophone, and every time the music stopped, one of them would crank the lever and reposition the needle, until they'd listened to the song at least a dozen times. And sometimes they applauded Jelly Roll and told him to sing it again.

Seda had admitted she wasn't feeling her best lately. Her headaches had gotten worse. But that night her head felt fine and she was in good spirits, and the wine, compliments of Tanner, who made nettle and elderberry wine too, went down sweet and smooth.

They played a record by Billie Holiday—"My Man"—and then another called "Solitude." Abby said, more than anything else, a song could make her cry. She remembered walking down a sidewalk in Calumet, leaves blowing in her path. The air had the nippy chill of a day in late fall. Music played from speakers outside a shop—a pawnshop, a used book store—Abby couldn't remember for sure. She saw her reflection in the storefront window, the music was playing—saxophone and bass and brass, leaves were circling around her ankles, and she felt so much—the pure emotion of being alive on this planet. The store was closing. She turned to go. She continued down the empty sidewalk. She could have cried, but she was happy—it was all a very complicated feeling.

She and Seda lay back on the rug, the music still playing. Seda reached for Abby's hand. "Are you sad now?"

"No, I don't feel sad," Abby said.

"That's good," Seda said.

The record stopped, but this time they didn't choose another one.

"There's something about this place," Abby continued.

"It's the comma, the pause," Seda told her.

But Abby said, "I think it's more than that. I think there's a spirit here, a kind of companion."

Seda said, "I can tell you, I don't have the dreams anymore."

"What dreams?" Abby asked.

"The same dreams I had when I was small. A school counselor once asked me about them. I guess my dad told her I was having nightmares. I was really angry he did that. He'd never brought them up to me before. All that time, he knew I was having trouble sleeping, but he was too drunk to do anything about it."

"He talked to the counselor. He tried to get her to help you," Abby said.

"I thought you were on my side."

"I know, I'm sorry. I didn't mean it like that. But maybe he didn't know *how* to help you. Maybe him talking to the counselor was the only thing he knew how to do."

Seda said, "I didn't talk to the counselor. I didn't tell her anything. She had these pens on her desk with red silk flowers on the top. They were in a cup, and the cup was yellow with a smiley face. The counselor was sitting behind her desk. 'Tell me about the dreams you've been having. Your dad says you've been having night terrors.' That's what she called them."

"What did you say?"

"I told her I wanted my dad. She said your dad's not coming. I said, 'No shit.'

"But that was all I wanted, you know? I wanted my dad to stop drinking. I wanted him to check on me in the night. To do *something*."

Abby said, "You want to make peace with your dad. You don't actually come out and say it, but that's what you want. I want to absolve myself for something I hope to God I didn't do."

They fell quiet, until Seda said, "Maybe I do want peace with my dad. Maybe we're here to help each other. I really hope you find what you're looking for."

• • • • • • • • •

By Monday, the heat wave broke. Abby was sitting on the porch, her back against the old logs. On her lap was a book about all kinds of forest edibles written by a botanist in Canada. She discovered the book on one of the shelves in the cabin. The book was full of pictures of wild fruits and vegetables, and each picture was covered with a page of tissue paper. She was making a mental list of food she and Seda might forage in the woods: blueberries and blackberries, sumac berries, elderflower, Joe Pye weed—when Seda exclaimed, "She was a painter! Come and see!"

Abby felt disoriented. "Who was a painter?"

"The woman who lived here. She was an artist."

Abby followed Seda inside the cabin. The gramophone and records were on the floor, and the trunk was pulled out away from the wall. Scattered all around the trunk were dried-up tubes of paint and paintbrushes and sketch notebooks, and a painter's palette covered in a mosaic of color.

"Look at this one," Seda said, showing Abby a pencil drawing from one of the notebooks. "And this one," she said.

They were looking at sketches made of the cabin—trailing flowers growing from window boxes, a wreath of dried hydrangeas on the cabin door, a well-tended vegetable and flower garden next to the water pump.

Abby sat on the floor with Seda as they picked up one notebook after another. There were detailed drawings of plants in the woods and others of birds and wildlife—a finch perched upon a rock, a male robin teaching his young how to forage for worms beneath the wet grass.

Abby thought of the woman living out here by herself—there was no evidence of anyone having lived here with her—drawing and painting and reading about wild edibles and studying the scientific names of the naturally occurring vegetation.

Seda continued to explore the items in the trunk and withdrew a large canvas bag with wooden handles. Inside the bag were embroidery threads and different sized needles, as well as embroidery hoops and a magnifying glass. And then Seda was on her knees and moving toward one of the bookshelves. She pulled a volume off a shelf and flipped through the pages. It was a needlepoint encyclopedia full of patterns and detailed instructions about the eyelet and beaded stitch and so many others.

Abby may have been fascinated by the woman who'd walked these woods and observed and studied its community of flora and fauna, who'd so painstakingly captured these images in sketches and paintings, but for Seda the connection was for the woman's sensibilities—the comforts, the intricate designs on the teacups, the mason jars and vases that Seda filled with fresh water and wild columbines and roses, the handmade quilts on the bed, the throw pillows with their embroidered images and patterns.

And then Abby was struck by a thought. She stood and went to one of the paintings on the wall—the one that hung above the small trestle table—of a colony of marsh marigolds growing along a rocky shore. On the lower left corner of the work was a name painted in silver. The signature was in cursive and was difficult to decipher.

"She has a name," Abby said. "But I can't read it."

Seda retrieved the magnifying glass and held it over the signature.

"Charlotte. Her name was Charlotte," Seda said. But neither of them could make out the woman's last name.

The atmosphere of the cabin took on that of a museum. Abby and Seda moved slowly from one canvas painting to another, thoughtfully examining each work. There was the small painting of a vase of crocuses atop a stack of clothbound books that stood on an easel on one of the bookshelves; another of four sandpipers along the water's edge that hung next to the front door; the panorama of the two Summer Islands, as viewed from Anderson Point, that hung next to the wardrobe in the bedroom; and the largest of the paintings, which hung above the mantel, of a forest with a teal-blue lake in the distance that blended into a blue horizon, and a cliff shadowed with evergreens. The canvas looked as if it had been damaged, the paint cracked along some of the edges and corners making it impossible to read the signature.

They moved to the kitchen. On the painting of a large ceramic bowl full of rhubarb that hung next to the window, they were able to read the signature more clearly. Yes, Seda was sure, the woman's name was Charlotte DeVore.

Abby and Seda stood there for some time staring at the woman's name, holding on to this new piece of information, as if they were making her acquaintance for the first time and they didn't want to rush it. Then Seda said, "Hello, Charlotte. It's very nice to meet you."

With their new knowledge of Charlotte's name, everything took on fresh meaning. They listened to Bessie Smith and Ethel Waters and Sippie Wallace sing the blues. They sat on the velvet sofa, beneath the knitted afghan of many colors, and held the framed photograph of the man who they thought looked so debonaire. Was he a boyfriend, or a husband who had died in a war, or a brother, or even a son? They searched the cabin for other photographs but didn't find any.

In everything they were gathering details—a brooch with a tiger's eye gemstone that Seda discovered in the pocket of a sweater, a bookmark made of bronze with a cameo of a dragonfly that Abby found tucked into *The Four Quartets* by T. S. Eliot, a tea ball shaped like a robin's egg that they found wedged behind a kitchen drawer.

There were other details they were gathering as well—the vesper song of tree sparrows and warblers and robins, an owl in the night, the screeching of a red fox, the slant of the morning light through the kitchen window and its warmth upon their faces, the mineral taste of the cold water from the well, the rich, smoky smell of the log walls, a shift of the wind across the porch, the flutter of the curtains—they gave their attention to each of these details, understanding that Charlotte had experienced all of these things too.

Even that night after they lit the hurricane lamp and crawled into bed, Seda preferred *Jane Eyre* over *Little Women* because it was written by Charlotte Brontë, as if the novel might offer them hidden clues into *their* Charlotte's life. They wondered what the name Charlotte meant and decided they could find out at the library. Abby was due back at work the following morning. They'd make the trip when she returned.

Abby picked up the book and resumed reading out loud. She had just begun a new chapter when Seda said, "Maybe she lived here during the war."

"Which one?" Abby asked.

"World War Two," Seda said.

Abby laid the book in her lap. "Maybe she was waiting for her boyfriend to return home to her."

"Maybe he never did."

"Maybe that's why she stayed here and lived alone in the cabin and spent the rest of her life painting and reading and planting gardens."

"And embroidering pillows that he would never rest his head on," Seda said. "And playing all those records of women singing the blues."

18

IT WAS EARLY THE NEXT day when Abby dragged the boat to the shoreline, climbed in, and pushed it off with the oar. Dust motes scampered over the water like pollen. She could get used to this, she thought. She felt the warmth of the morning light on her back as she headed toward Anderson Point. The treetops of the Summer Islands appeared a bright emerald lit with sparks of gold from the sun, as if they were on fire. To the east on her right, beyond the jetty, the land rose, and she could see not only the swaths of forest but also the parcels of farmland, the scattering of barns and houses—all of it such a striking image and charged with so much color.

She began to imagine what her life could be, as if this were her many years down the road, but perhaps not so many years, as if this were her life and she were on her way to a full-time job, commuting as she was over the water. She imagined Brew in her life and the two of them having morning coffee together. Maybe they'd cook eggs and bacon or make hot oatmeal. They'd pack their provisions, whatever they needed for their respective jobs. They'd leave each other with a kiss and a promise to see each other at the end of the day. When they returned in the evening, they'd talk of their work and their different encounters and their hopes and dreams, and they'd cook something together and do whatever chores needed to get done. They'd sit on the sofa and gather books to themselves and read, and every so often one of them would read something to the other, a particularly moving passage or a small bit of information one of them had found especially interesting, and there would be touches and sweet gestures.

Abby slowed the boat and steered it between the buoy markers and into the channel at Peterson's, seagulls mewing and squawking and screeching overhead. A lone fisherman stood on the jetty, his hands in his pockets and his eyes anchored on the horizon.

She cut the motor and drifted toward the mooring posts. The man helped her tie the boat. His face was wind-beaten and suntanned, his eyebrows bushy. "I thought you were Tanner," she said. He said his name was Ellis and that he was Tanner's uncle.

"You heading back out soon?" he asked.

"Probably not for a few days."

"Supposed to get a storm tonight," he said. "You got a rain cover?"

"In my truck." She climbed out of the boat and began walking along the jetty to get the cover.

Ellis said he had some extra lines and would help her tie it down.

After they fastened the cover over the small hull, she thanked him for his help, which he acknowledged with a tip of his cap, then began walking toward shore.

To the right of where the truck was parked, and up the hill, was a large gillnetter on lumber supports in a yard of tall grass. The boat was painted mostly white, with stripes of light blue and red. Painted in faded black along each side of the bow was the word *Kishkedee*. Abby wanted to ask Ellis the meaning behind the name, but he had already walked around the boat and disappeared inside the white-washed single-wide with an open garage door. In front of the garage were stacks of fishing crates, a refrigerator, and the red all-terrain vehicle that she'd seen Tanner driving when she first brought provisions out to the Falcon's Nest.

Driving back to the camp with the radio turned off, she noticed things for the first time—houses with lawn ornaments; windmills and flying geese; flowers pouring forth from hanging pots and window boxes; freshly tilled gardens with young plantings. She imagined she and Seda reclaiming one of the gardens at the cabin and later in the summer harvesting tomatoes and lettuce and squash. Maybe they'd even plant watermelon and cantaloupe. *This* was perfect, she thought to herself. All of *this*. And in four days she'd return to the Falcon's Nest, as if she could already feel the pattern of the rest of her summer and knew she never wanted these months to end.

It was still early, barely past six thirty. She wondered if Uncle Dennis would have already been in the woods. But when she pulled onto the dirt drive leading to the camp, he was sitting on the front steps. He wasn't drinking his coffee or loading his pack. He was just sitting there with his elbows on his knees.

Abby climbed out of the truck and walked toward him, her pack slung over her shoulder.

"Where you been?" he asked.

Abby sat next to him on the stoop, trying to decide how to answer him.

"You weren't at Nonna's," he said. "You weren't with Brew. Or with Reese or Jo-Jo."

"You checking up on me?" Abby asked.

"I'm just saying, nobody's seen you. Where have you been?"

"I was with a friend."

"Someone from Eagle River?"

"No, someone here. Why?"

"Remember that guy I went to school with?" Uncle Dennis said. "The one who stopped by? I saw him at the bar last night. Another camp got broken into. This time around Fairport, close to some of the tracts you've been working on. I was wondering if you might know something about it."

"Why would I know something about it?"

"I don't like bringing this stuff up with you, but I got to ask."

And then it hit Abby. "You think I had something to do with it."

She turned to look at her uncle.

He closed his eyes. "I hate this. I really do."

"Because of what happened? That was a long time ago. You know that."

"I'm not accusing you," Uncle Dennis said.

"Yes, you are. I don't know anything about the camp in Fairport getting broken into, or any of those other camps."

"That's all I needed to hear," Uncle Dennis said.

"It's not right."

"Abby, I'm sorry."

He tried to lay his hand on her shoulder, but she stood up. "I have to get to work," she told him.

Abby stepped inside the camp, letting in the tension like a back-draft, and moved around the small space to gather her things for the day. She spread peanut butter on bread. She filled a couple of water bottles. She grabbed an extra can of bug spray, everything done in haste.

Uncle Dennis was still sitting on the stoop when she left.

"See you later?" he said.

"See you," she said, but she didn't turn around.

19

WHEN ABBY WAS SIXTEEN AND attending the high school in Calumet, there was a route she often walked at the end of the day, to a diner where she sometimes read or did her homework, or just drank something warm and thought about things. The route cut down an alley and passed by a couple of abandoned trailer homes. It was true Abby had gone into one of the homes that day. The door had been open and the windows broken. She was curious, that was all. There was glass on the floor, and graffiti—*Dum vivimus, vivamus*—spray-painted on a paneled wall.

The afternoon was cold and the light dim when Abby left the trailer, and the alley was covered in icy snow. The wind blew, and she walked hunched over, winter coat down to her thighs, arms wrapped across her body, hat pulled over her head. A woman wheeled a green trash can behind a garage. Abby looked up and said hello. The woman said hello and asked Abby's name, and so Abby told her, and maybe she said something else, about how cold it was, and the woman nodded her head.

There were police the next day at the school. A can of white spray paint was found in the back of Abby's car. Abby stood in the parking lot and spoke with the officers, and other students huddled together close by. She had no idea how the paint can got in her car, and when she said this to the officers, the small group of students laughed and talked with one another and moved on. They'd set her up, she thought, but she had no way to prove it.

These were Abby's thoughts as she drove south on the peninsula and parked the truck probably no more than three miles from where she'd left Seda at the cabin. The air had completely changed. What had started out as a brisk morning on the water was now a stagnant pool of humidity.

Abby was starting a new tract that day. With her backpack over her shoulders, she left the truck and waded through the dense vegetation and boggy wetlands. Sweat rolled down her sides and dripped off her face and stung her eyes. The simplest of routines, mapping out a twenty-by-fifty-foot plot and hammering rebar stakes into the ground, felt impossible. She missed the breeze off the water from when she'd been riding so carefree in the boat, and really what she longed for was that last clear feeling she had, the sweet morning air through the truck's windows, flying geese and windmills and bright-emerald treetops.

The deeper she traveled into the woods, the muggier the air became. Clouds of insects hovered about her. Gnats stuck to the oily sweat on her exposed skin and flitted into her eyes and nose. She set her pack on a log and unzipped the main compartment with the intention of retrieving her bug net. Upon shifting things around, her hand came across something heavy and unfamiliar. As she withdrew the item, she found herself holding an expensive-looking pair of binoculars. She had no idea how the binoculars got into her bag. Her first inclination was that Uncle Dennis might have put them there, as some kind of peace offering. But Uncle Dennis didn't have access to her pack.

She retraced her steps from earlier at the camp, and she was certain she'd had her pack with her at all times. She removed the lens covers, held the binoculars to her eyes, tilted her head back. She adjusted the focus and could see clearly into the branches of the tallest tree where she spotted a nest, perhaps that of an eagle or an osprey or a hawk.

She straddled the log and sat down and rummaged through the rest of the bag, curious that she might find something else. There was nothing out of the ordinary that she could see. She removed the bug net and pulled it over her head and cinched it around her neck. The back of the pack contained a hydration sleeve with a zipper closure, which she never used, as she preferred to carry her water in bottles. It was sort of an afterthought, but she opened the sleeve and slid her hand into the compartment. She knew what she was touching, a wad of cash that didn't belong to her. She counted out the bills. There were five hundred and eleven dollars.

Her shoulders dipped forward. Seda was the only one who could have done this. Abby returned the money to the sleeve, praying Seda would have an explanation that made sense. Though she'd already stowed the binoculars back in her pack, she had this strange sensation that she should wipe them down and remove any of her prints.

She thought back to the afternoon in Calumet, when she'd stood in the trailer, her lace-up boots sticking to the orange shag carpeting; Latin words painted in white on a dark-paneled wall. She'd removed a glove and pressed a hand against the wall. She touched one of the letters. The paint felt cold and wet. Someone had just been there. She should have left then. But she didn't. Maybe she translated the words out loud—*While we live, let us live*. She knew the translation because of a poem read in her English class. What was the poem? She tried to recall it. And then she remembered, and it was sad, really. The poem was by Emily Dickinson, written to a young man on Valentine's Day only to later appear anonymously in a newspaper.

On the ground outside the trailer was a bottle cap—white with a red maple leaf—Molson Canadian Lager. She picked it up and pocketed it because she liked the red leaf. Already the light had dimmed, and soon it would be dark. She walked back down the alley and said hello to the woman taking out her trash.

• • • • • • • • •

Abby secured her pack over her shoulders and plodded through the heat and mosquitos and marshland. She'd worn the tall rubber boots she and Seda discovered at the cabin, anticipating that this new tract would be muddy. She believed she was moving in the right direction toward the area Uncle Dennis had assigned to her, though truthfully wasn't feeling certain of anything. The land had begun to open up, creating a large pocket of sunlight that felt out of place.

She studied the map, afraid she'd somehow veered off course, and used her compass to determine her coordinates. She was in the correct location and needed only to continue moving west another hundred yards or so before measuring out the plot and setting the stakes and flagging. On the other side of this clearing would be more wetlands, the same area she and Seda crossed when Abby first brought Seda to the cabin.

Abby entered the large pocket of sunlight. The reeds hid decaying stumps, one right after another, tripping up her footing. The area had been heavily logged at one time. She remembered the map spread out on the table at Bear Slide, her looking over Uncle Dennis's shoulder. He'd drawn a circle around a parcel of land, then tapped the pencil on the map for emphasis. "This area, right here," he said. "This is what I call Nate's Patch. We'll check it out, but we won't find much to inventory."

It was a parcel that had been clear-cut way back when but had failed to regenerate. Abby knew she was standing in what used to be a grouping of white and jack pine. Uncle Dennis had explained how when the trees were taken down, disease entered through a cut stump and moved through the root grafts, infecting the soil. His friend Nate, a biologist with the state, was the one who first discovered and treated the disease, stopping it from spreading beyond the stand. But the soil had yet to allow natural seeding and new age development.

As Abby began measuring out the plot and hammering stakes in the ground and tying string to the different stakes, she became aware of something taking hold of her—the understanding of how much Seda had come to mean to her.

Abby began to associate the disease that had struck this parcel of land with all the things that had happened in Seda's life. Abby knew then she didn't want to accuse Seda, as Uncle Dennis had done to Abby earlier that morning. What if Seda had nothing to do with the break-ins? What if Seda was just a young woman who'd had a hard life, a lonely girl trying to make a new start.

Kneeling in the open sunlight, Abby sketched out her findings using a set of colored pencils and rechecked her coordinates. Afterward, she packed up her supplies and continued to the other side of Nate's Patch, where the area thickened once more. There were bursts of green and sparrows chittering, and yet still no air current, so that as her body moved through the woods, she felt as if she were swimming.

Eventually the landscape became familiar—the small colony of yellow birch interspersed with red maple and pin cherry trees, the clubmoss and the princess pine that she'd come to love so well, that looked like miniature hemlock trees with their soft foliage and straight spines, and made Abby think of a fairy forest.

Abby spotted the clearing ahead, and in the distance, the cabin. She moved steadily toward it, the tall grass swishing against her boots, the Bear Buddha sitting erect like a shadow amid the tangled vegetation, and called Seda's name, but she didn't answer.

Once on the porch, Abby removed the bug net from her head

and shoved it into her side pocket. She pulled off her boots and set them aside. The door stuck in its jamb from the heat. Abby pushed harder until it gave, and when the door opened, she called Seda's name again.

The cabin felt muted. Abby missed Seda. What if she'd left for good, and put the money and binoculars in Abby's pack wanting her to have these things?

Sweat stuck to the hollow of Abby's back and pooled in the dip between her collarbones as she moved through the cabin looking for evidence of her friend—in the chair where Seda sat when she examined the unfinished needlepoint and attempted a new stitch, in front of the kitchen window where Seda drank a cup of ginger tea and watched a hummingbird. She sipped from the cup slowly and said she wished they had honey, and Abby said she'd bring some the next time she came. Seda then asked Abby what kind of bird she would be if she were a bird. Abby said she'd like to be a blue heron, and Seda wanted to know why.

"They look so peaceful standing by themselves along the water. Some Indigenous cultures believe they're messengers from the creator. They represent wisdom and grace."

Seda said she'd want to be a hummingbird. She liked their bright colors and how fast they beat their wings. But really, if she were a bird, she'd probably be a quail.

Abby laughed and said, "Why a quail?"

Seda said, "They're awkward and amusing, running around with those ridiculous hats. And they live on the ground, blending into their surroundings."

There was a plate, a cup, and a saucer in the sink. A broom had been left in the corner beside a cupboard.

"Seda?" Abby called. "Where are you?"

In the bedroom, the sheet and blanket were pulled back into a heap on the bed, as she and Seda had left them. Abby walked over to the window that was still open. She pulled it shut, remembering Ellis predicting rain. When she turned around, she noticed an empty glass on the nightstand and a bottle of acetaminophen. Abby wondered where the bottle had come from and if Seda had experienced another headache. Was that why Seda left? Could something have happened to her?

Abby returned to the living room and said Seda's name again. "I really need to talk to you."

She walked over to the chair where Seda sat that morning. There was the unfinished needlepoint—the stitches resembling the fiddleheads of young ferns and the trillium that grew in the woods. Beside the chair was a stack of hardcovers. Abby knelt on the floor and looked through their titles, then selected one that appealed to her because of its illustrations of different plants and flowers. She brought the book to the small sofa and stretched out lengthwise, thinking she would look through the book while she waited for Seda to return. But a few pages in, her eyes grew heavy, and her mind felt bogged down with too many scientific names of Latin origin. She must have nodded off, because by the time she awoke, the room was full of late-afternoon shadows, and when she checked her watch, it was almost five o'clock.

Abby rose from the sofa and grabbed her pack. She sat on the porch and pulled on the heavy boots, and with her feet planted on the step and her wrists hanging over her knees, she felt something wasn't right. The Bear Buddha was no longer raised on its haunches in the overgrown patch of grass and thorn brush.

Quickly she stood and looked around, and there he was, sitting on the far, right corner of the porch, wearing the pair of aviator sunglasses and looking out over the forest toward the water, just as serene as any Buddha might be. Abby knew then, Seda had been there while she slept.

20

ABBY LEFT THE CABIN AND made the trek back to the truck. She removed her boots and socks and slipped on her sandals, then inserted the key into the ignition. That's when she saw her orange field book that Uncle Dennis had given her for recording species of lichen, sitting on top of the dashboard. She thought it nothing more than an absent-minded gesture on her part—leaving the notebook where it was—and slipped it back into her pack.

Usually Uncle Dennis and she worked till almost sundown. It wasn't yet six o'clock and the sky wouldn't be dark for nearly four more hours. Abby didn't think Uncle Dennis would be back yet, but when she pulled up to the camp, his Subaru was there.

He was standing in the kitchen, hair wet from a shower, chopping cucumbers on a wooden cutting board. Beside the cucumbers was a bowl of chopped tomatoes.

"Hey," he said, looking up.

"Hey," Abby said.

"You hungry?"

"Yeah, actually." Abby set her bag on the floor. "Do you want some help?"

"You could get the corn ready."

Abby slipped out of her sandals and went to the sink and washed her hands. She shucked the corn over a paper bag and swept up the loose silks from the husks. Then she carried the bag to the compost pail they kept beside the back door.

As she turned on the stove to boil the water, Uncle Dennis said, "I owe you an apology."

"You already apologized," Abby said.

"I owe you another one."

"Why?"

"Because the Abby I know wouldn't do that."

"Do what?" Abby persisted.

"The Abby I know wouldn't break into those camps."

They ate outside—grilled chicken and cucumbers and tomatoes and corn, plates on their laps, bottles of root beer set on the ground beside their feet. If they remained still, they could feel a breeze that had just begun, which made the air outside feel cooler than inside the camp. As they ate, Abby told Uncle Dennis about coming upon Nate's Patch.

"What did it look like?" he asked.

"Like a lot of trees had been felled. Like the stumps were dead."

"Any new saplings?"

"I don't think so. Mostly just weeds and brambles."

But he was hopeful. "They'll come back," he said.

He picked up his bottle and held it in front of him for a second, then set it on his knee.

"What are you thinking about?" she asked him.

"Thinking about the day."

"What about it?"

"I didn't get a lot done."

Abby swatted a fly away from her food. She could have told him she didn't get a lot done either, but she'd managed to stake out the plot he'd assigned her, and she was glad for that.

The air smelled like pine resin and the lingering wafts of smoke from the grill instead of something earthy and metallic like before it rains. Maybe Tanner's uncle had been wrong.

"Bugs getting to you?" Uncle Dennis asked.

"Not too bad," Abby said.

"I found a large colony of pink lady's slippers," he told her. "Some people call them moccasin slippers. Did you know that?"

"I think I've heard that before."

Uncle Dennis said, "They're illegal to pick in Michigan. Illegal to transplant also. You can't pick them on federal lands either."

"I didn't know they were endangered," Abby said.

"I don't think they are. Not anymore. But they used to be. I spent a lot of time thinking about them today. *Cypripedium*. That's their genus name. It comes from the Greek word *cyprus* and the Latin word *pedium*. I thought you'd be interested in that, the way you like words. Do you know much about Greek mythology?"

"A little."

"Cyprus is the birthplace of Aphrodite," Uncle Dennis told her. "*Pedium* means sandal or slipper. So the flower represents the slipper of the goddess. Pretty cool, huh?"

"Pretty cool," Abby said.

"All of that's just an aside. What I was thinking about was how the lady's slippers, or the moccasin slippers, or the shoes of Aphrodite, however you want to call them, aren't like the other flowers. They can't survive without the wild. They're connected to it."

A mourning dove cooed from somewhere in the trees. The sunlight through the branches appeared like glitter, as if it had been scattered over the treetops. Abby's thoughts jumped to other thoughts, and she had the strange sensation of a person's ashes not being ashes at all, but rather particles of light, and when a loved one's ashes were spread, the dust fragments shimmered and glowed like glitter, like sunlight through these branches.

Uncle Dennis asked Abby if she was listening to him. Yes, she told him, she was.

"So there are some interesting things about these flowers," Uncle Dennis said. "First, they don't have any nectar, which gives them pretty slim odds of getting pollinated. Bees want nectar. And if the flowers are lucky enough to get pollinated, their seeds, like the plant, require the fungi beneath the soil's surface. The seed tissue adheres to the mycorrhizae. It's the fungi that germinate the seed. This goes on for several years before the plant's leaves appear above the ground."

Abby remembered planting seeds in egg cartons when she was small and waiting for the seeds to grow. "Three years is a long time," she said.

"It is," he agreed. "This may sound strange, but I was thinking of you."

Abby laughed. "What, I'm not sweet enough? I don't have any nectar?"

"Very funny," he said. He leaned forward, anchoring his arms above his knees. "What I'm trying to say is that these orchids need the woods to survive. They need to be in the wild. If someone tries to transplant them, not only will these plants fail to thrive, but they'll eventually wither and die." He straightened back in his chair. "This place suits you, Abby. You need it. That's what I'm trying to tell you. And I don't mean *this* place. I mean everything *about* this place. I hope I'm making sense."

"You're making sense," she said.

Uncle Dennis went on, "There's something else I got to thinking about today. It can take up to sixteen years for the cypripediums to mature and form flowers. What I'm saying is I was wrong to bring up what I did earlier today. I see the changes in you. I see the work you do. You're coming into your own, Abby. It's a really great thing to be part of."

"Thanks," she said. "But you still don't believe me. That's what

I realized today. You still don't believe me about the trailer. I wasn't responsible for the break-in. And you know what, it doesn't even matter anymore. I can't change your mind."

"Don't be so sure about that," Uncle Dennis said.

Abby sat with that last comment. Then she said, "So not only do I not have any nectar, but I'm a late bloomer as well."

Uncle Dennis laughed. "I'm never going to live this down, am I?"

"Nope." Abby smiled and drank the rest of her root beer.

Uncle Dennis was looking at the ground. He turned quiet all of a sudden. Then he said, "I talked to Nonna. I stopped by her house earlier today."

Abby fell silent.

"I asked her about the matches. She doesn't know what happened to them."

"Is that all she said?" Abby stared straight ahead, her body completely still.

"Abby, look at me."

"I can't," she said.

"Yes, you can."

Abby felt the tears behind her eyes.

"There were four matches missing," he went on.

"Why are you telling me this?"

"Because you wanted to know. But Abby, listen to me, that doesn't mean anything. You need to hear me when I say this."

She turned to face him now. "How do you know that?"

"You were a kid, Abby. My God, you were just a kid. You have to let it go."

"I can't," she said. Tears flowed down her face.

"You have to," Uncle Dennis said, as gentle as she'd ever heard him.

Abby said, "We'll never know, will we? We'll never have the answers."

"And that's okay."

"It's not okay, not to me."

"Abby, it has to be okay. You have to move on. You've got your whole life ahead of you. She'd want you to know that."

A car was pulling up to the front of the camp. The engine idled a second before shutting off.

"Around back," Uncle Dennis yelled over his shoulder.

At first Abby worried it was Travis. She stretched her neck over the back of the chair to look behind her. There was Brew rounding the corner, wearing his work boots, shoelaces untied and tucked inside. He gripped the rim of his cap and adjusted it a little.

"Pull up a seat," Uncle Dennis said, motioning to a couple of chairs leaning against the porch.

Brew grabbed a chair and carried it over to the other side of Uncle Dennis. He shook the chair open and sat down.

"Want me to fix you a plate? Not sure what we have left," Uncle Dennis said.

"No, I ate already," Brew said.

"Nonna send you to check on us?" Uncle Dennis asked.

Brew tucked his chin down and smiled and said no. "Thought I'd check on you myself. How's it been going anyway?"

"Oh, we're having a grand ole time. Gnats all over the place, mosquitos eating us alive. Just grand." Uncle Dennis was smiling. "Seriously, though, we're learning all kinds of things about these woods. Abby and I were just having a discussion about the *Cypripedium* and mycorrhiza and a whole lot of other great stuff."

"Sorry I missed it," Brew said.

"I'm sure she can fill you in."

By now Abby had wiped the tears from her face. "That's all right," she said.

"You got plans tonight?" Brew asked her. He was leaning over his chair, arms on his legs, hat pushed back on his head as if letting his forehead breathe a little.

"Do we have plans tonight?" she asked Uncle Dennis.

"Not as far as I know," Uncle Dennis said.

"I'm not interested in another party," Abby told Brew.

"It's not a party," he said. "Just thought we could hang out together."

Abby said she needed a shower first. She took the plates and empty bottles inside. Then she gathered her laundry, deciding she'd ask Brew to stop by Nonna's so she could start a load and pick it up on their way back. She removed some of the heavier items from her backpack—the rebar stakes and hammer, and some of the unnecessary items, like her lunch container with the sandwich she forgot to eat. She left the red sweatshirt rolled up at the bottom, in case it turned cold. The truth was, she wasn't comfortable leaving the pack behind. What if Uncle Dennis went looking for another can of bug spray or some flagging tape, or wanted to check over her notes, and came across the binoculars and the money?

She closed the bathroom door behind her and ran the shower until it turned warm. Then she stepped into the small stall and pulled the plastic liner across the metal rod, hot water running over her body, tears running down her face, the shower drowning her sounds.

• • • • • • • • •

Abby followed Brew out to his jeep. They agreed they'd stop at Nonna's first. "Then where to?" Abby asked.

"Thought we could head up to The Bluff. We haven't been up there in a while."

Abby was quiet.

"You okay?" Brew asked.

She didn't know what to say. Where would she even start?

Abby felt Brew looking at her. Then his eyes were back on the road. The windows were down on his jeep, the radio was playing.

Nonna wasn't home when they got there. The back door was open like it usually was. Abby started the load of laundry in the basement while Brew waited in the jeep. Upon returning to the kitchen, she noticed a pile of photos on the table—some of Abby, others of Abby's mom. Except for the difference in hair color, the two of them *did* resemble each other.

Abby picked up a photo of her mom wearing a pair of high-top basketball shoes and rolled-up jeans and a large flannel shirt. She was holding a stringer full of fish. Abby guessed the picture was taken sometime before she became pregnant. Her hair was long and pulled back in a ponytail and she was sticking out her tongue at the person behind the camera and squinching her eyes.

She had her whole life in front of her—that's what Abby thought. And there was the ache in Abby's throat again, rising to the surface. *What have I done?*

From the window she could see Brew sitting patiently in his jeep, window down, arm hanging over the side, head looking around as if he were following the occasional swallows swooping into his range of vision.

Abby retrieved a ziplock sandwich bag from one of the kitchen drawers. She placed the photo in the bag and sealed it shut.

She joined Brew back at the jeep. "Sorry it took me so long," she said.

"It's all good," he said.

Then she showed him the picture.

"Wow. Your mom sort of looks like you."

"That's what Aunt Jo-Jo and Nonna said."

Abby unzipped her backpack and slipped the photo inside the orange field journal.

Four matches were missing. You were just a kid. You have to let it go.

The matchbook was yellow with blue lettering. There was a basket of them next to a plastic toothpick dispenser and another basket filled with peppermint candies wrapped in clear cellophane. Her mom was paying. The woman wearing the apron said, "You ladies have a nice day." Abby's mom tucked her chin toward Abby and smiled, like she was saying, "Look at us, two ladies out on the town." Abby smiled back and slipped the matches in her coat pocket.

21

BREW DROVE UP THE UNEVEN road that led to The Bluff and parked the jeep. Abby told him they should roll up the windows in case it rained. He didn't think it would rain but said okay.

They walked a path through the woods, until the tree line opened enough for them to see the water. They were on the bay side of the peninsula, before Big Bay de Noc emptied into the northern end of Lake Michigan.

They sat on a slab of smooth rock and crossed their legs.

"This is nice," Abby said.

Brew said, "Yeah, it is."

But he seemed off.

"Everything okay?" Abby asked.

"Yeah."

"Now look who's being quiet," she said.

"Just wanting to make sure you're all right."

"I'm all right," she told him.

"You looked like you were upset back at the camp."

Abby shrugged. "Yeah, I know. Can we not talk about that right now?"

Brew picked up a small stick and scratched lines on the surface of the limestone. "Seems like there's a lot of things we haven't talked about lately. I was thinking about that when I saw you at the fireworks."

Brew tossed the stick over the ledge.

Then Abby said, "Hey, how did your orientation go?"

"It went all right. I met with an advisor and signed up for classes."

"What classes?" Abby asked.

"Was supposed to sign up for business classes."

"'Supposed to' meaning you didn't," Abby said.

"Did you know there's something called forensic archaeology?"

"Is that what you signed up for?"

"I have to take the introductory stuff first. Introduction to Archaeology. Introduction to Anthropology. Introduction to Sociocultural Anthropology."

"You did it, Brew." They'd talked about these things before—Brew wanting to be an archaeologist, him wanting to understand human history—where people were going and where they'd been.

"Family won't be too happy," he said.

"I wouldn't worry," Abby said. "The family will be okay."

"It was supposed to be Uncle Dennis taking over the fish house."

"I guess it wasn't in his DNA," Abby said.

"That's pretty funny, 'cause I'm not even blood related."

"It'll be all right."

Abby liked the idea of Brew digging in the dirt. She liked the idea of him piecing together humankind's existence.

"Kind of reminds me of the graveyard," Abby told him. "You digging for things."

"I guess it does."

Bugs darted about them. Abby swatted them away.

"You could study business and take over the fish house," Brew said.

Abby laughed.

"What's so funny?"

"I hate the smell."

"It's not so bad. You get used to it."

Then he asked, "What about you? You thought more about college?"

"Some."

"You still thinking about English?"

"Maybe."

Brew said, "But you're not there yet." His voice had a knowing quality.

Abby looked out at the water. "It's like when you're getting ready to go somewhere and you get your things together—the items you think you'll need. You leave and get in your car. You start to drive away, but then you get this feeling that you've left something behind. So you stop and turn around. You go back. And when you get there, you see you left the lights on. You realize you never turned the lights off. That's why you needed to go back, that's why you turned around."

Abby continued to look over the water. "Maybe I'm just trying to give words to something when there are no words."

Once more, she felt Brew watching her.

They'd been here before—when there were no words for the feelings she had.

"Can you tell me what it sounds like?" he said, because these were the kinds of questions he asked her when they'd get to this place.

Abby inhaled. She closed her eyes. "Like nighttime on the beach. Like water on the shore. It sounds like stars in the sky."

And then Brew asked her, "What does it feel like?"

Abby's eyes remained closed. "Like a night breeze. It stretches my heart. It's painful and beautiful. You know it will be morning soon, but you don't want the morning to come."

Brew spoke then, "When it does come, when the morning gets here, I want you to know, Abby, the rest of your life will be the best part."

Slowly, Abby opened her eyes. "I wish that were true, but you don't know that," she said.

"Yes, I do. I know you."

Brew went on, "I did some scouting a couple of weeks ago. I was looking for a place to set my blind. You know, it's kind of funny how these woods can feel so enormous when it's only a little piece of land. I was following a map, except I couldn't find a trail that was supposed to be there and got turned around. I thought, shit, what do I do now?"

"A compass might have been good."

"Well, I didn't have a compass, and then I thought to myself, get a grip. This is a peninsula. As long as you know east from west, you can just walk till you hit the water, so that's what I started heading for."

"East or west?" Abby said.

"I headed west because that was where the sun was falling and I could see my way through the trees better if I followed the sun."

"Makes sense."

"I had my spotting scope with me," Brew told her. "I thought I saw the sky opening up ahead. That's when I saw the cabin."

Abby went still.

"I saw you," Brew said. "You were sitting on the porch. Then you stood up and grabbed your backpack and headed off in another direction.

"You looked different that day. I liked seeing you that way. You had a girl-with-a-purpose kind of attitude."

Brew hadn't seen Abby talking to Seda. He didn't know about Abby and Seda staying at the cabin. For all he knew, Abby had just stopped to take a break.

Then Brew said, "Remember when you wanted to be a veterinarian? Remember when we found that injured bird?"

"The robin. I remember that. She flew into Nonna's picture window."

"No, I'm talking about the one by the beach. I think it was a titmouse."

"Titmice live in holes in the trees," Abby told him. "That's where they make their nests. Maybe it was trying to fly and fell out of the tree. But no, I don't remember."

"That's probably because the bird didn't make it. You fed it with a dropper and everything."

"Did we bury the bird?"

"I think we did. In a shoebox or something."

"Maybe I do remember that."

"It was a long time ago. But see, just listen to you, talking about the titmouse living in a hole in a tree. Who knows that sort of thing?" Then he said, "I think you still got bug spray in your hair."

"I washed it."

"I don't think you got it all out. It doesn't bother me. Smells kind of nice. You're a woods girl, that's what you are."

They stopped talking for a while.

Then Abby said, "I've been remembering something lately. It has to do with the things we've been talking about. I was with my mom. I'm not sure where we were living, but I remember this man coming by the house one morning. It was a Sunday, and I know that because my mom was getting me ready for church. The man had a bum lamb in his arms. You know what a bum lamb is, don't you?"

"I never lived on a farm, Abby. But I'm guessing a lamb nobody wants?"

"Yeah, that's exactly what it is. It's when the mom has more than two lambs, and she refuses to nurse the third one. She just abandons it. The farmer has to either find a sheep that only has one lamb and will adopt the bum as her own and let it nurse, or he has to find someone to bottle-feed the lamb until the bum is old enough to join the rest of the herd.

"So this farmer brought us the lamb. My mom and I took the lamb in. She and I bottle-fed him. He got bigger, and when he'd get cold, he'd crawl on top of Rudy."

"That's kind of sweet," Brew said.

Abby smiled, remembering. "Yeah, it was. Except the lamb was getting too big for Rudy, and one day it was time to bring the bum back to his herd. I remember my mom loading him in the back of the car. She drove us out to the man's farm where he had a bunch of sheep. Saying goodbye to the lamb wasn't what got to me. It was that the herd didn't want anything to do with the bum. I remember this long driveway that ran alongside the fenced-in pasture. We dropped the bum off and were driving away, and the lamb started running alongside the fence calling after us. I was staring out the back window. The lambs don't make a *baa baa* sound. When they cry it sounds like *maa maa*."

"You never told me that story before," Brew said. "What made you remember it now?"

"I've been thinking about the fire a lot lately," Abby said. "I never really belonged anywhere after that. We moved around a lot. I think that's why I read so much. There was always a library where we lived, or at the very least shelves in the back of a classroom with books I could check out and bring home."

Brew said, "It's like you could belong to all the characters in those books."

"Yeah, I could relate to them, you know? Then I found the bookstore in Copper Harbor, and I got to know Ian and Helen and the people up there, and that's been nice. But it's just a temporary job. What I'm trying to say—"

"I think I know what you're saying," Brew said. "You look good, Abby. You look like things are agreeing with you. Maybe all of this that you're doing here this summer is a way of belonging."

"I think you're right."

Abby fell silent.

Then she said, "That's a big word, isn't it?—*Belonging*."

She continued her thought, "There are relationships all around me in these woods. That's what I'm learning. I feel like I'm a part of those relationships. I don't know how else to describe it. It's something inside of me. Sometimes I get the idea of my mom when she was pregnant with me drinking water right out of the lake and eating the shoots and fireweed and foraging wild berries, and that somehow all of that got passed on to me."

"Well, she *did* eat the fish, and I'd be surprised if she didn't eat a venison steak or two. I wouldn't count on her drinking the water right out of the lake, though. But Nonna's house has a well, so I guess that counts for something."

"You're making fun of me."

"No, I'm not making fun of you. I think you're making perfect sense."

They turned quiet again, until Abby said, "I've missed you."

Brew reached over and rubbed Abby's shoulder, back and forth, then dropped his arm by his side. "I've missed you too."

She felt possessive of her time with Brew, and possessive of other things as well, like this ledge, and the *Little Daline*, and all the mornings Brew and she had gone fishing. Even the sounds felt uniquely theirs: the scraping of the aluminum hull over the rocky shore; the whine of their lines spooling out as they cast; the gentle plunking as their bait hit the water; the click and cranking of their spin reels; the conversations—"You got a bite," or "Should we try another spot?"; fish popping their heads to the surface; a gull barking overhead. They'd drift a little, try another spot, catch a snag, sometimes a fish, small perch or bass. The afternoons were theirs too, as was the rocky shore. They looked for smooth stones. Some they pocketed, others they sent over the water with a side-arm swing and counted their skips. They collected driftwood and built fires, and the grown-ups joined them—Aunt Jo-Jo with her guitar, playing folk songs they all knew the words to, about answers blowing in the wind and flowers that had gone to graveyards. They held sticks over the fire and roasted marshmallows, and once Brew reached out with his thumb and wiped sticky marshmallow off Abby's lip.

These were her thoughts when a pair of honking geese flew over the water.

Brew said, "Remember the loons?"

"I remember." Abby wanted to write words on Brew's forehead, words like *loons*, and *geese*, and *Little Daline*, and *The Bluff*. She wanted to write the word *marshmallow* across his lips. She wanted to claim him as her own.

The light had grown somber and still, suspended over the water and the treetops and the two of them sitting together on the ledge.

Brew said, "I made something for you, for your birthday."

He reached in his left pocket and pulled out a small arrowhead hanging from a necklace of black leather. "I carved it from an antler."

"Whitetail?" Abby said.

"Yep, a young buck. I found the antler along a fence line."

Abby was glad the antler hadn't come from a deer he shot. She placed the necklace over her head and then grabbed her hair and whipped it out from under the string. She couldn't believe he'd taken the time to make this for her. "It's perfect," she said.

He was looking out over the water, squinting under the brim of his cap, his eyelashes catching the sun.

"I'm heading off to college soon," he said. "I'm not sure where I'll be going from there. We won't always have a summer like this one. The way I see it, you'll be coming back less and less. You'll have your own things to do. But that doesn't mean this place won't always be with you. I was thinking about that when I carved the antler. I thought it could remind you of this place when you're not here."

"It makes me sad to hear you talk like that."

"Maybe so, but there's some truth to it, don't you think? Look at Uncle Dennis. Look at him going off to Alaska. If it hadn't been for you, he might still be in Alaska."

"He wouldn't be in Alaska," Abby said. "He's here because of his doctoral study."

"I just think he's trying to give you some direction, that's all."

"What are you saying?"

"I'm not saying anything."

"Yes, you are. Did someone put him up to it, what, like my dad? Was this whole thing orchestrated?"

"Come on, Abby, why do you have to make such a big deal about it?"

"Because it *is* a big deal."

"I'm sorry I said anything." He took off his hat, swiped it on the ground, stood up, anchored his hands on his hips, cap still in one hand, then took a few paces. "Tonight was supposed to be something special. I thought—" He took a few more steps away.

"So now what, you're leaving? Go ahead, but I'm not leaving. I'm staying right here." Abby returned her gaze to the water, all the while listening for Brew walking away, but instead she heard him moving back toward her, the sandy particles beneath his leather boots, the brushing of the denim on his pants legs. He bent down and touched her shoulder. Abby's eyes remained fixed on the horizon. The sky looked less blue. The lake appeared gray. Clouds were moving in.

Abby wasn't supposed to take any matches, but that day her mom was distracted. Behind the cashier there were mugs for sale with pictures of moose on them. Her mom was interested in purchasing one. "What do you think, Abby? For Uncle Dennis?" His birthday was two weeks away.

Brew's hand was no longer on Abby's shoulder, but she knew that if he touched her again, in that incredibly gentle way of his, the tears would come.

"I'm sorry what I said hurt you," he told her. "I've missed you. I guess I thought tonight could be different. That we could come up here, just the two of us, no party with a bunch of people you don't know, and things would be like they used to be."

"I didn't know Uncle Dennis would rather be in Alaska."

Brew said, "I think Uncle Dennis is exactly where he's supposed to be. I think this summer is about both of you. I don't think I realized that till just now, but yeah, that's it. Like we all got things to work out. I think he's got things to work out too."

There was truth to what Brew said. Uncle Dennis had his own things to sort through.

"People love you, Abby. What's so wrong about that?"

Abby wrapped her fingers around the arrowhead that hung above her breastbone. "You were thinking of the cave when you carved this."

"Yeah, I was."

"Have you been back?" she asked.

"A few times."

"We could hike down there," Abby said. "We still have a couple of hours before sundown."

"It's a harder climb now. Some of the steps are gone."

"Some of the steps were gone the last time we were down there."

"Yeah, well, it's worse now," Brew said.

Abby stood. "That stopping you?"

"No, that's not stopping me." Brew looked around, then gestured off to their left. "I think I went this way the last time."

22

TECHNICALLY, ABBY AND BREW WERE on parkland. The cave was on parkland too. Before the land was sold to the state, the private owner built steps that descended the one hundred and fifty feet to the beach. The park was closed for the day, and the cave was closed to the public. That never stopped Abby and Brew before.

Shadows pooled around the trees. Wood pigeons clattered above them, flushed from their roosts. A female cardinal, the muted color of salmon, perched solemnly in one of the birches, a beautiful contrast against the white bark and green foliage. Abby pointed her out to Brew, and when she did, the bird flew quickly to another tree, hidden from their sight.

Brew was right. Many of the steps were missing. Others were covered in moss and softened by moisture and rot, flexing precariously beneath their feet. The sound of the water grew louder. Waves furled and broke below them. They spotted the trail along a narrow ledge that led south to a number of rock shelters. The ledge used to be a beach when the water was higher, and imagine that, they said, and how many more fish might still be in the lake if the water had remained that high.

They followed the ledge along a wall of shaggy cedar until they came to the largest of the shelters, known as Spider Cave. Outside the shelter's southern wall was the image of a humanoid figure, painted in red ocher, mostly faded, and a spiderlike shape that sent up a swirling cord arcing over the figure's head and connecting to his body. Some believed the cave used to be a sweat lodge. Some believed the figure was a shaman and that the spiderlike shape wasn't a spider at all, but the logs of a fire. And perhaps one of the logs wasn't a log but a messenger stone heated by the fire and sprinkled with water creating steam for the purpose of bringing the shaman a message from the spiritual world. Brew and Abby had debated this topic, pointing and speculating, and Brew had said perhaps the logs were sending up prayers, like incense.

Brew didn't have his jeep the first time they came here. But he had his license and borrowed his dad's truck, a blue Chevy Silverado, with pockmarks on the hood from too much pine pitch.

He and Abby had been a little jumpy standing on the ledge that first time. Someone had built a cairn of rocks, almost two feet tall, commemorating J.P., Abby's biological dad, who'd plunged to his death from this spot. Over the years, people had left fishing lures, jigs and spinners and spoons, all different colors. Yellows and greens and reds, gold and silver and bronze, treble hooks, neon casters, and shiny minnow lures, so that the cairn resembled a miniature Christmas tree, brightly decorated.

Her dad's death was an accident, people said—just a bunch of teenagers messing around. He was sixteen years old. He was going to be a dad.

That first day at the shelter, Abby and Brew explored every inch of the cave. Brew found the skull of a bat, and there were animal droppings of one kind or another, and fish bones left by a seagull. The cave was over four thousand years old. The archaeologists who excavated it didn't find any artifacts indicating that humans had ever lived there, but they found over a hundred arrowheads and harpoon points, suggesting, along with the painting, that the space held some kind of magical or spiritual significance. Legend was known of native hunters in canoes shooting arrows into certain rock shelters as a ritual for obtaining good fortune. Brew and Abby had looked for arrowheads and harpoon points but didn't find any. After they hiked back to the truck, they lay on their backs in the pickup bed and looked at the sky until dark.

They were both sixteen then, the same age Abby's dad had been. As they lay in the truck, Abby asked Brew if he missed his mom, if he missed his stepbrothers.

"Sure, I miss them. But if I were there, I'd miss my dad. And I'd miss you."

"I guess we got that in common, not having our moms," Abby told him.

"It's not so hard for me. I can talk to my mom. I can go see her."

Abby said, "Sometimes I feel like my mom's with me."

Then Brew told Abby to hold out her hand, and when she did, he laid a yellow and green fishing lure in her palm. "Maybe your dad's with you too," he said.

• • • • • • • • •

Brew and Abby were now about twenty feet above the water, with a steady breeze off the bay. They stepped into the cave, the air warm, then cool. The ceiling, about fifteen feet high, had eroded over the years, leaving chunks of limestone scattered across the shelter's floor. Abby found a smooth spot and sat down. Brew moved a couple of rocks aside and joined her. It was Brew who finally broke the silence.

"Nice to see the cairn still there," Brew said. "Nice to see the fishing lures. I think there might be a few more than last time."

"I think you're right."

And then in one breath, Brew said, "It was Reese. Your being here this summer was her idea. Sometimes she misses your mom, that's all. I guess it was just her way of looking after you."

"It's okay," Abby said.

"You're not mad at Reese then? Because I don't think she wanted me to say anything."

"I'm not mad."

And that was true. The thought of being mad, and all feelings associated with being mad, had already left Abby. Being on the peninsula was a good thing, and eventually Uncle Dennis would write his dissertation. Abby thought of herself in a college library one day, perusing books along the shelves. She'd be running her fingers along the spines, reading titles that had to do with trees and carbon mass, and other words, like snow forest and boreal and taiga, and there would be Uncle Dennis's name. She'd stand beneath the fluorescent lights and pull the book from its shelf and read about all the work they'd done. Maybe there'd be an acknowledgments page before the bibliography, where he thanked his advisor and all the faculty he'd ever worked with, and there would be Abby's name too.

She and Brew sat in silence for a long time after that, until Abby said, "I've been asking a lot of questions lately. I'm not sure why I didn't ask them before."

"What kind of questions?"

"Questions about the fire."

"Maybe things are coming back to you, with your being here and all."

"Maybe. I keep seeing this light, like a zap, like a flash. I never saw that before—never had that thought. It feels important, but I don't know why."

"That's something, Abby. Maybe more will come to you."

"I'm scared, Brew."

"What do you think you're scared of?"

"I'm scared I started the fire."

"Hey, I thought we already talked about this. I thought we decided that wasn't what happened."

"But what if we were wrong?"

"Not a chance. This is what I think—I think someone was watching over you that night—maybe J.P. or one of your great ancestors, or maybe God. I don't know, but there's a reason you're here. There's a reason you got out alive, and that should mean something to you. I just wish you'd focus on that, you know, put all your energy into the fact that you're here."

"Then why weren't they watching over my mom too? I know you're looking out for me, Brew. But I'm not sure that's the best thing for me right now. I feel something. It's hard to explain. Maybe God or a great ancestor or J.P. got me out of the fire, but maybe they're calling me back."

"Be careful, Abby."

"There you go again. Who says I'm the one who needs protecting? Maybe you need protecting too."

"From what?"

"The big, wide world. I don't know."

Brew laughed at that. "I'm good, Abby. I swear it." He tilted his head so that he was looking at her, and there was an impish smile on his face.

And then Abby was curious. "You said you'd been back to The Bluff. Did you come down to the cave?"

"Been down here a couple of times. Thought maybe I'd get lucky and find an arrowhead. I was hoping I'd find one for you."

"Seriously?"

"Yeah, but I didn't have any luck. That's why I carved you the antler."

Abby reached for the pendant. She brought it to her lips like a rosary, ran her thumb over the smooth edges.

"Do you hear that?" she asked.

"Hear what?"

"Do you hear the quiet?" Abby could no longer pick up the sound of the water breaking on the shore, or the birds calling to one another, not even a seagull. "I think it's going to rain."

There was the smell too, like a damp basement, when nothing more can evaporate because there's no more room at the inn, the molecules are all full. These were Abby's thoughts. And Ellis, she thought of him also, the way he'd been looking at the sky that morning, and the two of them pulling the cover over the *Little Daline*.

"We should get going," Brew said.

They made their way back along the ridge in a single file with Abby out front. The stillness they'd experienced was quickly changing. A storm was blowing in. Abby looked down once and felt a little dizzy. She saw small whitecaps appearing on the water. The wind picked up, flapping their T-shirts against their chests, and though Abby wore her hair pulled back, messy strands kept blowing in her eyes.

By the time they approached the steps, the sky was quickly becoming darker. They were definitely just ahead of a downpour, but Abby thought they still had time to make it to the top and back to the jeep. Except Brew was wearing his heavy boots, which were still untied, and Abby was sure were slowing them down.

Then a strong gust of wind seemed to arise from out of nowhere and Brew's hat went flying. He must have reached out to catch it, because he was yelling, "Shit!" When Abby turned around, he lost his balance. He grabbed on to a limb and righted himself and scrambled back onto the steps.

"You okay?" Abby yelled.

"I'm fine," Brew shouted. "Keep going!"

They started to move more quickly. Abby told him it was a dumb idea him wearing those boots, and he yelled back, "Abby, I can't hear you!" And of course he couldn't hear anything she was saying—he was behind her and the wind was getting louder, as were the waves and the band of quaking birch trees.

Abby looked over her shoulder at the clouds that were swirling overhead as if they might rupture soon. Then they did, just like that, they burst into heavy sheets of rain. And because there was so much noise, and now so much rain, and the steps had become slick with rainwater, Abby didn't hear the step give way beneath Brew's weight or hear him fall. All she heard was the splash after he'd hit the water.

Abby looped her arm around a tree and pivoted quickly. Brew's head was bobbing on the surface. The waves were scooping down and the water appeared black. She let go of the tree trunk, and without any thought, jumped in after him. She came up sputtering, shocked at how cold the water was, and feeling the weight of the wet backpack pulling down on her shoulders.

She could no longer see Brew's head, only water. She reached for the buckle of the backpack, ready to drop her pack, but then a wave broke and she saw a large rock within a few feet. She hoisted herself onto the rock, wrapped both arms around it, screamed for Brew. The water was cold, her arms were fatigued, and she wasn't sure whether to keep holding on or to swim for dear life.

Something grabbed her leg. She screamed again until she saw it was Brew. He leveraged himself onto the rock beside her—both of them breathing heavily. Abby was shaking and her arms were becoming numb.

"Come on," Brew said. He reached an arm around her waist and pulled her off the rock. Together they swam to the shore. They grabbed a roothold from a cedar, then another, until they slowly pulled their shivering bodies from the water. From there they were able to negotiate the terrain, moving between rock cliff and cedars, giving careful consideration to handholds and footholds. Brew was moving much more fluidly than he had earlier, which Abby realized was because he was no longer wearing his boots.

Eventually they were back on the ledge that led to the cave. Both of them were all right, they could see that. Abby said, "What should we do now?" She was wondering if they should try again to make it to the top, but the steps were greased with mud, and Brew said they should head back to the shelter and wait out the storm. Already, the wind had died down. They weren't in any more danger. Then Brew started laughing and said, "Shit, that was something." Because he was laughing so hard, Abby started to laugh too, because he just looked so ridiculous standing there soaked, his face dripping rivers, his ruddy hair plastered like paste to his head. They kept on laughing as they walked along the ridge and back to the shelter.

He flopped down on the dusty floor of the cave and pulled off his wet socks and wrung them out. Then he lay back and drew up his knees and clasped his hands over his wet T-shirt. His laughter was winding down and his eyes were staring off skyward through the cave, as if he were still thinking about everything that had happened. Abby unbuckled her backpack, slid it off her shoulders, and flopped down beside him. "You lost your boots," she said.

"Yeah, I seem to be aware of that." And then he started laughing again and let out a whoop. "We're a couple of crazy idiots."

"You're the crazy one," Abby said, "wearing those heavy boots of yours."

"You're crazier than I am. You jumped in after me."

"What was I supposed to do, let you drown?"

Then they stopped laughing, rain slapping down hard outside the cave.

"You cold?" Brew asked.

"Not sure I can feel my toes." Abby sat up and pulled off her shoes and set them aside. Then she pulled off her socks and crossed her legs, tucking her toes into the crooks of her bent knees.

Brew sat up as well. "Come here," he said. He scooted himself so that he was sitting behind her. Abby adjusted her position, and he began rubbing his hands up and down her arms.

Daylight was quickly fading. Soon they'd be sitting in complete darkness.

"Are you scared?" Brew asked.

"No. What about you?"

"Maybe I am a little," he said.

"What are you scared of?"

"Bats mostly."

Abby laughed. "Bats are nothing to be afraid of. It's insects they're after."

"Bats carry rabies. Don't care to get rabies."

"You aren't going to get rabies unless a bat bites you."

"Don't care to get bitten either."

Abby didn't have to look at Brew to know the abashed grin on his face. Nonna used to tell them to cover their heads when the bats were out, that they'd get caught in their hair and make a nest. Abby wanted to tell Brew that none of it was true, but the moment passed and she could tell his mind was onto other things.

"What are you thinking?" she asked him.

"Not sure if this place is sacred or haunted. It's more of an unsettled feeling."

"That's probably because it's so dark," she said.

"We're not going to make it back tonight, you know. There's no way with the rain. Even if it stops, we won't be able to see our way out of here, not unless you have a waterproof headlamp or flashlight in your pack."

"I took the flashlight out before I left," Abby told him. "Wouldn't matter anyway. It's not waterproof."

"Going to get cold," he said.

"I'm already cold," Abby said.

"Doesn't help that we've got wet clothing on."

"No, it doesn't," she said.

"Probably should take our wet clothes off."

"Probably not a bad idea."

Brew pushed himself back and took off his shirt. Then Abby heard him undo the buckle on his jeans.

Abby lifted her shirt over her head. The light continued to fall so that their bodies appeared as nothing more than muted shadows. Abby could hear Brew whipping his legs out of the wet denim. She could hear him shivering. She shivered too.

"Come here," he said again, and he wrapped his arms around her. "You didn't get hurt, right? You're okay?"

Abby closed her eyes as her brain struggled with words and her heart fired back at his touch.

"I'm fine," she said. "You okay?"

"Yeah, I'm fine."

And then Abby worried that she'd lost the antler he'd carved for her, but when she reached up, the pendant was still there.

Brew's stomach rumbled. "I should have taken Uncle Dennis up on his offer and had something to eat."

"Hey, I've got trail mix," Abby said. "I just remembered. And Vernors—I picked up a couple of bottles at Nonna's."

Abby crawled over to her backpack. Except for the stash of money that was still in the hydration sleeve, she laid out the items to dry: the red hooded sweatshirt, the binoculars, some flagging tape, the orange field notebook with the photograph of her mom in the ziplock. She stood the book up on its spine and propped it open. Then she handed Brew one of the Vernors and a bag of trail mix.

"Thanks," he said. He used his teeth to open the bag and poured some into his mouth.

By now the light was gone and they were sitting in darkness, and even though they were no longer touching, Abby could feel the heat from Brew's body. "It won't be that cold tonight," she said.

"It's not so bad," he agreed.

They ate the trail mix and drank down the ginger ale.

Brew said, "I'm glad you're okay."

"We're both fine. Don't worry about it."

"I've always liked that about you," Brew said.

"Liked what?"

"Just the way you are."

"That doesn't tell me a whole lot, but okay," Abby said.

The sky kept raining. They were still sitting beside each other, Abby with her legs crossed, Brew with his legs pulled up in front of him. Small bumps of gooseflesh ran up and down Abby's arms and legs. She wished Brew would rub her arms again or hug her against his body.

Abby finished her trail mix and took their empty bags and bottles over to where her pack was propped against the cave wall.

When she moved back to Brew, he was lying on his side, with an arm raised over his head and his head resting on his arm. "We should try and get some sleep," he said.

Abby lay down beside him, turning her back to him, and when she did, he draped his other arm over hers, but he seemed tentative this time when he touched her.

"Is this okay?" he asked.

"This is nice," she said.

They were in new territory here, slow and strange, and yet newly familiar. Older bodies moving closer still. Brew's warm breath against Abby's drying hair—the whole thing a dance in this dark cave—precipitous and daring. But they were cautious, they had grown up together. They were cousins, they were friends. They were more than all the swirling sensations beneath Abby's skin. Still, there was this, this moment, and it felt like everything to her.

23

ABBY AWOKE SOMETIME AFTER THE rain stopped. Gray light filtered in from the wide opening of the cave allowing her to see her belongings laid about—and Brew, this very gentle, very warm body beside her. She watched his face and listened to his even breathing. She could no longer sleep, try as she might. Her hips were sore and her back ached.

She rose quietly, so quietly that Brew didn't stir, and went outside the shelter to relieve herself. The sky was magnificent—violet and magical and shimmering. And in the trees above the cave there was skittering life, squirrels and chipmunks and other moving things, which led Abby to believe that the sun would be up soon, or at the very least, within the next couple of hours.

When she returned to the cave, Brew had rolled onto his back, but he was still asleep, his sun-browned arms with their farmer's tan, now extended alongside him. He wasn't a football player or a basketball player. He was just Brew, medium height and slight of build.

Abby moved over to her belongings and knelt to inspect them. Her clothes were still damp but wearable. Surprisingly the sweatshirt was the driest, perhaps because it had been inside the backpack which, though not waterproof, was water resistant. She pulled the sweatshirt over her head, and trying not to make a sound, stepped into her jeans.

The photo of her mom had remained dry, and she was glad she'd thought to put it inside the ziplock bag. She picked up the field notebook and swept off the layer of fine dust from its pages. She looked over her writings—observations of the different lichens in each of the plots she mapped: the burnt orange of the crustose on the buff-gray dolomite and green-tinted limestone; the silvery sage of the foliose, with their ruffled edges, in patches along the trunks of old maples and white pine; the fruticose, which she called the fruit of the woods because some of them appeared like wildflowers with brightly colored ends as red as raspberries or vine-ripe tomatoes. She not only described the lichens in detail but had also illustrated them using colored pencils.

She flipped through the pages, admiring her work. But the pale orange of the *Lecanora polytropa* crustose was not exactly right, and the *Cladonia cristatella* fruticose needed a brighter red, and she was sure the sage green of the *Parmelia saxatilis* foliose had more of a bluish silver to its edges. She'd ask Uncle Dennis if he knew of an art supply store in Escanaba that might have a larger selection of illustration pencils, because even when she blended the pencils she had, the colors weren't exactly right.

There was the quiet flipping of one page and then another, and the gentle inhale and exhale of Brew's breathing close by. There were her words written in their careful script, and the drawings she'd made with precise lines and delicate shading. She turned another page and instantly held the book closer, examining lines of poetry written in blue ink in unfamiliar handwriting:

THE CRY OF THE CICADA
GIVES US NO SIGN
THAT PRESENTLY IT WILL DIE.

The only person who could have had access to the notebook, aside from Uncle Dennis, was Seda. Abby looked at the handwriting with its slight deviation to the right, and the words written in all capital letters. She recognized the poem from the anthology her father gave her. She had the book with her the first night she slept at the cabin, and she wondered if Seda had discovered the poem then. Abby read the words again. She contemplated everything—the words, the handwriting, their last night at the Falcon's Nest, before they turned in to read *Jane Eyre*. Seda went to the kitchen to refill her glass with water from the pitcher. Her hands were wet with the condensation from the glass. The glass was slippery, and when it slipped from her hands and hit the porcelain sink, it broke into thick, chunky shards. But this is what Abby remembered—joining Seda at the sink, standing there with her, glancing down at the shard Seda held in her left hand, and was Seda's right arm suspended over the sink? Is this what Abby recalled now?

"What are you doing?" Abby asked her.

Seda seemed startled and laughed.

"Sorry, Charlotte," she said. "I broke one of your glasses."

They cleaned up the glass, and Seda's mood seemed fine, but had Abby missed something in that moment? Abby returned all of her belongings to her pack. She slipped her feet into her damp sneakers and double knotted the laces. She was chilled and ready to get back to camp. She was ready to check on Seda.

She crept over to Brew and shook him gently on the shoulder. He stirred and opened his eyes and turned his head toward her.

"Hey," he said, his voice groggy. "Good morning."

"It's not morning yet," Abby said. "I mean, technically it's morning, but the sun hasn't risen."

"Is everything okay?"

"I think we should get going," Abby said.

He sat up and looked around. "Is it light enough?"

"I think so," she said.

He reached for his jeans and shook them out, then stood and pulled them on. In his bare feet, he navigated his way around the strewn rocks and stepped out of the cave and onto the ledge.

"There's enough light over the bay, but everything's going to be dark once we're in the woods," he told her.

Abby knew he was right. The brightness of the sky was an illusion from the stars and moon reflecting off the water.

"I think we can make it," she said.

He turned and looked at her with such earnestness. "What's going on?" he asked.

"Please, Brew. It's important."

"You don't want to tell me?"

"I can't," she said.

"What happened between last night and this morning?"

Abby could feel every part of her drowning in his questions. She wanted to tell him, she really did, but she wasn't ready—not yet—because doing so would betray Seda.

"You can't say," he said.

He rubbed a hand through his hair, let out a deep breath, and looked away from her.

"Okay," he said.

He grabbed his damp T-shirt and pulled it on over his head. He shoved a sock in each of his back pockets.

"Let's go," he told her.

They made their way along the ledge and back to the steps that would lead them up the side of the cliff and into the woods. They were careful as they ascended the stairs, testing each step before applying their full weight, reaching for handholds on nearby limbs and roots, checking them as well. They shook rainwater from branches, neither of them speaking a word.

Abby listened to the birds—a seagull, a raven, the *dzee, dzee, dzee, dzeeet, dzeeet* of what sounded like an Eastern kingfisher. And there was the sound of their bodies, their grunting breaths, the rubbing of Abby's pack on her shoulders. "Be careful," she wanted to say to Brew, who was leading the way this time, in bare feet that were no doubt slippery and cold, but she didn't say it. He was upset with her. She couldn't blame him. They'd never held so many secrets between them before.

And then Brew said, "Would you look at that." Caught in one of the low-hanging branches was his hat, the same hat he'd had for what seemed like a hundred years. Carefully balancing himself on the steps and holding on to the trunk of a young sapling, he reached for the cap and pulled it over his head.

The sky had lightened, and everything around them glistened—the droplets of water, the fine gossamer, mica-flecked rocks here and there, the tiny, white blossoms of miterwort that appeared like minuscule pin lights in bunches close to the ground.

Abby felt hugely relieved when they got to the top and could see the jeep. "We made it," she said.

"There's fresh tire tracks," Brew said. "Someone was right here."

The tracks belonged to a truck and led up to the side of the jeep. They could even see where the truck had turned around.

"Maybe it was the park services," Abby said. "It's not a private road."

They climbed into the jeep, and Abby said, "I guess you're glad I told you to roll up the windows."

Brew leaned over the console so that his face was only inches from Abby's. "I had a good time last night," he said.

"Me too." Their faces remained close. "Thanks," Abby said. "You weren't ready to get going this morning, but you did." She hesitated, wanting to tell him more but knowing she couldn't. "Just thanks."

"Abby, listen, I'm going away this coming weekend. I'll be visiting my mom for a couple of weeks. If there's anything you want to tell me before I leave, I want you to know you can talk to me."

Two weeks suddenly felt like an incredibly long time. "It'll be good you getting to see your mom," she said.

"Did you hear what I said?"

"I heard you," Abby said. "I know I can talk to you. It's just this is something I can't tell you right now."

"Okay," he said.

He started the jeep, and they rode in silence—no radio, no words—back down the all-terrain trail. Once they were on the pavement, Brew reached over and took Abby's hand, interlaced his fingers with hers so that their hands rested on her left thigh.

It was still early. There weren't many cars on the road. They passed the turnoff for the camp. Brew said, "I'm sure it'll feel good to put on some dry clothes. A hot shower's going to feel good too."

Abby realized she'd forgotten all about the load of wash she started at Nonna's. "It's a strange feeling how you can lose all sense of time," she said. "Hard to believe that was just yesterday."

"Are we going to tell anyone about what happened?" he asked.

"Probably not," Abby said.

"Just want to make sure we get our stories straight. No need to get everybody worried."

Then Abby said, "Are you going to tell Tracy?"

Brew was passing the corner market and about to make the opposite left-hand turn when Abby saw a dark-gray coupe with a rear spoiler that looked like the car Piper was driving the night at the bar.

Brew hadn't noticed the car, hadn't seen the look on Abby's face. He was in his head considering things. "Abby, I want you to know—"

But then he hesitated. They were approaching Nonna's house. He made the turn into Nonna's driveway, and there was Uncle Dennis's car and Aunt Reese's truck and a Delta County Sheriff cruiser that Abby had a strong feeling belonged to Travis, and a green pickup truck that neither she nor Brew recognized.

24

THIS IS WHAT HAPPENED. A state park ranger by the name of Gary Ecklund had been making routine checks throughout the park. Although the road leading to The Bluff—if it were indeed to be called a road, because in truth it wasn't much more than an all-terrain vehicular trail—wasn't one of Ranger Ecklund's regular checkpoints, he noticed fresh tracks just before dark. Because the parkland, aside from designated campsites, was closed after dark, he decided to have a look. When he got to the top of the road and found the jeep, his first inclination was that either an individual or a party of hikers hadn't made it back to their vehicle yet, but given the imminent weather, would be back soon. And on second thought, he couldn't be certain there was in fact a passenger or passengers up there, as someone could have just left the jeep and ridden with someone else, even though Ecklund was sure he hadn't seen a second set of vehicle tracks. But mostly Ecklund was anticipating getting home to his wife and seeing his young daughter and having a warm meal.

It wasn't until the next morning, after a good night's sleep and a cup of strong coffee and a fresh day ahead with a glistening morning sun, that he took a turn up the mud-slick road, and by God, the jeep was still there, even after all that rain. He made an attempt to look for foot tracks, but given the heavy rainfall the night before, there were none to be found. Ecklund had no way of knowing in which direction the passenger or passengers of the jeep had gone, and again he told himself he couldn't be one hundred percent certain there had in fact been any passengers.

And yet, deep down Ecklund experienced a real sense of alarm and foreboding. Hadn't a young boy died up there years before? He suddenly felt guilty for his good night's sleep and the roasted chicken and mashed potatoes and blueberry pie he'd eaten and the television he'd watched before drifting off.

This was Abby's impression of things, especially given Ranger Ecklund's sheepish look when he talked about having seen the jeep the night before.

What Ecklund proceeded to do upon finding the jeep that morning was call in the license plate number. He then tried to reach Uncle Ronnie, who was listed as Brew's closest of kin, but Uncle Ronnie was driving a shipment of fish to Marquette, and so Aunt Reese answered the phone.

Because there were no phones at Bear Slide, Aunt Reese drove in record speed out to the camp, with the hopeful idea that perhaps Abby and Brew had taken Grandpa Pete's truck and had simply left the jeep at The Bluff and were in fact in no harm's way.

Given the heavy rain the night before and the tricky roads leading back to the camp, Uncle Dennis, upon waking early that morning to find Abby wasn't there, just assumed she'd stayed at Nonna's. It wasn't until Aunt Reese showed up in a state of panic that he too became alarmed, and his mind began to go down many dark roads, which he would later confide to Abby, and they'd have a good, long talk about.

Uncle Dennis followed Aunt Reese back to Nonna's house, all the while hoping that by the time they got there, Brew's jeep would be in the driveway, and he and Abby would be safe and sound. When that wasn't the case, he called his friend Travis.

The details of an organized search were being thrown together just as Brew and Abby pulled in behind the other vehicles. Like a flock of birds, all the bodies in the kitchen rose from where they'd been sitting around the table, and everyone's eyes stared back at the two teenagers through the big gallery window.

Brew and Abby joined the others at the table. Nonna poured them each some coffee, and the questions ensued. Where had they been? What were they thinking? And where were Brew's shoes? And then, "Thank God you're all right," and "You had us worried sick." Though Brew and Abby admitted their trip to the cave, they didn't tell anyone about Brew's fall into the water and Abby's subsequent jump in after him. There was no point in creating more of a stir.

Gary Ecklund said, well, everything had worked out and that he'd be on his way, and Travis said he'd be on his way too.

Ranger Ecklund said, "Best to stay off parkland after it closes."

Brew said, "Yes, sir."

Travis laid a hand on Brew's shoulder and said, "Everything's all right. We've all done stupid things before. They were just being kids."

Reese said, "Kids or no kids, I don't like it." She glanced at Uncle Dennis, and there was an understanding in that look, but he didn't lift his eyes from the table. He was sitting all to himself, his jaw pulled back and set firmly in place. Aunt Reese said, "Let it go," and there wasn't any mistake that she was talking to her brother.

Aunt Reese took in a deep breath and blew it out. There was a second that followed when everything was as quiet as Uncle Dennis, where even the air seemed wound tight.

Aunt Reese broke the silence and said, "Brew, they're expecting you at the fish house." There were boats coming in and there'd be fish to clean.

Nonna said, "Dennis," and there was authority in her voice.

Uncle Dennis stood from the table. "Let's go, Abby. Let's get you back to camp."

He was silent as they drove, and Abby was so encased in all that silence that she forgot to look for Piper's car when they passed the market and as they drove through town.

When they got to the camp, Uncle Dennis said he had some meetings at the high school, which was next to the cemetery. "I'm not sure when I'll be back," he went on to say. "You might want to get some rest." It was a Wednesday, when they'd usually be in the field.

Abby told him she thought she'd mark a couple more plots on the southern end of the peninsula and that she had some inventory she wanted to finish, which was her way of putting herself in close proximity to the cabin without drawing any unnecessary attention from Uncle Dennis. She set her pack on the counter and was just standing there trying to decide what to do next, as if waiting for him to make her next move apparent to her.

"Suit yourself," he said. He was packing some folders into his backpack, and then he closed his laptop and unplugged it and slid it into his pack with the other items.

Abby truly planned on exploring a couple of the plots she'd already marked and completing an inventory list, but first she wanted to find Seda. She also planned on staying the night at the cabin, given her concerns about Seda and the cicada poem and all the other details that had unsettled her. That said, it was only Wednesday. The reason this proved to be a problem was that Abby made it a habit of only staying away from Bear Slide on the nights she had off. So she said to Uncle Dennis, "I have a friend in Fairport. I'm thinking I may stay with her, if that's all right."

"You don't need my permission," he said.

"I just didn't want you worrying," she said.

This was not a betrayal of Seda. Abby needed to offer Uncle Dennis something as to where she'd be staying. The cabin wasn't in Fairport, but truthfully, Fairport was the last unincorporated community before arriving at the Falcon's Nest, and Uncle Dennis would know that it would put her close to the boat and the area where her work was. But he was still upset, or concerned, or what have you, and so she said, "I'm really sorry."

"How about we forget it," he said. "I'm just glad you're all right."

She stood at the screen door as Uncle Dennis backed out of the driveway and drove away, as she lifted her hand and gave him a wave, even though he didn't see her. Then she returned to the kitchen and poured orange juice and made toast. There was a radio on the kitchen counter, and she listened to an announcer declare sunny skies and light winds out of the southwest. She was glad for the forecast and hoped for a smooth ride to Point Detour. She showered quickly, gathered fresh clothes and a few grocery items, and left for Peterson's.

As she pulled up to the boat launch and parked the truck, she noticed Tanner standing along the shore. Beside him was the boxy-shaped dog. Though not an unusual sight, Tanner and his uncle lived just beyond where Abby was parked, they moored their boat here, they fished these waters. What caught Abby's attention was the purity of the image before her, a perfect moment between a man and his dog, in rays of sunlight.

She shut off the engine and watched the two of them, Tanner bending over and playing with the dog, then tossing a bright-green object over the lake, and the dog bounding into the water and swimming clumsily after it. The dog retrieved the toy and splashed back toward shore. She sprang out of the water and dropped the toy beside Tanner, and shook her short coat, and Tanner raised his arms as if to protect himself from the spray and was laughing. The two of them moved on down the shore, the dog prancing beside Tanner and lifting her head and smelling the wind. There was something very arresting and beautiful watching the two of them, while Abby remained the silent observer hidden away.

And this—Abby in the *Little Daline*, navigating her way through the buoy markers, then accelerating the engine and steering the boat in a parallel line to the land, maybe a few hundred feet out on the water, and there was Tanner and his dog making their way along the rocky shoreline, and Tanner raising his arm in a wave, and Abby waving back at him.

• • • • • • • • •

By the time Abby arrived at the cabin, it was later than she'd hoped. There it was, picture perfect—the straw hat hanging on the door, the Bear Buddha still perched on the corner of the porch. As she stepped onto the porch boards and dropped her backpack by her side, she noticed a necklace hanging around the Bear Buddha's neck, and she laughed at that, the colorful beads another item Seda had no doubt come across, perhaps in the back of a drawer or tucked in a pocket of one of the items of clothing.

Everything looked bright and cheerful in the sunlight, and the light breeze was fragrant with the sweetness of tiny sunflowers and blooming grasses. Seda and Abby had worn a path to the cabin by now, like that made by wildlife, and all around the cabin were other paths, one to an outhouse, another to the well pump—their own little arterial highways. But the cabin was quiet, and to be honest, Abby had worried it might be. Seda was like a wild animal that couldn't be contained. "Who are you?" was the question that kept recurring in Abby's mind. And in another breath, "I'm worried about you."

Abby had brought provisions from the camp—a loaf of bread, a couple of apples, some beef jerky, a jar of peanuts, the honey she promised, half a carton of eggs, a pint of blueberries, some chocolate bars. She hoped Seda would be right where she'd left her—sitting on the sofa in the warm glow from the hurricane lamp, with a cup of coffee and the afghan of many colors pulled over her lap.

But Seda wasn't at the cabin, and it was as if all the familiar colors and pieces began to shift, and Abby was entering into a new landscape. Abby made the bed and gathered the nightgown and a couple of the blouses Seda insisted on wearing—she'd bring them to Nonna's and wash them the next time she did laundry; she wiped down the kitchen and swept off the porch. Despite having told Uncle Dennis she might mark a couple of new plots at the southern end of the peninsula, she decided instead to stay at the cabin in case Seda showed.

She opened the windows and lay back on the sofa. In her mind she was a young girl again, and Brew was standing beside her, and there was Rudy, leaping and bounding in fields of timothy, sunlight and wind, grasses blowing like waves on the horizon.

Lying perfectly still, she could feel the gentle cross breeze. She closed her eyes and imagined Brew beside her, imagined his breathing, his warm breath against her hair.

She slept soundly, and when she awoke, light poured through the west-facing windows. It was already half past seven. She'd missed an entire afternoon. There was still no sign of Seda, and she was hungry, not having eaten anything since the toast she made that morning.

The sun wouldn't set until almost ten o'clock. She set up the cookstove on the porch and heated a can of minestrone soup and fried a couple of slices of bread. She dipped the toasted bread into the soup and spoke to Brew as if he could hear her, as if he knew about Seda. *Where is she, Brew? Where has she disappeared to?*

The cabin felt chamber-like, a void, even as Abby sat outside on the porch and ate her food. She missed company, both Seda's and Brew's. And just like that, her heart shifted, became vulnerable and afraid. What if Brew were with Tracy now? The cave, all of it, suddenly felt far away. And there had been the car that looked like Piper's. What if Seda had gone back to him? What if her life really *was* in danger, like the cicada that gave no sign? Only Seda *had* given a sign. She left the poem. And there was the night Seda dropped the empty tumbler in the sink—was that a sign also?

Abby had noticed when making the bed that the bottle of acetaminophen was no longer on the side table. And earlier that day, when Abby looked inside the console of the truck—for what? a pen? a piece of paper to write on?—the bottle of aspirin was no longer there either.

• • • • • • • • •

The next day, Seda still didn't show. Abby returned to the cabin after completing another assignment in the woods. She filled a pail with water from the cistern and heated the water over the woodstove, as she'd done the night before and on other nights she'd stayed at the cabin, and gave herself a bath. She cooked dinner—eggs over toast—and ate the rest of the blueberries.

Abby stepped onto the porch, because she heard a high-pitched whistle, incessant and piercing. A broad-winged hawk, Abby thought. The calls continued. The hawk sounded close. Abby searched, and there he was, soaring high, then lighting on a branch in a pine. From the silhouette of his body against the sky, Abby could see that the hawk was facing her, she and the bird regarding each other in absolute stillness. "*What is it?*" Abby whispered, as if he had come to tell her something.

A movement of Abby's head, and the hawk was gone, but still she heard his whistles in the distance. Abby stayed on the porch, staring at the sky, feeling as though she were poised at the edge of a world. She felt something warm and peaceful under her skin. Her life was taking a particular shape, and she liked the shape. Everything was going to be all right.

Abby moved off the porch and walked the perimeter, looking for stones. Some she carried, others she rolled into position. She built a fire ring about thirty yards from the cabin. Then she brought out the two chairs from the small dining table, which Seda and she rarely used. She lit a fire and sat in one of the chairs and imagined everyone she ever loved, one by one, taking their turn sitting next to her. She wanted to tell them things—about the hawk she'd heard, and the hoof-clacket of a beautiful buck she spotted on the beach the other evening. She wanted to tell them not to worry about her. She wanted them to witness her life.

Many people came to mind: her father back in Eagle River, her beautiful mother, Catherine and Gracie and her uncles and aunts, Nonna and Grandpa Pete. There were other people, like Helen and Ian at the bookstore in Copper Harbor, and Cal at the corner market in Garden, whom Abby had known since she was a little girl. And there was Geri, who sold fresh eggs and corn at the end of her driveway on Abby's way to Anderson Point. Abby liked how Geri named her chickens after the presidents' wives—Rosalynn, Jacqueline, Eleanor, Martha, and so on.

Abby imagined Rudy, too, mouth hanging open, brown eyes content, lifting his paw to say he wanted her to pet him. And lastly, she imagined Brew, knees turned out, cap pulled over his head, wearing a new pair of leather boots.

At different times she pressed her palm over the pendant he made for her, simply held her hand against it, and stopped whatever it was she was doing for a second or two.

And what was it that he was going to say to her—"Abby, I want you to know—"? What were his next words? Round and round she went over that in her mind.

She decided to bring the boat back to Peterson's the next day after she finished her work. She'd talk to Brew before he left to see his mom. She'd ask him to finish his sentence. What was it that he wanted her to know?

Maybe she'd even tell him about Seda. Maybe she'd tell him everything.

25

AFTER ABBY FINISHED WORK THE next day and was driving through the Garden village on her way to find Brew, she saw his jeep—spruce green, top down, brown upholstery that he treated like leather—in front of Millie's Fish Fry.

The jeep where Brew had taken Abby's hand and held on to it for the duration of their ride back to Nonna's house. And even then, when they pulled in behind the vehicles in Nonna's driveway, Brew continued to hold Abby's hand a second longer, giving her a knowing glance that said, "We're here, let's do this, we'll do it together," and then a gentle squeeze before they both released their grip.

Abby slowed the truck and was about to park and get out when she saw Brew and Tracy walking toward the restaurant door, their backs to Abby.

It was the little things Abby noticed—Brew wasn't wearing his hat; he looked freshly showered with his hair neatly combed; he was wearing a long-sleeved, collared shirt. And there was the way he opened the door for Tracy, with his right hand on the doorknob and his left hand on her back.

The door swung shut behind them. The hopeful jolt upon first seeing his jeep dissolved in seconds. This is how things really were.

Abby drove on. All that mattered was to be elsewhere. She tried to quell her thoughts of how vulnerable she'd made herself the night in the cave. They'd just been two bodies trying to stay warm.

She pulled into the parking lot at St. John's and turned the truck around. Then she headed south and drove back through the village. She didn't look through her side window as she passed the restaurant another time, thoughts probing every moment in the cave, the pendant, Brew's arm wrapped over her body, and the next morning, watching him sleeping, moonlight casting a gray light over him, his body a silhouette, rising and falling with each of his breaths.

How long had she stood at the cave's entrance that morning watching him—long enough to be sure the two of them were real, the two of them tangible in each other's hands.

Abby remembered the spring before she turned thirteen. She and her dad had just moved to Eagle River. She'd gone for a walk through a neighborhood and down a dead-end street that ended at the town beach. It was still freezing on Lake Superior. She wore her long, black coat that looked like sheep's wool and her pink knit hat. A portable radio was in one of the large pockets. She could only pick up three stations where they lived, and the only one that came in well played country music. But she'd discovered that if she got away from the trees and houses and was standing on the beach, she could pick up a station out of Houghton that played classic rock.

She turned the dial on the radio to tune in the station out of Houghton, then pushed her hat above her ears and positioned the headphones. She must have accidentally switched the band from FM to AM, because she picked up an oldies station from a town in Canada.

She walked down the beach to a log tucked away from the shoreline, and sat looking out over the water, when a song by Otis Redding came on about how strong a man's love was for the woman he called darling. Abby closed her eyes, imagining Brew singing the words to her, that he would be the moon in her life when the sun went down because that was how strong his love was.

She became filled with so much love and longing that she began to cry. The song was still playing and she was still crying when someone tapped her on the shoulder. Abby flinched and opened her eyes, and saw a man bent over from his waist, staring down at her. When she lowered the headphones, the man asked, "Miss, are you all right?" Abby wiped her eyes quickly and said, "Yes, I'm fine." Then she fumbled with the radio in her pocket, trying to turn it off because she could still hear the music playing through the headphones.

These were Abby's thoughts as she drove back to Peterson's, all the years she'd carried her love for Brew. "Enough," she said to herself. "Enough now."

26

ABBY RETURNED TO THE FALCON'S Nest and filled the next two days catching up on her assignments. Saturday came and went, and Sunday passed by her, as she marked plot VS1042 and sketched the details of a fallen pine and lichen growing in bunches like clover, and on her way back to the cabin one night, watched two baby foxes tumbling and playing. Beyond them, two more baby foxes lay in the shadow of their den where, on the slope of a hill, the soil and sand had washed away from the roots of a cedar.

She read books and poems, and in the mornings walked deep into the woods, mug of hot coffee warming her fingers, dew like gossamer, daylight shaking through the leaves—all of this, because she was looking for a path that would bring her back to the peaceful feeling she had the night she listened to the hawk and sat by the fire.

She saw bluebead lilies growing on the forest floor, with berries as blue and ripe and plump as the blueberries sold at the store. And sometimes she would sit cross-legged on a path laden with fir needles, or on a bed of moss, or on a rock or a log, witnessing and listening, her thoughts growing deep.

By Monday afternoon, she thought it might rain. A haze hung

over everything. She wandered down to the cove, a cup of tea in hand, backpack slung over her shoulders. She kept her pack close to her these days—a book of poetry—W. H. Auden or Edna St. Vincent Millay, collections she found at the cabin—along with her field journal and notes.

But at the cove, the water and air felt stagnant, and the bugs got to her, landing in her tea and skimming the surface. She emptied the cup on the ground, then untied the boat and climbed in, and pushed off using one of the oars. She puttered along the shore, and perhaps the haze would burn off, perhaps it wouldn't rain, and the bugs would return to wherever it was they returned to.

As she rounded the point, she saw a fisherman and his boat making a slow, even wake. She waved to the fisherman, who waved back to her. Only then did she realize he was Tanner, and on the boat with him was the dog. She followed Tanner through the buoys, both of them lowering their speed as they approached the dock and the jetty.

There was a strange kind of holiness to all of this—the idling and shutting down of engines, boats rocking and water lapping, the stepping over fendering timbers, lines tied over mooring posts, the grit of the jetty's sand and earth and rock beneath their feet.

"Any catch?" Abby said.

"Not today. Was setting nets."

The dog barked a couple of times and ran toward Abby.

"Willow!" Tanner called.

"Is she friendly?" Abby asked.

"She is."

Abby knelt beside Willow and rubbed her short coat, damp from lake spray. The dog's chest was deep and her legs were stocky. "I like her name. Very fitting."

Tanner laughed. "Yes, like the tree."

"So I gathered," Abby said. "How long have you had her?"

"Almost eight years."

The haze was burning off. Tanner raised his arm and wiped the sweat from his forehead. There were bottles of water in a cooler on his boat, and some bottles of beer as well, he said. They decided they'd have a beer, because it was already late in the day, almost four, and Abby had nowhere she needed to be, only here.

Tanner was old enough to buy beer, but not much older than Abby. He retrieved the two bottles, and they walked to the end of the jetty and down the wooden dock. They sat along the edge of the dock, cold beer in their hands, Willow walking around sniffing the plank boards.

"Do you want to hear a story?" Tanner asked.

"I'd love to hear a story."

"Once there was a dog," Tanner began. "She was a very brave dog. She had to fend for herself because she didn't have a master. She had no one to feed her at night or give her shelter. And the dog was about to give birth to a litter. But the coyotes weren't kind to her when her pups were born, and one by one, they snatched them away, until only one of the pups was left. So the mother carried the pup by the scruff of her neck and looked for a place where it would be safe. There was metal and rebar and old appliances—refrigerators and car doors, stacked beneath a willow tree. The mother found a tunnel into the large pile of metal and hid the pup away from the coyotes. But sometimes during the day, the mother would bring the pup out to play, and sometimes they would rest in the shade of the willow tree. Then one day, a fisherman walked by the willow tree and saw the mother and her pup running back into their shelter. He brought them food and water until they trusted him and he was able to bring them home."

"That's a sad story," Abby said. "And a beautiful one. What happened to Willow's mom?"

"She lived out a good life. My uncle took her in. She never left his side."

They drank their beers. Willow lay down in the little bit of shade from the shadow of their backs. Abby could feel the dog's warm breath against her.

"Do you have a dog?" Tanner asked.

"Not at the moment. I'd like to get another one sometime."

"What was your dog's name?"

"Rudy. He disappeared the night of the fire. I always hoped he got away."

Tanner clinked his bottle against Abby's. "To Rudy," he said. Then he set his bottle beside him and reached for Abby's wrist. He turned her arm over so that he could see the underside, where with a permanent marker, she'd written the words *"Here such a passion is / As stretcheth me apart."*

His eyes looked inquisitively at Abby while his hands still held on to her arm.

"It's from a poem," Abby said.

Then Tanner let go of her arm, and drank more of his beer and looked out at the water. She felt she needed to explain something to him—these words, on her arm, this poem called "God's World." She had read the poem the other night on the porch at evensong, from a collection by Edna St. Vincent Millay. A hermit thrush was singing, and she thought the bird sounded like her heart—if her heart could sing, this is what it would sound like, because the song was sad and beautiful. She felt such passion then, in the song of the bird, in the night air that felt warm, then cool, the same passion she felt so many times in the woods, or on the water, and it *stretcheth* her heart apart. This was prayer, she decided. This was everything she wanted to say to God.

And here was Tanner, and he was happy, and she just wanted to sit with him for a while—on this dock, with Willow's warm body and breath behind her, beside all that happiness.

"Do you think you'll always stay here—on the peninsula?" Abby asked.

"Don't have anywhere to go," Tanner said.

"What if you did have somewhere to go?"

Tanner shrugged. "No reason to leave. No reason to go missing something I like."

As the beer went down cool, and their bottles were almost empty, Abby knew for her it was different. She knew for Brew it was different also, like waking up in a dark room, and you can't quite see, and you're hungry, and you need to see; you need to eat, and you know you've been asleep for a very long time. You get up and walk into the kitchen. You turn on the light and make yourself something to eat. And there's this voice out there—it sounds like a voice, and it's saying to you, "Well, all right then. Come on, let's get going."

Then Tanner said, "What about you? You plan on sticking around at the end of the summer?"

"I'm not sure what's next," Abby said. "I'll go back to Eagle River and check on my dad. But I don't know what's after that."

"You should get a dog," Tanner said.

Abby smiled and said maybe she would, and she knew she'd said those words so many times before.

27

ABBY MIGHT HAVE GONE BACK to the Falcon's Nest, but there were her field notes and inventories from the past week that Uncle Dennis would need, and she had to pick up her next assignments from him. There was also the fact that she was low on groceries. But mostly, she didn't want to be alone.

Uncle Dennis was getting out of his car when Abby pulled up to the camp. She was quick to notice that, like Brew when she'd seen him the other night with Tracy, he appeared different than he normally did, wearing a yellow button-down shirt and a newer pair of jeans, and, like Brew, he didn't have his cap on.

He'd been at the school, he told her, helping them with their science curriculum.

He wasn't angry anymore, that's what Abby realized. He'd moved on to other things.

"We should get out of here," he said. "Are you hungry? There's a new restaurant at the end of Vans Harbor."

Yes, Abby told him, she was starving.

Uncle Dennis drove, which required Abby to shuffle things around—folders and notebooks to the backseat and a science textbook that had been on the passenger floor.

At the restaurant, Uncle Dennis strode in, hands in his pockets, stopping to talk to others, gesturing to Abby—"You remember my niece?" he said.

They were seated at a table on the deck and ordered whitefish sandwiches and beer-battered fries, and Abby listened to Uncle Dennis talk about the new curriculum at the school.

Students would take part in the work he and Abby were doing by monitoring a couple of the more accessible plots. The students would get to know the different plant species and then learn about those species in more depth back in the classroom.

And he talked about the teacher he was working with, who spent a summer riding a bike around Lake Superior and taking photographs of birds—who spotted a northern hawk owl and a white-winged tern, some of the rarest birds to inhabit the UP. The teacher was from Illinois but used to visit the UP with her grandfather when she was young. She was growing sweet corn and would give them some when the ears were ready.

There was the tilt of Abby's chin and an amused smile.

"What?" he said.

"Are you more interested in the curriculum or the teacher?"

"That obvious?"

"A little," Abby said, stealing some fries from his plate.

"So, you and Brew had quite the adventure the other night." But his comment didn't seem to affect his mood in any way.

Abby nodded. She dipped a fry in ketchup. "Can I ask you something?" she said.

"Go ahead."

"You seemed really upset the other morning." Then she looked up meeting his eyes.

"Well, sure. I was worried about you two. We all were."

"There's a cairn up there, and fishing lures."

"Yeah, I know about that."

"Did you build it?"

"I had some help. But yeah, I had something to do with that."

His expression seemed to pause. His eyes remained on Abby.

After a couple more seconds he said, "I wasn't reacting to you and Brew. I was reacting to what happened up there with J.P. I should have recognized that. I shouldn't have responded the way I did."

"You weren't so bad. You just seemed a bit overconcerned, that's all."

"Well, that's true. I *was* concerned. But how I reacted wasn't fair to you or Brew."

He reached in his back pocket for his wallet and opened it to the photo of him and J.P., standing side by side with their fishing rods.

"That was taken the month before he died," Uncle Dennis said.

Abby searched J.P.'s face. He was just a boy—barely sixteen. He wasn't old enough to be a father. And yet she thought there might be something—in the way he stood, his long legs, or in the way he held his head, a little to the side, the way he smiled. Might those things belong to Abby—might they have been passed down to her?

Uncle Dennis returned his wallet to his pocket.

"I was with him the night it happened," he said. "There were a bunch of us there. We'd gone up to The Bluff and hiked down to the cave. It was in July, just like it is now. We were having a good time, nothing out of the ordinary, until one of the guys made a dare for us to jump off the ledge. There's a ladder that goes to the water, but maybe you already know that. I think the idea was that we could jump off and swim over to the ladder and climb back up. I don't even know who first made the dare. But there was J.P. saying he'd do it. He pulled off his sweatshirt, the same one you found in the attic, and tossed it to me. And that was it. Next thing we knew, he'd gone over the edge. We were laughing, wondering who'd be next. At some point we sobered up from all our laughing. I leaned over and yelled for him. I didn't see him at first, and then I did, just floating there in the water.

I lowered myself down the ladder as fast as I could. I swam out to him and brought him onto the beach."

Uncle Dennis looked away briefly, just for a second before meeting Abby's eyes again. "One minute he was with me, Abby, and one foolhardy mistake later he was gone."

"I'm really sorry," Abby said.

"So am I."

For a brief instant she had the sickening feeling that this could have been Brew—the cold, clammy weight of that thought.

Uncle Dennis was leaning over the table now and had pushed his plate aside. "You know, someone dies, and we all want to claim our stake in the person, we want to talk about how we knew this or that person and what the person had meant to us. But Abby, I'll tell you, J.P. was my best friend. You don't get a second chance at a friend like that."

Abby thought of the sweatshirt she now held in her possession. She thought of her uncle as a younger man. She thought of him swimming to his best friend and bringing him to shore, and what that would feel like to hold the lifeless body of someone you loved.

Eventually they scooted out their chairs and stood to leave. Abby noticed the orange poppies and red geraniums in long, rectangular planters, and a half dozen hummingbirds hovering over their blossoms, just batting their wings a kazillion times. Uncle Dennis stopped to talk to a couple of people he knew and introduced Abby, and he was laughing at one thing or another. His talking to Abby about J.P. hadn't altered their evening. He told her what happened, and now they were getting on with things. And there was that little smile that settled around his eyes when he was talking about bike rides and Lake Superior, and photographs of white-winged terns, and ears of sweet corn.

After they got in the car, Abby asked him when he was going to see the teacher again. He wasn't sure, he said. She had something going on over the weekend at the bird observatory in Whitefish.

"Does the teacher have a name?"

"Gale," he said. "Spelled like the wind."

"You should ask her out," Abby told him.

There was that smile settling around his eyes again, subtle and gentle, but it was there. And he said, "You know, Abby, I think maybe I will."

28

THE NEXT MORNING, ABBY RETURNED to Fairport. She wanted to spend the weekend at the Falcon's Nest. Maybe Seda would show.

With her backpack over her shoulders and bags of groceries in each of her hands, she pushed the truck door shut with her foot.

Tanner was riding up the hill on his ATV. He pulled up beside her. "Looks like you could use a hand." He'd just come back from delivering his morning catch at the fish house. A red-and-white cooler was strapped to the back of his four-wheeler.

"Follow me up to the garage," he told her. "I'll give you some fish. Then we'll get your things down to the boat."

Abby left the bags of groceries at the truck and walked the hundred or so yards around a cluster of birch trees and the gillnetter named *Kishkedee*, the sun so bright she had to shield her eyes.

Tanner pulled the ATV up to the single-wide and parked in front of the raised garage door.

"Is this your boat?" Abby asked, standing a few paces in front of the gillnetter.

"It belonged to my grandfather," he said. "Giving her a fresh coat of paint. Hope to have her back in the water soon."

"What does the name mean?" she asked.

"It's Ojibwe for 'beautiful bird or tree.' I like to think it means beautiful bird."

Tanner unstrapped the cooler from the back of the four-wheeler. Abby walked with him into the garage. The space was full of fishing crates, plastic bins, all sorts of tools, and large fishing nets that hung from the rafters. To their right was a chest freezer.

"Got some smoked fish too," Tanner said.

He opened the refrigerator and took out a package of smoked whitefish wrapped in newspaper. Inside the refrigerator were at least three days' worth of fish fillets, as well as maybe a dozen bottles of water and sports drinks. Tanner opened the cooler and took out a large trout he'd caught that morning and that had already been cleaned and filleted and packed on ice. "Don't get much fresher than this," he said. And then he told Abby, "Got some perch in the freezer." He lifted the lid to the freezer, which was full of more fish, and several frozen pizzas.

Abby told him the whitefish and trout were plenty. She asked how much she owed him, but he wouldn't take any money. He made a sweeping gesture with his arm and said they had plenty. "As long as the fishing's good, we eat good."

He wrapped the trout fillets in newspaper and laid them and the smoked whitefish in a grocery bag, along with four bottles of frozen water. "That should keep them fresh," he said.

"I got blackberries and eggs," Abby said. "I'll swap you out."

"Keep your blackberries and eggs," Tanner said.

They stepped back into the sunlight. For a minute or so they were quiet. Abby looked at Tanner, hands hanging down at his sides, paint on his T-shirt, head tilted a little to the side as if he were trying to get away from the glare of the sun. She'd bring him cantaloupe and blackberries and corn next time. She'd bring him a blueberry pie. She didn't feel so alone, standing there with Tanner, both their lives in that instant.

• • • • • • • • •

When Abby got back to the cabin, she left the fish on the bottles of ice and set aside a couple of potatoes, a bag of cherries, a ripe tomato. Then she grabbed a bucket and brought it out to the cistern to collect more water.

Beyond the cistern pump were daisies, black-eyed Susans, clusters of purple coneflowers, and something else that caught Abby's attention—a copper and bronze pinwheel, staked among the flowers and spinning in the breeze. She left the bucket and waded through the wild growth and the buzzing bees. "Seda, no," she said. Because deep in the pit of herself, she knew—Seda broke into the camps. The money. The binoculars. And now this—an antique that was reported missing.

Water sloshed from the bucket as Abby carried it inside. She went straight for the kitchen and filled two pitchers. She set the bucket on the floor and reached for a towel to wipe up the spillage.

"Need some help?"

Abby started—there was Seda, casual and calm as if nothing had been amiss, nothing at all.

A bag of groceries was balanced on Seda's hip. She set the bag on the counter and went for the towel. Then she knelt and wiped the water from the floor.

"I saw Piper," Seda said.

She stood and tossed the towel onto the counter. "I met him at the corner market. I called him from town last week and asked him to meet me there. I wish I'd done it weeks ago. You were right, you know."

"Right about what?" Abby said.

"About giving him his money back."

Abby walked over to her backpack beside the front door. "Then how do you explain this?" She picked up her pack and unzipped the hydration sleeve. But when she reached inside to pull out the cash, there were only the two fifty-dollar bills.

"Where is it?" Abby's voice rose. "It was right *here*."

"I told you. I gave it back to him, all four hundred and eleven dollars of it. The two fifties are yours."

And then Abby knew—the hundred dollars her dad gave her for her birthday. She'd tucked the bills into the poetry anthology, the one Seda copied the poem from. "You took my money? How could you do that?"

"Abby, I'm sorry."

"And why did you put it in my backpack?"

"It's the only place I thought you wouldn't look."

"Are you serious?"

Abby sank onto the floor. She pulled her knees up in front of her and leaned her back against the door with a heavy thud. She thought of the binoculars. The pinwheel.

"It was you, wasn't it," Abby said. "You broke into the camps."

"What are you talking about?"

"The camps in Fairport. The break-ins. Uncle Dennis blamed me. He thought I was responsible."

"Abby, I don't know what you're talking about. And why would he blame you?"

Abby reminded Seda of the trailer incident and the police showing up at her school. She and Seda had already talked about this.

Seda sat with Abby, back against the door. "Abby, I'm sorry about your uncle, but I didn't break into the camps. I didn't even know about them."

"What about the binoculars? How did they end up in my pack?"

"You found them? I totally forgot about them."

Abby shook her head.

"They were Charlotte's," Seda told her. "I wanted to surprise you. I thought you could use them."

Abby fell silent.

"They're pretty sweet, though, right?" Seda said.

"Feels kind of like stealing."

"Who would it be stealing from? Charlotte's not here. Besides, you weren't against wearing her boots or that shirt you like, or reading her books."

Then Abby said, "When I was getting water, I saw a pinwheel in the back garden. I thought you'd taken that too."

"That's always been there."

"You're sure?"

"Yeah, I'm sure."

"Then why didn't I see it before?"

"Because you weren't looking for it. Now you're all paranoid or something."

"You took my money," Abby said.

"I know."

An angle of light caught a small pool of water on the floor. Seda dabbed a finger in it. She made an *x* on one of the plank boards in front of them. "I was here," she said. She made another *x* several inches from the first. "And now I'm here. I've changed. And you know what's weird—Piper came all this way, thinking that we'd start hanging out again, like he was coming to rescue me or something. But when I saw him, I didn't feel anything. I couldn't believe I'd ever been with him, like he was some guy I knew in a different life. And now I can't believe I took your money. I think I was angry, mad about your dad—him giving you money and books, the two of you getting along—"

"I saw the poem," Abby told her. "The one you copied from the book. You had me worried."

"Why were you worried?"

Abby closed her eyes. She shook her head lightly. "I saw you in the kitchen, the night you broke the glass. You were holding a broken piece in your hand."

Seda pressed her head against the door and laughed. Then she got to her feet and grabbed Abby's hand. "Come here," she said.

She led Abby to the kitchen. She pointed to the right of the windowsill, to the log above the red countertop, to the pale undertone of the wood where words, barely an inch in height, had been carved—*Seda and Abby were here.*

So Seda wasn't planning to take her life. But why had she copied the poem? The cicadas always appeared about that time of year—the dog-day ones, making all kinds of noise, and then just like that they'd be gone, like the poem said.

"I know you were at the truck," Abby said. "I know you left the journal out so I would find it."

"That's true," Seda said. "And I *did* copy the poem. I *did* want you to have it."

"It talks about dying."

"I don't think it talks about dying."

"The cry of the cicada / Gives us no sign / That presently it will die," Abby recited.

"I was thinking about the summer, Abby. Soon it will be over. The summer will be gone. None of this will be ours anymore."

"I thought—"

"I wasn't thinking about dying," Seda said. "I didn't read the poem that way. I heard the cicadas. Their time's almost up. Still, they just go on making all that noise, like they could care less about not being here one day. They made me think of the two of us singing to Jelly Roll Morton, or the night we danced the Charleston. They made me think of summer, like you and those clouds that first day we were at Anderson Point. I don't think the poem's about death. I think it's about living."

"The Piccadilly Revels Band," Abby said, remembering dancing the Charleston with Seda, remembering swinging their arms and kicking their legs, and laughing so hard they were crying. "I think we'd been drinking Tanner's wine that night."

"I think you're right. Which reminds me—"

Seda reached into the grocery bag on the counter and took out a bottle of bourbon and a six-pack of Coke. "Compliments of Piper, for returning his money."

"So you and Piper are on good terms? No more altercations?" Abby said.

"Let's just say we've made our peace. Things are better that way."

"It's too bad you can't do the same thing with your dad."

Seda fell silent. Then she said, "Maybe one day I will. But I'm not there yet."

Abby and Seda mixed the bourbon and Coke and brought their drinks outside. The two chairs were still by the firepit where Abby left them. She hadn't expected to be gone as long as she was. She and Seda entered the edge of the woods and scouted for more wood and starter bark. They took their time, drinking their bourbon and Coke, passing along conversation, leaning against trees. Abby talked about Tanner and the fish fillets and the *Kishkedee* that meant beautiful bird. She talked about Uncle Dennis and his new girlfriend.

Before she and Seda knew it, two hours had gone by. The Coke and bourbon were gone from their cups. They hadn't picked up any firewood or sheets of bark.

Then Abby wanted to know, had Seda ever slept with Piper?

Sleeping and sex were two different things, Seda said, and no, she never had sex with Piper, though they made out a few times.

"Did you ever have sex with Brew?" Seda asked.

Abby almost laughed. No, she never had.

"He has a girlfriend," Abby said, because she needed to remind herself.

A second passed before Seda answered. "I know," and her voice was kind when she said it.

They stepped here and there, twigs snapping, detritus bunching underfoot. Abby found a long sheet of birch bark. She rolled it up and slid it into her empty glass.

Seda picked up a dead limb and snapped the branches and gathered them under her free arm.

"I think I started the fire," Abby said.

Seda was at first confused.

"The night my mom died," Abby said.

Seda touched Abby's arm. "Wait." She stopped walking. "We need to talk about this."

"I asked Uncle Dennis. He said there were four matches missing."

"Abby, that may not mean anything. You can't jump to conclusions."

"But you said—"

"I know what I said. But maybe there's an explanation. You have to think. Do you remember anything at all?"

"No, that's just it. I don't think I do."

"But you're not certain. Maybe there's something you remember."

"I was at Nonna's the other day. She had some old photos on the table. There was a picture of Brew and me with Uncle Dennis. There was a birthday cake. Uncle Dennis was getting ready to blow out the candles. His birthday is right after Christmas. Brew and I were seven. That would have been a couple of weeks before the fire.

"I remember there was a book of matches on the table. After Uncle Dennis blew out the candles, Brew said he had a trick to show me. He tore off one of the matches. Then he flipped the matchbook cover to the back. He squeezed the match between the cover and the striker pad. When he pulled the match free, it lit. 'Here, you try,' he said. We just kept lighting matches and blowing them out until someone saw what we were doing and took the matchbook from us."

"So you were seven years old and you knew how to light a match."

"We were playing with matches, Seda. It all makes sense. That's why I picked up the matches at the restaurant. Then days later the house caught on fire."

"But you're not sure, are you? You're not sure you caused the fire."

"I'm not sure because I can't remember."

• • • • • • • • •

The evening was warm but not hot. Abby tore pieces of the birch bark and built the fire inside the circle of stones. Once the fire was going, she returned to the kitchen. She washed the potatoes and prepared the salad. Seda unwrapped the fillets of fish and set them on a sheet of aluminum foil. As she gathered the sheet of newspaper to bring out to the fire pit, she began to laugh. Across the newspaper was the headline "Two Schoolcraft County Teens Arrested for the Burglaries of Summer Property on Garden Peninsula."

"I wonder if Uncle Dennis has seen this," Abby said.

"You should save it and put it on the front seat of his car," Seda told her.

"Why would I do that? His car would stink like fish."

"That's my point."

But Uncle Dennis had already apologized. Abby didn't want to stir things up again. She knew sooner or later Travis would get around to letting Uncle Dennis know about the arrests.

Once the fire was going strong, Abby added the potatoes wrapped in aluminum foil, pushing them deep into the coals with a long stick. She and Seda mixed another bourbon and Coke. They sat by the fire and watched the glow of the trees. The sun still had a ways to set, but the light was fading, and the few clouds in the sky were beginning to turn color, the faintest of pink, like a newborn's skin.

"Reminds me of the yellow birch trees," Abby said. "The young ones look like rods of gold or brass. As they get older, their bark turns a whitish color and begins to peel. They almost look like the white birch trees. But I can always tell the difference. At the bottom of their trunks, the bark takes on a rosy hue."

"I was never into trees the way you are," Seda said. "I like the cabin for other reasons."

A number of images came to Abby's mind—Seda running her hands over the needlepoint on the throw pillows, her inhaling the rich scent of cedar each time she opened the wardrobe to decide what to wear, or her filling the mason jars with flowers—butterfly weed, with its bright-orange clusters, and big bunches of yarrow and black-eyed Susan.

After Abby and Seda filled themselves with the potatoes and salad and smoked fish and trout, and the sky turned to night, and the fire burned down to embers, Seda suggested they go for a swim. The moon was practically full and lit up the sky, and the bourbon buzzed beneath their skin.

They walked down the path that led to the water, their sandals flapping against their heels. The cove was perfect for swimming—a small pocket of water with a sandy beach, and beyond the beach, a hedge of cedar trees.

Abby peeled off her T-shirt and slid out of her jeans. Half-drunk, she stepped into the water, numbing cold. Seda ran in, cold sprays kicking up behind her. Pretty soon they were both submerged. They bobbed up and down, giddy with laughter, squealing and splashing.

That's when they heard something moving in the woods.

Abby tried to remain still, toes sinking into the sediment. Little, undulating waves rose against her chin. She was certain she heard a branch break and what sounded like something or someone moving farther away from them. She strained her eyes toward the tree line along the beach.

Seda thought they should dunk under water, so they dipped their heads and held their breath for as long as they could, then slowly came back up for air. There were all the night sounds that they were used to—a hundred different peepers and insects, and the gentle lapping of the water on the shore, but other than that, the woods were quiet.

Then Seda shouted, "We can't see you!" and "Go back where you came from!" and "Leave us alone!"

She and Abby waited awhile longer, until Seda swam farther out and began to float on her back. She started humming to herself, quietly at first, and eventually began to sing the words to "Michael, Row the Boat Ashore." Abby recognized the song as one Aunt Jo-Jo used to play and remembered the chorus, but Seda knew the words to every verse, about boats and trumpets and unknown lands, and rivers being deep and wide, and meeting my mother on the other side. Seda was afraid, that's what Abby realized. She was singing to ward off any intruders. Make noise when you hear a bear, or a wolf, or any large animal, for that matter.

Later that night when they were in bed reading *Jane Eyre*, Seda asked Abby how she'd made out all by herself at the cabin without anyone to read to. Abby didn't tell her about the loved ones whom she imagined sitting with her one by one, but she did tell her about how once the sun had set and the moon was out, she had enough light to read by the fire and read out loud to whomever would listen—to the bears and the barred owls and the bobcats and foxes. She didn't read from *Jane Eyre* that night. She read from *Animal Dreams*, the library book she checked out for herself, about two sisters who were so completely opposite each other in temperament that Abby was reminded of Seda and herself, especially given the way the novel first introduced them from the point of view of their father. He remembered the girls from when they were small, *curled together like animals*.

"I think it was a bear we heard," Seda said. "I think he smelled the fish."

Abby didn't think it was a bear but didn't say that to Seda. Nor did she tell her about the flash of red Abby was sure she saw moving between the trees, as she didn't want to cause alarm. Abby told herself it could have been a bird—a male cardinal or a redheaded woodpecker or a scarlet tanager. Yes, she told herself. Perhaps it was a bird.

Heron

29

ABBY'S MOOD CHANGED, AND THOUGH it felt sudden, perhaps it was a long time coming, like pressure that is building, an accumulation of all the little things—smells and comforts and places, memories and cello music off a lonely road at night, an overgrown tractor trail leading to the burn site that Abby passed almost every day, the *Little Daline* and Brew, the smell of silage and the whiff of gasoline when an engine turns over—all of those things bringing Abby closer—the hug of her grandmother, the smell of her grandmother's lotion, like rose blossoms, her grandmother's kitchen, the smell of fresh coffee, campfires and smoked fish, her grandfather's truck, the woods—always there were the woods. But Abby had managed to hold it all back, until the night she no longer could.

She and Seda wanted to make tea. Abby opened the kitchen window and set up the cookstove on the counter—and no, she wasn't supposed to burn the propane indoors, but the water would only take seconds to boil, and a fresh breeze was blowing in through the window. Up until the night her mood changed, Abby had used a lighter with a long neck to light the cookstove, or to start a fire in the firepit outside, or to light one of the hurricane lamps or a candle. Except the lighter was out of fuel, and she didn't have another one.

Seda said, "I think there are some matches in the drawer." She rummaged through a drawer of twist ties, a pen, a corkscrew, a couple of buttons, a recipe card for making hot buttered rum and brought out a small matchbox. She shook it to make sure there were matches inside, then handed the box to Abby.

Abby slid the box open and withdrew a wooden match no longer than half her index finger, or maybe no longer than half her thumb. She struck the match and opened the valve on the stove, and lit the flame, then lifted the match toward her face to blow it out, and when she did, suddenly she felt afraid. She looked up and saw Seda's reflection in the windowpane. Seda had washed her hair a little earlier. Her hair was still wet, and a drop of water was sliding down her face from her wet hair so that it looked like she was crying. Seda met Abby's stare in the reflection, the two of them standing there for a time just being silent, until the match burned down to Abby's thumb, and she cursed and cursed, though the pain was only minor, and shook out the match, extinguishing the flame, and dropped the match on the counter.

Abby felt cold, though the temperature in the cabin was pleasant. Her hands felt clammy, and she tucked them beneath her arms while she waited for the water to boil.

Seda said she'd take it from there, she'd make the tea, that obviously Abby was shaken. She'd make the tea and they'd talk about it, they'd talk about whatever Abby needed to talk about.

They sat with their tea made with orange spice and honey, on the red velvet sofa, and Seda draped the afghan over Abby's lap. "What is it?" Seda asked.

Abby said, "What is déjà vu, what is it really?"

"It's an illusion. It's not real," Seda told her.

"But what if it's not an illusion?"

"Did you remember something?"

What was it that Abby remembered? The sulfur smell from the burnt match? The quick burst of light? A darkness all around her, even though the cabin wasn't dark. No, this darkness was from someplace else.

Nothing was clear. It was just this—the match, the smell of sulfur dioxide, the chill, the dark, the spark of light. And she was cold, so cold. She wanted Brew then, she wanted to push against him to be warm. She wanted his reassurance that she hadn't started the fire, that mice had chewed on the electrical wires, that Abby was never to blame.

"Abby, listen to me." Seda was shaking her.

"Brew said I didn't start the fire. He was so sure of it. How could he be so sure? This was a mistake, all of it. Coming here this summer."

"You're angry," Seda said.

"I did what you said. I asked about the matches. Maybe I am angry. I have no right to be angry. But I don't know." Abby held the hot tea in her lap, both hands wrapped around the mug, her fingers still cold, numb more like it—her fingertips tingly, like sharp needle pricks.

"My dad used to work at the paper mill," Abby said. "He'd work on the machines after everyone clocked out. He was gone most nights. Sometimes his clothes smelled like the paper mill. Mom would wash his clothes, and I'd take them out of the dryer, and then they'd smell sweet, like the dryer sheets she used, or the fabric softener. Sometimes when I'm in Escanaba and I drive near the plant, I get that whiff. I think of my dad. Him walking in the door after he'd been working, and the sun starting to rise, and the cold draft coming in. Mom would be drinking coffee in the kitchen, and then he'd be drinking coffee, leaning against the counter, with me tucked in against him hugging his legs. Sometimes his clothes had that smell, not exactly, but that whiff—"

Seda understood. "Like a burnt match," she said.

"One day everything's perfect. That's what I remember. My parents are drinking coffee. My dad is home. I'm in my bare feet and the floor is cold. There's a box of cereal on the table. Soon I'll be getting ready for school. Brew will be at the school, his desk next to mine, and his breath will smell like maple syrup, and then we'll be waiting our turns at the pencil sharpener."

"And the next day?" Seda asked.

"And the next day I'm lying on a sofa, and there's a quilt over me, and the pillowcase smells like my grandmother's lotion, like rose blossoms. People are crying and talking. They're in the kitchen. They're pouring coffee, chairs are scuffing against the floor. Someone walks in the room to check on me. I hear footsteps on the carpet. The person is wearing dark pants. I shut my eyes."

Abby drank the tea, sweet and warm. She swallowed again. "Do I even want to know the truth? Isn't it better just to go on living, moving my life forward like everyone else?"

"I don't think it works that way."

"Why can't it work that way?"

"It's like everyone's on this great big bus going places, except one night the bus stopped, and you got off, and the bus drove on, and you got left behind. But life still means something to you. It means a whole lot. And pretty soon your life's going to start up again in a really promising way. I think it's something like that. I think you need the truth. I think that's what your life is waiting for. It's not the same for everyone else."

"They weren't the ones with the matches," Abby said knowingly.

Abby cried then, tilting her head to the ceiling. "I think I did something really terrible. I think I did something so terrible I'll never be free from what I've done. All this time I've wanted to say, 'No, Dad, I didn't start the fire. No, Nonna, I wasn't responsible.'"

Seda lifted the corner of the afghan and wiped Abby's face. "Remember the girl with the douchebag father?"

"Yeah, I remember."

"She was maybe six or seven."

"I think so."

"Just a girl," Seda said.

"Yeah, just a girl."

"You don't have to prove yourself to anyone. You were just seven years old."

Abby could feel her heart beating in her chest—the same heart that beat in her chest when she was seven years old, the same heart that beat inside her before she was born—just this one heart, connecting everything she'd ever been, everything she'd ever done. She wondered why she hadn't understood that before, hadn't always known it.

Seda was talking again, just saying the words that came out of her. "We make mistakes. We hurt people. We try to leave something behind. Take off our clothes, drop them on the floor, wash our skin. Step into something new. And the day after, take off our clothes, drop them on the floor, wash our skin. We really want to try this time. We want to make ourselves right in the world. We can't wash away the past, but we go on trying."

Abby wanted to tell Seda she loved her. But for some reason, she didn't say the words.

There was light in the sky, a stripe of blue over the treetops. They built a fire outside and read by the fire until it was too dark to see the words, and then read in bed until sometime in the wee hours when they finished *Jane Eyre*. They would make a trip to Escanaba after breakfast the next day. They would check out more books.

Sometime in the night Abby heard her name, over and over and over—a young woman's voice, a worried voice. When she opened her eyes, Seda was there. "You had a dream," she said.

Seda brought Abby a glass of water. Abby remembered the dream, bits and pieces of it, a room painted avocado green with posters on the ceiling, her grandfather's shoes—steel toe, black leather, scuffed and creased, his army-green trousers. They were going home, he said. "And Mom?" Abby asked. "Did she make it out of the fire?" The sheet of white paper beneath her crinkled. Then everything was cold, and she was in her grandfather's truck. The sun was coming up. White light through the windshield. Abby couldn't see a thing.

• • • • • • • • •

The next morning, Abby and Seda drove to Escanaba, stomachs empty because they'd passed on having another breakfast of instant oatmeal. They pulled into a drive-through at a fast-food restaurant and ordered sausage and egg biscuits, greasy hash browns, and Seda wanted a large coffee because another one of her headaches was coming on. Her bottle of acetaminophen was empty, as was the bottle of aspirin in the console. There was a drugstore a couple of blocks away. They'd get Seda whatever she needed, Abby told her.

The drugstore belonged to a chain of many. The analgesics were toward the back, past sunglasses and cosmetics and plastic sand buckets and shovels. Seda looked at her reflection in the mirror above the sunglass carousel. "I look pale," Seda said. "I always look pale when I get a headache." She picked out a tube of lipstick from the wall of cosmetics—Coral Crush—and removed the plastic wrapper.

"You can't do that," Abby said.

Seda swiped the color over her cheeks and rubbed it in. Then she applied it to her lips.

"Relax," Seda said. "I'll pay for it."

Seda paid for a bottle of Excedrin, the lipstick, a couple of candy bars, because she said she was craving chocolate.

There was a picnic table next to the parking lot. They brought the grease-stained bags with their breakfasts to the table, and Seda took the pain medicine with her coffee.

"Are the headaches getting worse?" Abby asked.

"I don't think so."

"You seem to be getting more of them."

Seda shrugged.

"Have you seen a doctor?"

"Once I did."

"What did he say?"

"*She* wanted to put me on birth control pills. Dad wasn't a fan of the idea, so she prescribed something else."

Seda squeezed a packet of ketchup on a wrapper. She dipped the hash browns in the ketchup. "The medicine made me sick. And moody. I swear, I wanted to hit somebody."

"Was that when you smashed the TV?"

"No, that was all me," Seda said.

The girl who'd rung up Seda's purchase was now standing outside leaning against the building, one leg drawn up, the sole of her shoe pressed against the brick. She placed a cigarette in her mouth and leaned her head down to light it.

"We probably took her seat," Seda said. On the ground were cigarette butts, a couple of bottle caps, dandelions and patches of dirt, little red strings of cellophane from cigarette packages.

"My mom and dad met at a place like this," Abby said. "She worked at a drugstore, about a mile from here. I don't think it's there anymore. My dad says him getting his hand caught on a machine blade was meant to be. Mom was working her shift, and he stopped in to buy first aid supplies. When he laid the items on the counter, she noticed the rag tied around his left hand. He told her it wasn't bad, that he'd gotten his hand somewhere it shouldn't be. But when she left her shift for a break and went outside to have a smoke, she saw him sitting at the picnic table with his supplies spread out in front of him. She offered to help. She'd brought a bottle of water outside with her and poured some over his wound. She thought he should get stitches, but he said it was just a small cut. Then she applied the ointment and made a bandage with the gauze and tape. He asked her if she'd ever thought of becoming a nurse.

"He told her his name was John Francis McDermott, but people called him Jack. He'd been taking classes toward a certificate at the heavy equipment school down the road. He was hoping to pick up enough work to pay his way through school. He wanted to study industrial maintenance.

"Then he asked her if she was in school. She told him she had a child at home and didn't have much time. He didn't judge her, or say she was too young to have a kid. Instead, he told her he'd like to see her again. She was crazy about him, Nonna says. And after they moved to Garden, Mom started taking classes at the community college. She was studying to be a nurse."

Abby liked to tell the story—how her parents met. She liked to remember how they loved each other. She saw her dad back then, heavy-seeming, blue eyes that sparkled and were given to smiling. She saw her mom standing with him, at a checkout counter, groceries on a conveyor belt, her fingers making zig-zags over his back while they waited their turn in line. Things were never more complicated than that—two people in love who refused to find fault with each other, as if already they knew life was too short for that.

• • • • • • • • •

At the library, Abby went to peruse books. She was carrying a stack of them when she realized Seda wasn't with her. She found Seda sitting in front of a large microfilm reader set up on a table in one of the back rooms. A woman named Donna brought in another newspaper reel and loaded it into the machine.

Seda explained that the reels consisted of quarterly newspaper installments by year. She was now viewing April through June of 1973. She was looking for information about Charlotte—an obituary, some mention of her artwork, some mention of her name.

"You could be here for hours," Abby said.

Seda looked at the clock hanging above the door. "I've been here for two hours already."

Abby couldn't believe that much time had passed.

"I started with 1975 and am working in reverse," Seda told her.

"Why 1975?"

"I found a tin of baking powder at the cabin. Its expiration date was for that same year. Maybe she died in the seventies. It's a long shot, but I needed to start somewhere."

Donna brought in another reel and loaded it into the machine. Seda advanced the reel. She and Abby looked through headlines and articles—the Hiawatha pulpwood production increase, the smelt feed at the American Legion, good food at the Buck Inn. Abby got distracted by a story about eight canoeists who retraced the trip of Father Jacques Marquette, and later by a crossword puzzle, and a three-letter-word for a literary collection. Seda became distracted as well, with *Blondie* and *Andy Capp* and *Beetle Bailey* comic strips, or grocery store advertisements. "Look at this," she said. "A person could buy ten grapefruits for sixty-nine cents at Elmer's, and an entire watermelon for under a dollar."

Another headline announced the Hilltop Theater showing *Lady Sings the Blues* about Billie Holiday, and didn't Charlotte have a Billie Holiday record?

And then there it was, under the death notices, "Mary Charlotte DeVore, artist and naturalist, passed away at her home on Saturday, from natural causes. She was 67."

There, beside the article, was a photo of Charlotte. Abby and Seda were looking into the face of the woman whose special place in the woods—just a little cabin tucked at the bottom of a peninsula where, according to the article, she had whiled away her summers studying and painting the flora and fauna—had become their sanctuary as well, their comma, their chrysalis, their cocoon.

The photo was in black and white. Abby thought Charlotte's hair might be blond, but perhaps it was gray, and was cut just below her ears and pushed away from her face. She was wearing dark-framed glasses and a white, billowy blouse. Her right elbow was supported on a table, and in her lap was a midsize, scruffy-looking dog. Charlotte's left palm was resting on the dog's head. The dog looked as if he was smiling. Charlotte's eyes were on the dog, and like the dog, she was smiling, and it was a wistful smile, that is what Abby thought.

Upon reading the article, Abby and Seda learned that the dog's name was Cooper, after Stanley Cooper, a beloved friend of Charlotte's who passed away when she was young, and Abby thought certainly now she and Seda knew the name of the handsome man in the framed photograph at the cabin. They went on to learn other things about Charlotte. She was born in Gary, Indiana, and studied biology as well as art at the University of Wisconsin. She earned a master of fine arts at Eastern Michigan University in Ypsilanti. She created a path of her own, doing what she loved, and had worked tirelessly as an educator at the community college and as a facilitator of cultural enrichment. The article went on to list many community programs she'd been a part of, and said that her legacy would live on in the artists and students she'd inspired, and Abby felt in her heart that Charlotte would live on in the lives of Seda and her as well.

For ten cents a page, they could print a copy, so that's what Abby did. She went to pick up the page from the printer and then stopped to show Donna. It was only after she returned to her chair that she became aware of Seda staring at the far-right column on the viewing screen, to a picture of a softball team. "Ten straight wins for the Miss Demeanors," the headline read. The girls on the team looked to be no older than thirteen or fourteen. Their names were printed at the bottom of the photo: Debbie Bourdeau, Beverly Beauchamp, Jeanne Swetkis, and then, Abby couldn't believe it, there was her mom's name—Cathy Treadwell. She was standing in the back row, fourth from the left. Though her mom's eyes were hidden from the brim of her cap, Abby recognized the smile.

"I can't believe you found this. We could have easily missed it."

"I can't believe your mom's picture is on the same page as Charlotte's."

"I'm seriously having chills right now," Abby said.

"Maybe it's the air-conditioning."

"It's not the air-conditioning."

"I know," Seda said. "I'm having chills too."

Abby looked at the page she'd printed on legal-sized paper. "I swear, I'm going to frame this."

"You should," Seda said.

Abby rolled up the page and put it in her backpack. She picked up the stack of books she wanted to check out—*The Handmaid's Tale*, *A Prayer for Owen Meany*, and a nonfiction book about a rock hound's journey across the UP.

Then she remembered something and walked back to the desk where Donna was working. Where could they find a book on the meaning of people's names? Donna led them to the parenting section. Abby withdrew a book and flipped the pages until she came upon *Charlotte: Of French origin, meaning free woman, derived from Charly, which means free man.*

She then looked up the name Seda: *Of Arabic origin meaning a voice or an echo, and of Portuguese origin meaning silk. In Armenian, Seda means spirit of the forest.*

30

BY THE TIME ABBY AND Seda left the library, the sky had turned from partly sunny to a flat white, and the windshield was covered in mist. They were mostly quiet as they drove out the highway leaving town, past a cornfield and a cantaloupe field and the Escanaba River.

Abby thought of her parents—a small wedding at the courthouse, the adoption papers, the sublet in Marquette. Abby's mom worked behind the counter at a pharmacy and pressed linens for a Catholic parish. Her dad operated large machines and went to school. There were other towns and other apartments, and a dairy farm in Baraga County, where her dad managed the equipment, and her mom milked cows and waitressed on the weekends.

This is what came to Abby as she was driving—an image of her kicking a bucket, making all sorts of racket. It was early morning. Abby was in a barn, and her mom was off in the barn doing something. Abby could see herself as she was then—blond hair cut short around her face. She must have been four or five.

Abby tried to remember her mom exactly as she was that day—what she was doing, what she looked like. Gradually, an impression came to mind—her mom wearing gray-colored pants that were baggy in the legs and tucked into big rubber boots, and a dark-colored coat, perhaps a raincoat, hanging below her hips. Her hair was long and brown and pulled into a ponytail, and she was setting something on the ground or picking something up. As Abby drove, she had a sense of her mom feeling tired, that's what Abby recalled, as if she could feel her mom's body.

Abby drove past a billboard for the local college, which led her to consider other things.

"I'm thinking about getting another dog."

"What would you name her?" Seda asked.

"What do you think of the name Taiga?" Abby said. "It means snow forest."

"Maybe you could name her Charlotte."

And so that was how they fell into conversation again.

• • • • • • • • •

They dragged the boat onto the beach, the weather moody and misty, their clothes and hair and skin damp. Abby felt like walking and Seda had the idea of exploring the shoreline around the point.

There was the sound of water lapping the shore, the clack of loose stones beneath their sandals. Abby said, "Brew gets back today. Probably sometime tonight."

"You going to see him?" Seda asked.

"I don't think so."

They walked a quarter mile or so. The wind was getting stronger. "I should be heading back," Abby said. They'd already decided it would be best if Abby didn't stay the night—the water would be too rough in the morning for her to be out in the boat.

They were about to turn around when Abby noticed a cream-colored object ahead of them. It looked like a bone. She first thought it was human. She crouched down and inspected it more closely. "I think it belongs to a deer, maybe even a bear."

"It looks old," Seda said.

Abby waded into the water and washed the bone thoroughly. It was fairly weighty with a golden hue, and triangular in shape, with pockets and ridges. Maybe a pelvis bone, Abby thought, though really she had no idea. She dried it off with the hem of her T-shirt and then placed it in her pack.

• • • • • • • • • •

By the time Abby returned to Bear Slide, the rain was coming down in torrents. Uncle Dennis was working at the table. He set his work aside and moved over to the sofa. Abby grabbed a towel and sat in the blue recliner across from him, the bottoms of her jeans wet, her hair beaded with moisture.

"How's your friend?" Uncle Dennis asked.

"She's fine," Abby said. Then she asked, "How's *your* friend? Did you see her again?"

"Now that you mention it, she was just here."

Abby's smile broadened. "How did it go?"

"I think she had a good time. I cooked her pasta, and you know what a good cook I am."

"The best," Abby said.

"No, seriously, we get along well. We have lots of things to talk about."

Then Uncle Dennis said, "I almost forgot. Brew stopped by. He was looking for you. He just got back in town. Come to think of it, he stopped by a couple of weeks ago too. He wanted to see you before he left."

The rush hit her.

"What did you tell him?" she asked.

"I told him you were staying with your friend down in Fairport."

The conversation moved on and they were talking about other things—the Whitefish Point Bird Observatory, where the teacher Gale had just been, because these were the things Uncle Dennis wanted to talk about. Abby understood this is what you do when you're interested in someone, you talk about the things that remind you of that person. And yet all the while they were talking, Abby was thinking of Brew. She thought about him stopping by two weeks ago—two weeks ago was when she and Seda went swimming. Abby assured herself no one had seen them that night, and once more told herself that the flash of red was just that, a flash of red, like the color of a bird. But still, she wondered why Brew had stopped by.

31

ABBY WALKED DOWN A LONG, muddy road, a couple of miles at least, before stepping into a field, grass swishing high against her pants. The ground remained soft, and then there were woods and lush ferns resembling rolling meadows. A little deeper into the woods was a small bog, about fifty yards across.

She went about her business, measuring out a new plot, and sat squat down, ready to hammer a stake, when she heard a splash—something small, like when a fish is caught and is reeled in and at last breaks the water's surface. She became very still and searched the bog. Standing on its far side was a sandhill crane. The crane was an adult, mostly gray with a red crown. Sandhill cranes weren't typically solitary creatures, Abby knew, unless they wandered away from their group, scavenging for food, as this one must have done.

Abby moved closer, crouched in a stealth position, footsteps hitting the ground lightly. That's when she discovered the bench, made out of two-by-fours and weathered the same color as the grayish brown of the crane. She sat on the bench, watching the bird dip her bill into the marsh. After a brief time, the crane must have decided she'd had enough of Abby's presence, because she made a rattling bugle sound and disappeared into the trees.

Abby was sitting with her body perched slightly forward and her hands on the edge of the bench. She leaned back a little and lifted her right hand to shield her eyes from the sun and stared off into the trees, looking for the crane. After a brief time and no sighting, her eyes happened to glance down and notice several sets of initials etched into the wood. In the exact spot where her right hand had been was the fairly deep carving of *J.P. and Kee Kee.* Abby had never known anyone to have the same nickname as her mom, and now here was her mother's name carved into the bench where Abby was sitting, along with the initials of Abby's biological father.

Abby felt tethered in that moment to a time so long ago, when a young couple in love sat in this same spot. Had Abby already been conceived? Was something of her with her parents then? Two people in love, her mother and her father, both gone now—and this—their names in the bench where Abby was sitting. She ran a fingernail along the grooves, pressed her palm against the grain of the wood. *You were here, Mom. You were here, Dad.* Calling him Dad felt strange at first. *My dad,* she thought. *My mom.* She felt flushed—warm all over, a pocket of warmth in the air. She'd felt these warm spots before, like the heat off a car radiator after the engine is shut off.

There was another time, after her mom died, when Abby was walking along the water in front of Nonna's house, loose stones beneath her feet, the air cooled from the water, but then this—a warm spot settling over her. And something else—the crisp smell of denim, the soft tuck of flannel against her skin—Abby's mom was there. Then she was gone, the air was cool again, the wind tossed Abby's hair and smelled of lake water and wet bark.

And there was the night after the party on the beach, when Abby chose to walk back to the camp alone. The cello music, the rain mostly a drizzle then, the moon behind the clouds. One more step, another, the warm pocket, the smell of coffee and fresh air, like the breeze through Nonna's kitchen window.

Abby's language arts teacher introduced the class to writers such as Emerson and Thoreau, and perhaps the warm spots Abby experienced were something transcendental. She thought about all the energy that made its way from one living thing to another, all the energy that went on living even after it passed to the *Oversoul* as Emerson called it, so that when a person died, they simply transcended, but were never too far away.

In a single instant, the day had suddenly become something more to Abby—this one day, this one girl—not really a girl, but a woman growing up—sitting in this spot with no intention but to watch a sandhill crane. But the girl wasn't alone, that's what Abby knew. Her parents were with her also. This expression of biological life and spiritual life and something big and eternal. In that one instant, boundaries and margins and ceilings vanished. Gone were the frozen lakes trapping her in their darkness. This is what the broad-winged hawk was saying to her, this is what his high-pitched whistle spoke—you are free, don't be afraid.

In her mind she imagined herself as a young child, and her mother and J.P. standing on either side of her, holding her hands, swinging her back and forth. She could see her own face, beaming and bright, legs kicking out, eyes catching glimpses of her doting parents. Higher and higher she went until she was soaring like a child jumping from a swing. The moment felt like a movie frame that has paused—sky and air and sunlight all around Abby. Her parents had let go, but she knew they were still there, watching her, each one clasping their hands together and smiling. This was the horizon. This was the eternal. This great mystery. This great unity of everything.

• • • • • • • • •

That night back at Bear Slide, as the nighttime temperature dropped and the cool air wafted into the camp from the open windows, Abby pulled the red hooded sweatshirt over her head and tucked her hands into the front pocket.

She didn't mention to Uncle Dennis about finding the bench, and she wondered if in all his wanderings in those woods he'd ever come upon it. She would tell him eventually, but for now, she wanted to keep it to herself.

She sat with Uncle Dennis at the table and listened to him go over their assignments for the rest of the week. He gave her a new map, and when she went to put it in her backpack, she remembered the bone she found on the beach and brought it out to show him. He turned it over in his hand several times. What she'd found, he felt certain, was the sacrum of a caribou. "I bet it's almost a hundred years old."

"You're serious? You're sure it belonged to a caribou?" Abby was incredulous.

"I can tell by the size. I've got a friend who saves the sacrum when hunting deer. He's got a sacrum from a moose too."

"Why the sacrum?"

"The sacrum is considered the holy bone. Some Indigenous cultures believe it's where the soul resides." He then pointed out the eight holes in the bone. "These are the sacrum houses. They draw energy from the earth. I think when an animal comes to you like this, like the caribou has done, it's trying to teach you something. It's giving its energy back to you."

Uncle Dennis smiled. "You're the caribou girl," he said.

"What does the caribou teach you?" Abby asked.

He handed the bone back to her. "It teaches the same lessons as the earth. Endurance and adaptation. It can also teach us about duality and regeneration. Both the males and females have antlers and shed their antlers in the spring."

"Then why didn't they adapt and regenerate in Michigan?"

"Because we didn't take care of them," Uncle Dennis said. "We did this to them."

"What about disease and wolves?"

"Disease and wolves took them because we destroyed the caribou's habitat."

32

IT WAS ALREADY AUGUST. AUNT Jo-Jo had started a new job working at the restaurant in Nahma. Gracie adopted a kitten she'd named Petals. Brew had gone with Uncle Ronnie to Chicago to make a shipment. They were going to stay over and catch a baseball game. These were the things Abby learned when she stopped at Nonna's to do laundry.

And that last piece of information—the mention of Brew's name, that little skip or falter in Abby's chest.

"You two haven't seen much of each other," Nonna said.

"No, not really."

Abby's clean clothes were in a heap on the table. She smoothed out a T-shirt, folded in the sleeves. Nonna picked up a pair of jeans, snapped them out straight, folded them at the waistline, then hung them on the back of a chair.

They continued to fold clothes. Abby said little.

"What's on your mind?" Nonna asked.

Abby searched through the clothes for socks. She matched them together. She was thinking about things—Brew and Tracy, J.P. and her mom. "I saw something in the woods the other day. There was a bench."

Abby went on to describe the bench—her mother's nickname, Jimmy Pruitt's initials.

Nonna set a folded shirt on top of the others. Her hand remained on top of the shirts. She smiled then. "He was a good kid. They both were."

"Does it ever get easier for you?"

"No, not easier."

Nonna paused. She wasn't looking at Abby. "It changes. The initial shock goes away."

"Do you ever talk to her?" Abby asked, because she was thinking of the words she'd spoken to her mother—*Are you there, Mom? Can you hear me? Mom, I'm so sorry.*

"Every day," Nonna said.

• • • • • • • • •

Abby was dressed in jeans and a couple of shirt layers under a windbreaker. Beneath her clothes she wore a swimsuit. Seda was dressed the same. The wind stung cold on the open water. The bow of the *Little Daline* rode up hard on the rolling waves and slapped down harder.

Little Summer Island was an unpopulated parcel of land just two and a half miles from shore, off Anderson Point. Abby's time on the peninsula would wrap up soon, and more and more she and Seda were feeling the imminence of that, like the song of the cicada. They were remembering things—the night dancing on the beach, Seda's riding on top of Alex's car—"You were crazy that night," Abby said. And Seda replied, "You were crazy, walking home alone." They remembered driving to Anderson Point and sitting in the truck in front of the jetty and looking out at the islands. Seda had said they should go there sometime.

As they approached the island, Abby decelerated. Twenty feet out she cut the motor and the boat surfaced the bottom, gritty sand scraping the hull. She and Seda jumped onto the beach, shoes and jean cuffs barely getting wet, and pulled the boat farther ashore.

They'd packed a blanket from the cabin and food and water, as well as beach towels, and chose a spot where they spread out the blanket. Off the open water, the air was calm and the sun warm. They stepped out of their jeans, removed their shirts, slathered their bodies in sunscreen. Abby brought a transistor radio and was able to pick up a country station out of Escanaba. She and Seda tapped their feet on the blanket and sang lines from some of the lyrics. When they got hot under the sun, they went for a swim, not too far out, because there were riptides, Abby said. They ate tuna fish sandwiches and ripple potato chips and dried mango.

After lunch, they walked down the beach, sand and sweat sticking to their bodies. That's when they heard a croaking sound coming from a large bird a little farther down the shore. The cry sounded plaintive and pitiful. "Something's wrong," Abby whispered.

She and Seda took their next steps slowly, approaching the bird with caution. A few paces closer Abby identified the long gray legs and yellow eyes, the gray plumage and the downy white tufts on its chest, the gray crown. Its long neck was folded into itself. The bird was a young blue heron, not even a year old, Abby was sure.

"This is probably close enough," Abby said.

She and Seda crouched down about ten feet away from the heron. "It's okay, we're not going to hurt you," Abby said. The bird seemed weak and disoriented. Her legs stumbled a little as she tried to move away, until she seemed to resign herself to their presence.

"We should get the blanket and try and move her onto the boat. We need to get her help," Abby said.

When they returned with the blanket, Abby draped it carefully and quickly over the heron. She wrapped her arm around the bird's wings, holding them against the bird's body, and grasped the beak through the blanket with her other hand, knowing how dangerous the beak could be. The heron was surprisingly light, and Abby remembered Uncle Dennis telling her that birds had hollow bones, which is what allowed them to fly. Abby could feel the bird quivering beneath her arms, but for the most part the heron didn't try to struggle. "She's really sick," Abby said. "If she wasn't, I think she'd be making more of an effort to get away."

"Or maybe she's just too frightened to move," Seda said.

Abby drove the boat slowly back to Peterson's, trying not to disrupt the bird any more than they had to. Ellis and Tanner were standing on the jetty when they got there, rinsing their fish trays and stacking them.

Tanner waved. "Whatcha got there?" he asked.

Abby told him about the heron. He knelt down and extended his arms to take her so that Abby and Seda could climb out of the boat. Ever so carefully he pulled the blanket over the bird's head. The bird opened her bill a couple of times. Tanner was quick to move his hand over her head and hold her beak closed.

"You should get her to the bird rescue," he said.

Abby wasn't familiar with the place he was talking about.

"I think I know where that is," Seda said. "I've seen a sign for it."

Ellis finished what he was doing and came over to join them. "Her name's Gale," Ellis said. "She runs a wild bird rehabilitation center out of her house."

Abby thought it might be a coincidence but asked if Gale was a schoolteacher.

"She teaches science at the high school," Ellis said.

"My uncle knows her," Abby told him.

Ellis laid his hand on the bird's head, just held it there for a second or two. Then he told them he'd head up to the house and give Gale a call. "She'll probably want to transport the bird herself."

Abby and Seda walked with Ellis and Tanner down the jetty and the short distance to the truck, Tanner still cradling the heron against his chest. Abby lowered the tailgate and set her things in the truck bed.

Tanner said if Gale couldn't come down, he could drive them to the center.

Abby thought they'd be okay. "She stayed pretty calm on the boat ride over."

"Maybe so, but you don't know what she'll be like once you get on the road. She could be in shock right now."

Abby could see Ellis standing in front of the open garage, holding a cordless phone. He held the phone to his side and called to them. "She's on her way."

Seda and Abby climbed onto the tailgate to wait. Ellis walked back down the hill and rejoined them. Already he'd talked more than Abby had heard him talk all summer. He told them about a loon he'd found a couple of years ago. The bird had swallowed a lead weight. "You don't think of a bird getting lead poisoning." He hoped that wasn't the case with the heron.

"What happened to the loon?" Abby asked.

Ellis shook his head. "Not good," he said.

Brew and Abby had fished with lead sinkers. She never thought of them causing any harm. She was also thinking about the hooks and bobbers and fishing weights they'd scavenged at the graveyard, and all the plovers and seagulls that lollygagged along the shoreline pecking away at this and that.

Ellis went on to tell them that the birds would swallow the sinker, thinking it was a stone. "They need the gravel in their gizzards to grind their food. Doesn't take much lead to make a bird sick."

"Can anything be done when that happens?" Seda asked.

"Depends on the toxicity level," Ellis said. "Not a whole lot they can do. Maybe surgery. Maybe get the bird to pass the weight. Give the bird fluids and medicine."

Tanner had climbed onto the tailgate. Abby reached over and

stroked the bird's head. The heron's eyes didn't look as alert as they had earlier and were starting to close. "I hope she's just tired," Abby said.

"I can still feel her heartbeat," Tanner said. "Her heartbeat feels strong."

About that time a red pickup truck with a white camper shell turned off the road. Ellis lifted his hand, gesturing to the driver.

The woman parked her truck beside Abby's and climbed out. She had on a red cap and was wearing a pair of light-colored trousers and a dark tank top. Beneath her cap, her hair was braided off to the side. Abby scooted off the tailgate and walked over to meet her.

"I'm Gale," the woman said, extending her hand. She was the same woman Abby saw when she brought Seda to Anderson Point that first time, and whom Abby saw again at the market.

"You know my uncle," Abby said, and introduced herself.

Gale's eyes widened. "You're Dennis's niece. He told me about you. That's really great the work you two are doing. And now you're rescuing birds."

Gale turned her attention to the heron. "So what do we have here?" She pushed back the blanket and examined the heron's plumage. Then, holding on to the bird's beak, she examined her eyes.

"Mind if I hold her?" she said to Tanner.

Gale unwrapped the bird, and supporting her, stood her up on the ground to determine the strength in her legs. "Hey, sweet girl. You're a young, little thing."

"How old do you think she is?" Abby asked.

"She hasn't even gone through her first molt yet. I'd say she's about four months. Hard to tell exactly." Gale finished examining the bird and said, "I can get some fluids and nutrients in her. But we should probably get an X-ray and run some blood tests. I've got a vet I can put in a call to. He's really good about this sort of thing."

She picked the heron back up and held her close in her arms. "You mind helping me, Ellis?" Gale said.

Abby could tell they'd done this sort of thing before. Ellis lifted the back window of the camper shell and lowered the tailgate. Gale had brought a large plastic dog crate. Ellis opened the crate, and Gale brought the heron over and set her inside.

"Dennis can give you my number," Gale said. "Call anytime. I'm happy to give you updates."

"Do you have any idea what's wrong with her?" Abby asked.

"Hard to tell. Could be lead poisoning. Could be mercury. Maybe it's just parasites and malnutrition."

She hesitated for a second. "Do I know you from somewhere? You look really familiar."

Abby wasn't sure if she was speaking to her or to Seda. Seda shook her head. Abby said, "Maybe just around town."

Gale turned away, but then turned toward them again and was regarding Abby. She gave a little side motion of her head, a slight lifting of her shoulder. "I'll think of it." She closed the back of her truck. "Thanks for the call." She held up her hand with her fingers crossed and a hopeful smile.

After she left, Abby said, "Gale seems really knowledgeable."

Ellis said, "She's been doing this for years. Your heron's in good hands."

33

A WOMAN STOOD OPPOSITE THE priest and began reciting names of people in the congregation who were on the prayer list. Abby wasn't listening to the names. She was thinking of other things—the injured heron, Seda and Tanner and Ellis. She was remembering something Ellis said about herons only raising one or two of their hatchlings. The babies fledged a couple of months after that but usually stayed around the nest for a few more weeks so their parents could feed them. He thought their heron's nest was somewhere on the island, but she'd been too sick to fly when it was her time to move on.

Abby was attending mass with her grandmother. They'd driven separately, meeting at the church. The room was mostly filled with women and older men, a few children. Abby looked around, recognizing faces. Ellis was there, on the other side of the aisle, and a few rows back.

When the service concluded, some women approached Nonna, forming a horseshoe in front of her. Abby stepped into the aisle and caught up to Ellis. He was doing all right. These were the pleasantries they spoke to one another, and Abby was going to check on the heron, she told him. Then she asked Ellis how he knew Gale. He said he did some teaching at the school, filled in when someone couldn't make it.

"What about the fishing?"

"I leave that mostly to Tanner."

They spoke to the priest and moved onto the sidewalk, both of them squinting at the bright, sunless sky.

An older man approached and shook Ellis's hand.

"Good to see you, Don." Ellis was just heading out. "You take care, Abby."

As Ellis began to leave, the man then turned to Abby. "I think the last I saw you was at your grandfather's funeral. What was that, four years ago?"

He wore charcoal working pants, working boots, a blue knit shirt. His gray hair lay flat where his hat had been. Abby didn't know him.

Perhaps he read the confusion on Abby's face.

"You don't remember me. I'm Don Pelletier. My wife and me—"

Abby nodded. "Yes," she wanted to say. "I know who you are."

He and his wife wintered in Florida now, he told her. "We only get up here for the summers."

He said it was good to see Abby, he was glad she was doing well. And then he was gone, walking to his car.

On her drive to Nonna's, Abby thought of Mr. Pelletier—his blue eyes, were they familiar? And his knit shirt, the NHL logo neatly embroidered on the left side. So he was a hockey fan.

Abby looked out the rolled-down window at passing houses and children on bicycles, and vegetable gardens in people's yards—squash and potatoes and carrots. Her mind drifted to winter. Hot stew, a radio playing from her parents' bedroom—hockey announcers late into the night, her dad unable to sleep because it was the weekend and he was used to his night shift at the mill, and Abby in bed down the hall, eyes peacefully closed, the assurance knowing both her parents were there.

• • • • • • • • •

At the house, Nonna set out lunch meat and white bread and jars of mayonnaise and mustard. Abby picked up the receiver and gave Gale a call.

"She made it through her first night," Gale said. Her voice was upbeat. She went on to tell Abby that the heron wasn't suffering from lead poisoning, which had been Gale's greatest concern, but had shown elevated levels of mercury. The vet thought the mercury brought on the bird's poor weight and malnutrition. But the patient's prognosis was good, Gale said. "If she can regain her strength these next few weeks, we can release her back into the wild."

Abby continued to check in with Gale the next two days. The bird's weight and appetite were still a concern. "Most juvenile herons at her age would have reached eighty-five percent of their adult weight," Gale explained, "which would put them at around four pounds. Your little girl barely weighs three pounds. She was lucky you found her before one of her predators did, or before she died of malnutrition."

Abby wondered, "Do you name the birds you rescue?"

"I probably shouldn't," Gale said. "They're not mine to keep. But I do."

"What about ours? Did you give her a name?"

"I named her Thunder. I want her to be strong."

"I like that," Abby said.

"I could probably do better. Feel free to change it."

"Can I see her?" Abby asked.

"That wouldn't be a problem." She gave Abby directions to her house.

Gale lived in a log cabin, painted a deep salmon color, just south of the village. Her house sat at the end of a dirt road. Before the turnoff, Abby noticed a sign—*Wings of the Wild*—with an arrow indicating a right-hand turn.

Gale's mailbox was anchored into a whiskey barrel and designed to look like a Canada goose. Pots of purple and yellow million bells hung from the eaves of the house, and flower boxes overflowed with begonias and sweet alyssum.

Gale met Abby outside and led her down a slightly sloping hill to the door of her walkout basement. "This is where most of the rehabilitation takes place," she said.

The lot leveled into a backyard, where Gale had planted a row of raised vegetable beds. Toward the back of the lot were the flight cages, or playpens, as she referred to them. "That's where the birds hang out before I release them."

She had three pens adjacent to one another. The first pen housed a peregrine falcon who was recovering from a broken wing. The other occupied pen contained a large baby pool and housed a white pelican. Gale went on to tell Abby that the pelican had gotten caught in some fishing net. "Elbert wasn't badly injured, but by the time we found him, he was extremely malnourished. He's one of the first pelicans to be sighted in Michigan. There are others over the Wisconsin border."

Then Gale led Abby inside the basement area, which was filled with an assortment of crates and bird cages and shelves full of supplies. "This is where I keep the birds who need additional care," she said.

There was Thunder, still in the large crate she'd been rescued in, which had been set on a working table. Her eyes were alert. She took a couple of steps when she saw Gale and Abby.

"Hey, Thunder," Abby said.

Abby glanced back at Gale. "I think she looks stronger."

"I've been getting the calories in her," Gale said. "And the vet prescribed chelating injections. But she still has a ways to go. We've got to get her weight up."

Gale introduced Abby to some of her other patients—a sandpiper, a robin, a baby barn owl she'd named Prudence.

Posted next to the door was Gale's certificate for wildlife rehabilitation, yet she didn't charge for her services.

"How do you do it?" Abby asked. "How do you pay for all of this?"

"Mostly donations. Sometimes I get lucky and receive a grant."

A lot of noise was coming from the crates. Gale led Abby upstairs to her kitchen so that they could hear each other better and give the birds space.

She asked Abby questions—How was Abby's summer work going? What wildlife had she seen? And Abby told her about the foxes, the cranes, a porcupine, one time a buck, another time a doe. She heard coyotes playing at dusk. She hadn't seen a bear, but she'd seen their scrapings on the trees, and she'd seen the strands of their black fur snagged in the bark.

Gale said, "And tracks, I'm sure you've seen those."

Abby said, "Yes, plenty for sure."

There was a china cabinet filled with a plethora of bones with place cards neatly identifying them—silver-haired bat, hoary bat, deer mouse, ermine, marten.

"I keep those for my students," Gale said.

On the kitchen table were stacks of books with titles that had to do with ornithology and organic gardening, a bowl of grapes, a large jar of roasted cashews.

Gale poured them each a glass of water and joined Abby at the table. The two of them began pulling off the pale green grapes and popping them into their mouths and shaking out cashews into their palms.

Gale wasn't from the UP, she said. She'd grown up in Illinois. She'd taken the job as a schoolteacher right out of college. That was thirteen years ago, and she had no intention of ever leaving.

After being offered the job, she found this two-bedroom cabin to rent, which she said was surrounded by five wooded acres. In time, she convinced the owner to let her buy it. To the west of her parcel were more acres that eventually turned into cropland. She loved having the space for the birds, and she loved the acreage, which she said was perfect for owling.

She told Abby about going owling with her grandfather—or going on owl prowls, as he called it—when she was a young girl. And then she said, "Here, let me show you something." She pushed her chair out from the table and said she'd be right back.

When she returned, she handed Abby an eleven-by-fourteen-inch framed photo she'd taken of a snowy owl with an almost-five-foot wingspan. "That was taken up at Whitefish," she said. She was twelve years old at the time, and since then had seen several other snowy owls, but there was nothing like the allure of her first.

Abby was still looking at the picture when Gale said, "Abby, there's something I need to tell you. I know where I've seen you before. It all came back to me."

34

THE INFORMATION GALE RELAYED TO Abby was startling and strange—this schoolteacher and lover of birds, on that mythical night of which Abby had no recollection, walking through the woods after midnight, night-vision binoculars in hand. A great horned owl took flight. Then there was smoke and the sound of running. Abby's face looked in Gale's direction briefly, like a flash. And there was something else—a metallic, clinking noise, that is what Gale heard.

All these years, Abby searching for truth—What happened that night? Why had the fire occurred?—questions that became the story of Abby's life.

Now this new information, almost right, almost the truth, almost a memory. Abby had made it out of the house alive, she'd run through the woods, a schoolteacher was owling that night, the schoolteacher spotted Abby and called out to her and then ran toward the fire and from there ran to get help. And Abby, only seven years old, the same age as Abby's niece Catherine was now, alone on the side of a road, until a husband and wife found her—the Pelletiers, driving home from somewhere—they wintered in Florida now. He had blue eyes.

They were becoming cloudy with cataracts. He had a bad hip. He remembered Abby.

Once more the striking of a match felt close—almost real, almost certain. The feel of the slim, cardboard piece between her fingers, her tearing it from the matchbook—not just one, but two or three or four. Folding the matchbook over, the popping sound, the puff of light, the smell of sulfur.

Abby nodded when Gale finished talking to her. She wanted to think it all over. She sat quietly. She set the picture of the snowy owl on the table. She swallowed the last of a green grape in her mouth.

Later Abby would hold in her mind the bear scratches and rubbings she came upon in the woods—the exposed yellow-white flesh of the trees, the strands of black fur, like coarse threads, snagged in the bark. She'd remove a strand, rub it between her fingers, as she was doing now with each new piece of information, examining it for truth, looking for something familiar. That's the only way the night would come back to her. That's the only way it would become real. She would keep at it until she couldn't keep at it anymore. Relax, step back, she would tell herself, while remaining alert and receptive.

• • • • • • • • • •

Abby continued to check in with Gale over the next few days to see how Thunder was progressing, and sometimes Gale would hold the phone up so Abby could hear how vocal Thunder had become. Abby's heron was putting on weight. She was growing stronger.

"Another week and she'll be in the playpens," Gale said. "She and Elbert can become friends."

There was a brightness to Gale's voice, something hopeful, something *more*. It felt like everything Abby wanted to hold on to. And maybe she had it herself at times, when the clouds shifted. She'd felt it before, she was sure, but it escaped her—that love in a deeper sense—love that goes down to the very root of you.

All of this Abby kept to herself, though she wanted to seek out Seda. She wanted to tell her everything. They would celebrate Thunder's recovery. They'd open a bottle of Tanner's homemade wine, or mix the rest of the bourbon and Coke. They'd grow somber in their intoxication and piece together more clues to the fire. But Abby's work had taken her farther north and inland on the peninsula. She would have to wait until the weekend.

• • • • • • • • •

Abby completed her workweek on Friday. She and Uncle Dennis planned to make pizzas for dinner. He was standing in the kitchen with all the ingredients on the counter—pepperoni slices, fresh mozzarella, a jar of pizza sauce, peppers and olives. He told Abby that a friend of his from the graduate program would be joining them.

By the time Abby showered and dressed in a pair of jeans and a sweater, Uncle Dennis's friend arrived. His name was Seth Evers and he was a biologist for the state's Department of Natural Resources at the Shingleton office, about an hour's drive north of them.

Abby made a salad and set bottles of dressing on the table. Seth and Uncle Dennis opened bottles of beer.

"What's it been? A week since you found your heron?" Uncle Dennis asked Abby.

"About that."

"Gale's done a real wonder with that bird. She's really something," he said.

"Gale or the bird?" Seth asked.

Color rose to Uncle Dennis's face.

Uncle Dennis laughed. "Probably both."

So it was out there—Seth knew about Gale.

Seth asked Abby questions, and she relayed what she knew about Thunder's condition.

"We need to come at it from both directions," Seth said. "Help the heron and clean up the toxins."

He explained that the mercury that had made Thunder sick was the result of pollutants in the atmosphere that are carried by the wind and deposited into the water. From there, bacteria convert the pollutants into methylmercury. He said this form of mercury was the most toxic kind because of how it entered the food chain and accumulated in a body's organs and tissues. The fish eat the bacteria, and the herons eat the fish. He went on to say that the methylmercury becomes more and more concentrated the higher it moves up the food chain. That's why the state issued guidelines every year limiting the number of servings a person could consume a month. "Walleye, perch, trout, bass, just about every type of fish has some kind of restriction."

He mentioned mercury-loaded fish sickening dozens of tribal members in Canada when a paper mill poisoned a river that gave the members their livelihood. He mentioned the damage methylmercury caused to fetuses.

Uncle Dennis contributed information as well, bringing up the nearly two thousand people who'd died in Japan, and the two million more who'd suffered health issues, because they'd eaten the fish from Minamata Bay after a company had released methylmercury chloride into the water.

Abby thought of Tanner and Ellis and all the other fishers, and all the Indigenous people who relied so heavily on fish for their sustenance.

Then Seth began talking about a group of scientists who were studying the loons and trying to understand the reason for their decline, and how he believed the loons could provide important insight. "The loons seem to be particularly sensitive to the effects of methylmercury," he said. Not only was the toxin reducing their appetite and making them more susceptible to disease, it was also affecting their reproductive behaviors. "The mercury crosses the blood-brain barrier making it neurotoxic," he told Abby. "The loons are nesting less frequently, they're failing to incubate their eggs, they're slower to respond to predators. The whole thing has a cumulative effect."

"And the mercury levels are only going up," Uncle Dennis added.

"By four hundred percent in the last hundred and fifty years," Seth said.

Abby felt an urgency come over her. She felt uneasy and anxious. She felt as if the weight of the world were rising inside of her. She and Brew hadn't seen their nesting loons since that third year, despite the many times they looked for them, and now Abby wondered if what happened to Thunder was what happened to them.

Her panic began to escalate. She felt the enormity of something so big that she could do so little about. She wanted her heron to soar into a clean sky, and the loons to go on nesting and raising many more healthy chicks. She wanted Ellis and Tanner and all the people to be able to eat however many fish they chose to eat, and for the fish to be free of lead sinkers and methylmercury and all the terrible chemicals dumped into the rivers, and for the power plants to stop emitting mercury into the air and other toxins that were making people sick. She felt like she couldn't breathe.

Abby didn't understand the other things Uncle Dennis and Seth talked about—the scientific language of biomagnification and bioaccumulative environmental toxicants. But she understood the weight of the things they said. She'd held Thunder in her arms, and like Tanner, she'd felt Thunder's heartbeat. She'd listened to her plaintive cries—*frawnk, frawnk, frawnk*, her voice tired and weak.

Abby rose from the table and wrung out the dishrag and then swept the dishrag over the counter to wipe up the crumbs. She put the bottles of dressing away, wrapped up the leftover pizza. Uncle Dennis and Seth were caught up in other matters, plates pushed aside, elbows on the table, one of them hardly finishing a sentence before the other began saying something. Abby picked up their plates. She washed the dishes in the sink and set them on a towel to dry. The camp was small and there was nowhere to go, so she walked outside and looked at the stars, their quiet flickers of light against the deepening pastels. The summer was passing. Soon all of this would be gone. Each night darkness came earlier. Each night the air was cooler. Abby held her arms over herself. She wanted to speak softly in Thunder's ear and tell her it would all be okay. She wanted to make promises she couldn't keep.

She went inside to grab her jacket and pulled on her moss-green hat. She told Seth it was nice to meet him. He said he was glad her heron was doing better and that maybe one day he'd run into her in the wild.

Uncle Dennis said, "You going somewhere?" And then he smiled and said, "Don't worry, I won't wait up for you."

"I'm just going to find Brew," she told him, because she felt in that moment that if she didn't find Brew she might surely die of suffocation.

She didn't waste any time getting into the truck and driving into town. She passed the artisan gallery and the post office, and the bar where she'd witnessed Seda fighting with Piper, and how long ago that all seemed now. She passed Millie's restaurant and the Catholic church where she'd seen Mr. Pelletier. She made the left-hand turn for Nonna's at the corner market, and kept on driving past Nonna's and Uncle Buckley's. She then turned into the driveway of Uncle Ronnie and Aunt Reese's house and pulled up beside Brew's jeep.

He was standing along the left side of the house. He'd been coiling a garden hose. Though the sun had now set and he stood in the shadows, she was able to see him from the beam of her headlights. He stood still for a moment, shielding his eyes from the light, then set the hose on the ground and approached the truck. Abby switched off the ignition and turned off the headlights.

Her window was down. Brew walked over to the driver's side. His hands were in his pockets and his chest rose slightly, that little inhale of breath before someone says something, but Abby spoke first. "What did you want to see me about the other night when you stopped by the camp? And the night two weeks before that?"

He exhaled and did a laugh. "I had a nice time in Alabama with my mom. Thanks for asking."

"The loons are dying," Abby said.

Brew wasn't wearing his hat, that's what she realized. She could see his face. She could see the way he was looking at her. He took his right hand out of his pocket and tapped his palm on the doorframe of the truck, then walked around to the passenger side and climbed in.

"Hey," he said, after he shut the door and turned his body in the seat so that he was facing her.

"Hey," Abby said. She was still holding on to the steering wheel and looking through the windshield—at the garage door, at the gutter just below the roof.

Brew reached for her hand and brought it down to the seat and kept holding it.

The overhead light went out inside the cab and the truck was dark and quiet. Abby began to relax, and as she began to relax, she began to tell him things. She told Brew about Thunder and Ellis and Tanner and their freezer full of fish. She told him about Seth Evers and the banding of the loons and the blood samples and feather analyses. She told him about the mercury emissions that were contaminating the waters and all the people who had died from consuming fish.

She felt so helpless, that's what she told him, that it didn't matter how many trees Uncle Dennis and she counted, or how many lichens and saplings they identified. She couldn't stop the power plants from releasing toxins into the air, or the factories from dumping waste into the rivers. "And Brew," she told him, "we used lead sinkers. We could have poisoned the fish."

"Well, then let's get rid of our lead sinkers," he said. He tugged at Abby's hand. "Come here," he said. He wrapped his arms around her. "Don't become discouraged, Abby. You can't. If you become discouraged, you give up, and that's the worst thing you can do. As long as we're alive, there's the possibility that we'll stop making terrible mistakes."

"I don't even know where to start," Abby said.

"You saved a heron," he told her. "And we're not going to tie any more lead sinkers onto our fishing lines. You're helping Uncle Dennis save the forest."

"We're not saving the forest. We're just making maps and taking inventories."

"You're saving the forest," Brew said. Slowly they sat back in their seats again, their shoulders side by side. Brew's arm was over Abby's and he clasped her fingers between his.

"I want to show you something," he said.

"Now?" she asked.

"Not now," he said. "It has to be daylight. Can you meet me at the fish house tomorrow?"

"I think so."

"It'll have to be after the morning catch," he told her. "Meet me at one. They should let me out of there by then."

35

THE NEXT AFTERNOON, ABBY FOUND Brew behind the fish house. He was kneeling in the back of one of the aluminum boats Uncle Buckley kept for the guests staying at the cabins. He held a two-gallon container of fuel and was filling the outboard tank.

"Looks like we're going somewhere," Abby said.

The boat was smaller than the *Little Daline* by a couple of feet, and the outboard was only a fifteen horsepower, but Brew said that was all they needed, they weren't going far.

He and Abby fell into their old patterns. He handed her the fuel container, which she set along the side of the building. Then she climbed onto the boat. He untied the line at the stern. She untied the line toward the bow. Abby brought out a tube of sunscreen from her backpack and applied some to her face and arms. She tossed the tube to Brew and he applied the lotion as well.

Once they were away from the fish house, Brew opened the throttle. He led them into the open water and across the bay. At the far side of the bay, they began coasting westwardly along the shoreline at a low speed, until he steered them into the opening of a quiet cove with a shallow shelf of sediment and vegetation. He cut the motor and lifted it out of the water, and then reached for one of the oars. Abby took the other oar and the two of them paddled closer inland. Then they both stepped into the marshy water and dragged the boat onto the grassy bank.

"We'll have to walk from here," Brew said, and Abby knew in that instinctual way, Brew had come here to show her the loons.

"Over there," he said, pointing ahead of them. He took the lead, and Abby followed, water filling their sneakers despite their efforts to step from one clump of grass to another, and everywhere there were tall reeds making it difficult to judge their landings. But in a short time, he brought them to the spot he had in mind, a thick hassock wide enough for the two of them, and flattened by animals or the wind, or perhaps by Brew, who'd come here before and spent hours observing a family of loons, two parents and three loonlets, he told Abby.

"They know we're here," he said. "But once we settle in, they'll get used to us."

Abby sat cross-legged. Brew sat beside her. There was a gap in the reeds slightly to their left that let them see where the shoreline branched out into the cove.

"They're probably at the nest," Brew said. "If we stay here long enough, they'll come out."

"How old are they?"

"Not sure. Maybe seven to nine weeks."

For a couple of seconds, Abby looked at Brew, studied his profile. His face was tan, and she detected a light span of freckles, barely visible. Brew held Abby's hand as if there were barely any thought to it, just their two hands together, their palms resting side by side on this cushion of hassock. There was the sweet hint of suntan lotion and the earthy smell of the lake water and the sunbaked grass beneath them that smelled like hay. There was the smell of their skin, the salt of their perspiration, and Abby was sure she could detect in the fabric of their T-shirts the lake breeze and the spray off the water from their ride over.

"Do you think it's okay to talk?" she asked, her voice one step above a whisper. "Or will we scare them away?"

"They'll get used to us, no different than if we were just another bird minding our own business."

Then Abby said, "You never told me why you stopped by the camp."

"I was hoping to see you, for one, and I wanted to tell you about the loons."

"How did you know they were here?"

"I've been looking for them. I wanted to see if they'd come back."

Abby was trying to remember. "This isn't the same place—" Her words were more of a question.

"No, but it's close."

"What made you look for them?" she asked.

"It feels good coming out here, just skirting around the shore."

He said he spotted the loons before he left for Alabama. "Made me think of you," he said. He went on to tell Abby about other things, his trip to see his mom and how hot it was down there, and how his mom's family was doing—just small talk.

It was then that they heard the soft tremolo of one of the baby loons, and instinctively they both leaned forward, as if by doing so they'd be able to see things better. The little, gentle sounds continued and then there was a splashing in the water. One of the parent loons appeared with its pitch-black head and haunting, red eyes, its regal band of teal blue around its neck, its black-and-white-speckled plumage.

"Here they come," Brew whispered. "Look for the chicks."

He was right, there they were, two of them, like tiny, round blobs of brown fur. Abby let go of Brew's hand and quietly reached for her backpack to take out the binoculars. No sooner had she raised the binoculars and adjusted the focus than she saw one of the loon chicks swim up to the parent and tuck herself beneath the mother's wing and climb onto her back.

Brew chuckled quietly. "Here comes the other one."

Abby and Brew watched the second chick climb onto the mother's back.

"I thought you said there were three."

Brew pointed off to their left. "Over there," he said.

Here came chick number three, not far behind the others.

Abby handed Brew the binoculars.

He held them out a little ways, as if studying them. "These are nice," he said.

"They were a gift."

Brew didn't inquire further. His mind was on the loons.

Abby squinted against the sun and raised her hand to her forehead to block the glare.

Brew set the binoculars down. "Here," he said. He took off his cap, and using both hands, positioned it on Abby's head. "Actually," he said. He gathered Abby's hair off her neck, and pulled it through the opening in the back of the cap, then adjusted the band by a notch or two so that the hat fit more securely.

"That better?" he said.

"Perfect," Abby said.

They hadn't noticed the other parent emerge, but there he was, swimming with the rest of the family.

Then the male loon lifted a foot out of the water and started shaking it above the surface. When he was done, he submerged it and lifted the other one and shook it as well. "Well, would you look at that," Brew said, and he and Abby were trying not to laugh.

It was sometime after that when Brew said, "You know, it wasn't just about the loons. That wasn't the only reason I came by to see you."

Abby looked at him. "What was it, then?"

"I'm not with Tracy anymore, that's what I wanted to tell you."

Abby didn't respond right away.

"That's kind of an important thing I just told you," Brew said.

"It is."

"You going to say anything?"

"I saw you two going into Millie's the night before you left," Abby said.

"I took her to dinner so I could talk to her."

"If I were Tracy, I'm not sure I would have wanted you talking to me in a public place like that."

"Well, that's just it, Abby. You're not Tracy. She took it all right. I've seen her since then, just around, and it hasn't been bad. It's fine actually. I think the way I handled it was fine.

"But like I was saying, you're not Tracy, and she isn't you. I guess that's what I'm trying to say."

They both remained silent for a moment. Then Abby turned and looked at Brew. Their eyes locked on one another, their world—on the periphery of everything else, exactly as they used to be. Brew reached his arm around Abby's shoulders. His face came inches from hers, this little bit of space between them. "Is this all right, Abby? Is it all right if I kiss you?"

A subtle nod from Abby, their lips coming together, their mouths opening to each other. All of Abby's feelings were there, love and desire, everything she'd ever wanted with Brew.

His hands gently lifted the hem of her T-shirt, touched warmly against her bare skin. They pulled away only enough for their eyes to lock once more, both of them smiling, almost laughing.

A strand of Abby's hair blew alongside her face. Brew tucked it behind her ear and beneath the edge of the cap. "I'm always going to be here for you, Abby."

"You always have been," she said.

Then she asked Brew, "Remember that day at the graveyard?"

"I remember," he said.

"I've always wondered what you found."

Brew hesitated. He turned toward the water, arms now around his knees that were pulled up in front of him. "It was a dog, Abby. It wasn't Rudy. Nothing like that. But it was somebody's dog, and you'd just lost Rudy. I didn't think it would be good for you to see it."

Abby slid her arm beneath Brew's and laid her head on his shoulder. "You did the right thing."

Still, something unloosed itself inside of her hearing his words. The night of the fire. Rudy disappearing. No one ever found him. Abby continued to set food out for him wherever she was staying—Nonna's house, a couple of nights at Brew's—hoping Rudy would come back to her, but he never did.

She was carrying thoughts that hadn't been there before. A kaleidoscope of pieces to a story, and the story was hers, though others were a part of it—Brew and Nonna, Uncle Dennis and Aunt Jo-Jo and Aunt Reese, even Gale, this was her story too, and Rudy—somewhere there was Rudy. He'd be an old dog now, but anything was possible. He might still be alive.

"You're being quiet," Brew said.

"Just thinking about things."

"Want to talk about those things?"

"Remember the night of the party, when I was walking back to camp?"

"That wasn't one of our finest moments."

"It ended up all right."

"I guess it did."

"Remember me telling you about the dog I heard. What if that dog was Rudy? What if he's still out there somewhere? What if he knew it was me, and that's why he started howling?

"I know this is far-fetched," she said.

"Not so far-fetched."

"But highly unlikely."

"Maybe a little."

"I drove around the area, pulled off on some of the old logging roads, looked around the whole periphery of the burn site. Did I tell you that?"

"When was this?"

"A couple of weeks after hearing the music. I was coming in from the field. I just thought it was possible, you know. What if someone took him in? What if he's been alive all this time?"

"Did you find anything?"

"A small farm, a few houses."

"Any dogs?"

"I saw a dog, but the dog wasn't Rudy."

"Everybody looked for him, remember? We put up fliers."

"I know we did."

"Seems like there was a consensus."

"That he died in the fire, I know. But I'm not sure I ever believed it. If I got out of the house, then why didn't he? He slept in my room. He was always with me."

"You've been through a lot, Abby. I'd be lying if I said I understand."

Abby kept holding on to his arm. "It's okay," she said. "Everybody's got something."

"Has it been hard being back here this summer? With everything that happened to your mom?"

Abby tilted her head so that she was looking at Brew. Then she brought her chin back down and looked at the water again. The sound of the lake—the gentle lapping, rhythmic and calm. She sat perfectly still, not reticent, but *here,* as if she were finally, for a time, emptied out of all her thoughts, and this was all that was left, and it was perfect.

She could appreciate Brew asking, but Abby said, "Is it okay if we don't talk about my mom? Can it just be the two of us sitting here, watching the loons? I mean, we got to see a loon waggle his feet, and adorable little loonlets ride piggyback on their mother. Seriously, Brew, this has been the best summer of my life."

Brew brought his face around to Abby's. He kissed her again. He encircled her with his arms. He tucked his chin on top of her head. They couldn't see the loons anymore. Abby wasn't sure when that happened. Maybe the loons swam out of Abby and Brew's range of vision or returned to their nest.

Abby and Brew would need to get back. Brew was expected at the fish house.

They knew all of this, but they didn't get up right away. Abby heard the breeze for the first time. She heard the birds—the two-noted call of the chickadee, the high-pitched chirp of a warbler, a hawk somewhere in the distance. She hoped the baby loons weren't in danger.

36

ABBY WAS STILL WEARING BREW'S cap when they got back to the fish house. She tried to return it, but he was quick to stop her. "Keep it," he said. "It looks good on you." So that was how they left things, Abby wearing his cap that he'd had for as long as she could remember, him getting back to work at the fish house because there was a truck that needed to be loaded and someone had asked Brew to run the forklift.

Abby climbed into her grandfather's truck, drove back up the hill, arm on the rolled-down window, wind blowing her hair free. She felt the light of the day—felt it down deep, warmth buzzing beneath her skin like spring fever. She stopped by Nonna's house—to say hello, to call her dad.

Her grandmother was cleaning out the old leaves and buds from beneath her rhododendrons. Abby got out of the truck and joined her, worked alongside her, scooping up the dry leaves and buds and adding them to the five-gallon buckets. Then she helped carry the buckets to the compost pile beside the vegetable beds.

Nonna was heading over to Aunt Reese's, she said, to pick up mums. Did Abby want to go with her, but Abby wanted to call her dad. Nonna said the usual fare—tell him I said hello, tell him we're not sending you back.

Abby stepped into the kitchen. The storm door swung shut behind her—everything familiar, the squeaking of the hinges, the catch of the door closing, the kitchen air incensed with every meal ever prepared, coffeepot brewed, chocolate chip cookies baked—every scrubbing of the counter, dishes washed in the sink—lotion rubbed on hands—sun and cold and wind drafts through the big window—it was all there—reminiscent and permeating.

She picked up the phone receiver that had been left on the kitchen table, sat in one of the captain's chairs, her elbows on the yellow gingham oilcloth, and dialed her father's number.

"Hey, it's me," she said when he answered.

There was the small talk, how everyone was doing. And how was Abby, he wanted to know.

"Nonna said to tell you they're kidnapping me. They're not sending me back."

Her dad's voice was jovial. "Tell her they can't have you. Your old man misses you too much."

Their banter continued. Did he tell her about the Volkswagen he wanted to buy?

"Oh, she's a beauty," he said. "I've been looking for a yellow one. This one's practically vintage. Yukon yellow, 1961."

"Why yellow?" Abby asked.

"I don't know. Maybe my personality, maybe the stripe down my back."

He asked Abby about her car, how it was holding up.

"I thought I told you. I've been using Grandpa Pete's truck."

They talked about the truck and the car, and he said she should get her car out on the road or else the battery would run low.

"And check the oil," he said.

"I will."

"Make sure it's not leaking."

"Okay," she said.

"Hey, one more thing. Those writers you were talking about, the ones who wrote the book about the loons. They're going to be in Escanaba."

"When are they going to be here?"

She could hear her dad get up and move around the house, shuffle the pages of the newspaper. "Give me a minute."

Then he found it. "A week from this coming Friday. Book signing and discussion at the library."

"Thanks, Dad." She wasn't sure she could make it. She and Uncle Dennis were planning to wrap everything up that week.

And then, "Dad, can I ask you something?" Because she was still thinking about Rudy. "After the fire, you went back to the burn site, you looked through the ash. I think I remember that. You found some things."

"That's right. In the backyard I found the Christmas tree ornament, the one you made in kindergarten. You know the one."

Yes, Abby knew of it—a star cut out of gold cardboard with Abby's picture in the center. They hung it on the tree every year, along with the gold and silver and red glass balls they bought.

"What else did you find?"

He talked of other items she knew about—the andiron from the fireplace, that sat on top of his workbench in the garage.

And he'd saved nails—nails he kept in a jar that he could pick up and swirl around, their clinking like ice in a tumbler.

"What about Rudy's collar, Dad? We never found it."

"We never found a lot of things."

"Did we look for it?"

"We looked for it, Abby. We never found it."

"I want to believe he made it out with me," Abby said. "That he's alive somewhere, or if he isn't still alive, that he had a good life."

"I know you do."

Her dad couldn't control how she felt. Abby knew that. He could only try to work with it.

"As long as you don't go blaming yourself, Abby," he said. "Promise me that. If you're looking to blame someone, blame me. I wasn't there when I should have been."

"Dad, don't do that. You were working."

"Not that night, I wasn't. I'd plowed a few driveways, then I stopped at Jake's. The hockey game was on. I wanted to catch the end of it."

He worked four nights on and three nights off at the paper mill. He wasn't at the mill that night. There'd been a snowstorm earlier. He'd gone out to plow. He stopped at Jake's. A call came into the bar.

"Dad—" The air went out of Abby's voice. "Please don't," she wanted to say. "I love you. It's okay."

"Can I ask you something else?" she said. "I know this is going to sound weird, but what did we have for dinner that night?"

It was a sweet laugh that followed. "I don't recall, Abby. I wish I did."

• • • • • • • • •

Abby could never have imagined how things would play out after she left Nonna's house that day. Her grandmother's patio was covered with artificial turf. Abby walked across the turf, the gentle plinking of the wind chimes behind her. There were two vehicles parked in the driveway—Grandpa Pete's pickup and Abby's compact car that, as far as she knew, had been sitting there for almost an entire summer.

If Abby hadn't just spoken with her dad, she would have climbed into Grandpa Pete's truck, but she promised her dad she'd drive her car, so she walked down the sidewalk to the driveway and got in. There beneath the right corner of the floormat were her keys, just as she'd left them. The sun was shining brightly, so she lowered the visor.

Tucked into the band on the visor was the loon feather. She'd forgotten about it, but now, upon seeing the feather again, her thoughts were brought back to many things—to that day in June when she arrived on the peninsula and saw Brew at the fish house, and to the party later that night on the beach. She thought of her walk along the water, and the graveyard and the old gillnetter, and there had been the feather, caught in the rocks at the fish house dock. Her thoughts then turned to Seda and the dance and the rain.

It took Abby a few tries, but eventually the car started. She turned on the radio and drove toward town, singing along softly to the music, thinking of Brew, thinking of Seda, and the image of her dad at Jake's when the call came in.

The artisan gallery was on her right. She'd been wanting to buy something for Seda to commemorate their summer together.

The gallery was empty except for a woman occupied behind the counter. Abby perused the jewelry, the knitted hats and scarves, the quilts and watercolors and wooden spoons, the pottery bowls and ceramic mugs. She knelt beside a basket of needlepoint kits and chose one with flowers and butterflies and two hummingbirds.

After she paid for the kit and placed it in her pack, the bells over the door rang. When she turned around, there was Gale and Uncle Dennis.

"Well, what do you know, if it isn't my trusty sidekick," he said. They'd seen her car out front and wanted to stop in to say hello.

He looked nothing like himself, in a new button-down shirt that still had the creases from the packaging and a fedora hat—olive green, with a leather band.

"You clean up well," Abby said.

"What can I say." He smiled at Gale.

Gale looked different also—her hair in smooth waves tossed over her shoulders, a jean skirt that fell mid-thigh, a cream-colored sweater. She gave Abby the latest update on Thunder. She was in the flight cage now, preening and bill clapping. "She's either annoyed by Elbert or has a crush on him," Gale said.

Gale and Uncle Dennis wanted to look around the gallery. Abby returned to her car, but when she tried to start it, the battery was dead. She went back inside the gallery and asked Uncle Dennis for his help. She had jumper cables with her, she told him.

He moved his car alongside hers. They tucked their heads beneath their hoods and attached the cable clips. While their engines ran and the battery charged, Abby joined Gale on the sidewalk. She told her about the loons—the full story of them, from the first time Brew and Abby saw them nesting, to their long hiatus, and now their return, Gale interjecting with questions.

Gale said she thought of Abby the other day. She'd accompanied a friend in the woods, a scholar of spruce grouse—had Abby seen a spruce grouse that summer—the pattern of their feathers like lace? And yes, Abby had seen a couple of grouse, and weren't their behaviors hilarious, puffing out their chest feathers, stomping their feet and strutting around.

They talked about the trees—jack pine, red pine, white pine—their lisping branches, the heron rookery Gale spotted—multiple nest platforms made of sticks in a cluster of cedars along the water. Would Abby miss all of this? Gale asked.

Abby said there was the Copper Country Forest on the Keweenaw. She wanted to get to know those woods better. But yes, she would miss this—she would miss all of it.

Abby looked at Uncle Dennis, twenty strides away, leaning against his car, ankles crossed, arms folded over his chest, a bemused smile, not really looking at anything, giving Abby and Gale their space to talk.

Abby brought up the conversation she and Gale had when Abby was at her house, about the night of the fire. "When you talked about seeing me in the woods, you mentioned hearing the clinking of metal," Abby said.

Gale took her time, her mind going over the details from all those years ago. "There was the smoke. It was faint at first. And then the clinking sound," she said. "I'd just put my camera away. I remember standing still, listening. That's when I heard someone running. I raised my binoculars. You looked right at me. You wouldn't have seen me. I was wearing dark clothing."

"But the clinking sound—" Abby said.

Gale's eyes locked with Abby's. "Yes, I'm sure I heard it."

"I had a dog," Abby told her. "I never knew what happened to him. Everyone thought he died in the fire."

"Did the collar have tags?" Gale asked.

Abby thought of Rudy's *thump, thump, thumping* on the floor when he was scratching his neck, the clinking of his tags. Her eyes moistened with tears. She stared back at Gale. "He made it out of the fire."

Gale nodded affirmingly. "You've been wanting to say those words for a long time."

• • • • • • • • •

Uncle Dennis waved Abby over. "Give her a go," he said.

Abby climbed into the car. She pressed her foot on the brake and turned the key. The engine started.

"I'd drive her around for at least a half hour to get the amps back up," Uncle Dennis said. "And leave the radio off."

"I will," Abby said.

She climbed out of the car, leaving it running. Uncle Dennis unclipped the jumper cables and coiled them in a loop. He and Gale were on their way to the new restaurant at Vans Harbor. He'd catch up with Abby later. "You staying at your friend's again this weekend?" he asked.

"Yeah," Abby said. "Looks like it."

"You should bring her around sometime."

"Yeah, I will."

She waved as he and Gale drove away, thoughts still on Rudy, her love so deep it felt like a wound for him. She opened the passenger-side door of her car and went to slide the cables back under the seat. The cables knocked against something—the seat lever most likely, or a windshield scraper. But when she looked under the seat, she saw a cigar box, like the ones her grandfather used to have—Spanish cedar, with a tiny brass clasp.

She reached under the seat and retrieved it—curious, that was all. Then she ducked back out of the car and stood up straight. She opened the lid; she stared at the contents. "Oh, Seda," she said out loud. "What have you done?"

37

ABBY SANK ONTO THE CURB of the sidewalk, the car engine thrumming beside her, the open cigar box in her lap. She picked up the items one by one: the brooch with the tiger's eye gemstone that Seda found at the cabin—a keepsake, Abby understood, in the same way Abby had kept the bookmark made of bronze with the cameo of a dragonfly; a funeral card from Wayne Emerson's service, with the Twenty-Third Psalm; the crayon drawing of the boat and the fisherman that Abby's mom drew and Grandpa Pete kept in the glove compartment; the aviator sunglasses; a white beer bottle cap with a red maple leaf; a copy of Emily Dickinson's poem—"Sic Transit Gloria Mundi,"*All Glory Is Fleeting*; a handkerchief with a capital *P* embroidered with silver thread in one of the corners; a matchbook from the drive-in restaurant where Seda and Abby had lunch—yellow with blue lettering, the cardboard creased showing fine gray lines.

Abby opened the matchbook, fingers trembling, a cool sheen on her forehead. Her thumb traced the cardboard stubs—four matches were missing.

She set the matchbook down. She picked up the last item, a painful constriction behind her eyes and deep in her chest—Rudy's collar, royal blue, with his two tags—a rabies tag and the other, a tag shaped like a dog bone where a machine had engraved his name on one side, and on the opposite side, a telephone number. The royal blue was sun-faded. On the underside where the collar adjoined the clasp were tufts of Rudy's ruddy-colored fur. Tears fell from Abby's eyes. "Rudy, what happened to you?" she whispered to herself.

The car continued to idle. If she didn't drive it soon, the battery would die—she knew this sort of thing, like a person knows the sun will set at the end of the day—the thought distant and automatic—background noise. She laid Rudy's collar in the box and closed the lid. She placed the box inside her backpack. She stood from the curb. The passenger door was still open. She set her backpack on the floor and closed the door. She walked around to the driver's side and climbed in. She shifted the car into drive and pulled onto the road and kept on driving the fifteen miles to Peterson Brothers Fairport Fishery at Anderson Point.

There was no one at Peterson's—not Tanner or Ellis or Willow. Just Abby, alone, climbing into her boat, starting the motor, steering the *Little Daline* away and around the buoys, then skirting the shore to Point Detour.

She pulled the boat into the cove, killed the engine, and raised it from the water. The small waves from the wake rolled beneath her as she drifted sideways. She grabbed an oar, pushed it through the water and into the sediment, propelled the boat onto the shore, then jumped onto the beach. She grabbed the line and dragged the hull over the shell sand, and tied the line around the young cedar tree, the same tree around which she'd tied the line so many times before.

The pain in her chest was still there, pure heartbreak—and anger, there was that too. She would find Seda, she would insist Seda tell her everything. She adjusted her pack over her shoulders and gazed ahead at the footpath they'd worn down so visibly.

A pine warbler, with his bright-green chest, swooped in front of Abby and flitted to a higher branch. She listened to its trill, the sound she often heard at night when sleeping here at the cabin. Abby was just so sad—this missing in her heart, so big, so full—of her mom and her dad and Rudy—the farm, her home, the years her life might have been—all of it rising to the surface—a grief that up until now existed as only snatches of thoughts, a smattering of memories and images, of conversations in her head to a mother she used to know.

Abby didn't have to look for Seda. She was already there, as if she'd been waiting for this moment all along. They sat together on the red velvet sofa—the soft cushions they'd sat on so many days and evenings before, the afghan of many colors in a messy heap beside them. Abby unzipped her backpack and removed the cigar box, holding on to it as if it were a relic, and then placed it on her lap. Seda didn't seem surprised.

"We need to talk," Abby said.

38

ON A NIGHT IN THE middle of January, a fire broke out in Abby's home. She was seven years old. She spent the rest of her life with no recollection of the events around the fire, except for the purple synthetic fur of a stuffed animal she was holding in her arms, and the light-blue pattern of sheep on the comforter on her bed. She slept in an upstairs bedroom down the hall from her parents' room, and on the far side of her room, beside a little, white desk, was a night-light, which emitted enough light for her to make out those two items. She remembered being very focused on those items—the sheep pattern and the purple synthetic fur.

On a night in the middle of January, a terrible fire broke out in Abby's home. A young girl woke from the fire and smoke. She ran down the stairs and opened the back door where her dog was scratching to get out. That girl was Seda.

Seda was part of Abby. Though they were different from one another, and their experiences weren't the same—to those on the outside, they were the same person. The night of the fire, Abby suppressed the events so completely that another part of her emerged, assuming the persona of someone different from Abby, absorbing the terror that Abby couldn't bear. Abby was a seven-year-old girl who remembered buying new clothes with her dad and swimming in a pool on a hot, summer day with a girl named Nan. Together they rode a green blow-up float. The pool was above ground. There was redwood decking. There were poolside chairs. There was cedar-sided fencing around the deck.

This wasn't the case for Seda. For her, the aftershocks of the event were cataclysmic.

The years following the fire, Abby had no awareness of Seda. Abby simply allowed the episodes, as she called them, where she had no idea where the time went. There was the afternoon when she was lying on her bed reading a book. She looked at the numbers on the digital clock on her nightstand. The time was barely half past one. She thought she had all afternoon to read. But then it seemed only seconds later that she heard the opening of the garage door and the sound of her dad's truck pulling into the garage. Abby's bedroom was dark by then, and she was no farther along in the chapter she'd been reading than she was all those hours before.

She got used to this sort of thing. It was easy to find an explanation—she fell asleep, or her mind wandered and she became preoccupied. Other times, she'd get ready for bed at a normal hour and turn out the light, and the next morning her dad would say he heard her up late and wanted to know if she was all right. She'd stare at him blankly, having no idea what he was referring to.

Sometimes she'd be driving and wonder, *How did I end up here?* Other times she'd forget where she placed something, or find a paper cup from a drive-through restaurant on the floorboard of her car that she didn't recall leaving there. Once she found a shirt in her closet that she never would have worn—a black midriff. She had no idea how it got there.

She wasn't immune to these episodes, but rather she learned to live with them—until the party Brew invited her to on the beach—up until that night, she had no idea Seda existed.

The music had been playing. The air felt damp. Abby finished eating. She walked over to the fire and tucked her plate into the embers. Her body began to move, to sway to the music, as she might do when listening to music back home. And there was Seda—a different persona, moving her body with Abby's—the dance and the music and Seda muddled in Abby's head. There they were together—on the fringes of a group of people, a sense of assurance blending into Abby. It felt good, this strangeness. She wasn't alone.

Then there were the two of them getting into Alex's car.

That's when Seda took over, but this time Abby didn't disappear. Seda rolled down the window. She climbed on top of the car. She almost got them killed.

And there was the night at the bar when Piper appeared, and Seda yelled at Brew because he tried to intervene. Though the words were Seda's, it was Abby's voice Brew heard. It was Abby's body he saw.

When Seda said what she needed was a comma or a cocoon, Abby knew she had to come up with a place where Seda and she could co-exist together, where Abby could get a better handle on the things that had happened in her life, where she could get to know this part of herself, and what better place to do that than at the Falcon's Nest.

And yet, *they* could only suppress everything so long before too much pressure built—the trailer Seda vandalized, the lines from the Emily Dickinson poem—*dum vivamus vivamus*, "The Cry of the Cicada"—the headaches that were getting worse in their intensity, the loneliness, the isolation—the accumulation of years—the soundless abyss that lay between Abby and Seda for all the knowledge of what really happened the night their mother died.

Abby set the cigar box on the ottoman. She reached for the afghan of many colors and tucked it around Seda's and her shoulders. She was ready to hear whatever Seda had to tell her.

One night in January, a terrible fire broke out in the house. She awoke to Rudy standing in the doorway of her room barking and pacing. The room smelled of smoke, and the air was filled with a gray light, like a heavy fog.

She climbed out of bed and ran down the hall to her parents' bedroom. Smoke and heat poured forth from their doorway. Flames shot up from her parents' bed. "Mom!" she screamed. The fire was loud, crackling and roaring, and in the smoke, she saw her mother's arm. This is what she recalled, this is what she was sure of. She turned and ran, her eyes burning, the floor hot beneath her feet. From behind her, something exploded, glass shattering in her parents' room. She followed Rudy down the stairs. The red kettle was still on the stove, an open box of saltines on the kitchen counter. She shoved her feet into her boots and grabbed her winter coat. She turned the lock on the door and twisted the knob. When the door opened, Rudy took off running across the small yard, then cut across the field and disappeared into the adjacent woods on the right. She ran after him.

Memories from the house where Abby and her parents and Rudy lived suddenly resurfaced—a box of saltines, the red kettle. Then there was the layout of the house—*yes*, Abby thought, *I remember that*. Down the hall to her right was her parents' bedroom, and on the walls were family photos. There was wallpaper halfway up the wall. The pattern was something floral with vines, and maybe the flowers were small, perhaps purple or brown and white. To the left down the hallway was the staircase. At the bottom of the stairs was a small area with a bench and a couple of chairs and a big doorway that led into the kitchen. Abby remembered the layout of the kitchen, the sink in front of the window, and beside the sink the yellow canisters. Just off the kitchen was the back door. To the right of the door was a row of coat hooks, and below the coat hooks were plastic trays where the family left their shoes, which were always covered with snow or mud or clumps of grass when the field had been cut and turned into silage, or muck from the barn and the chickens. She remembered there being chickens. She remembered Rudy chasing them.

Abby reached for the cigar box and placed it on her lap. She opened the lid and took out Rudy's collar, held it with both her hands, ran a thumb over the tuft of his fur, still soft and smooth, still Rudy. "What happened to him?"

"You really don't remember, do you?"

Abby shook her head.

"There were four matches missing," Seda said.

"The matchbook—"

"You were in the woods. You couldn't hear Rudy anymore or see him running. You kept looking for him until you saw something ahead of you, a shadow in the snow. You walked closer. You knelt beside Rudy. His breathing was shallow and raspy. You took the matchbook from your pocket and struck a match. He tried to get up. You laid your hand on his head. The match blew out. You struck another one. Rudy's eyes looked wild. He couldn't breathe. He was gasping for air. The smoke had been too much for him. The match went out. You laid down beside him. You stayed with him until he was gone."

Abby's head moved back and forth in disbelief—radical and painful. "It's not possible. I don't remember any of this. I thought he was still alive. I was sure of it."

Seda continued, "Before you left, you took his collar. Your hands were cold. They could barely work the clasp. You put the collar in your pocket."

Abby's stomach cinched—nausea, disbelief, pain running deep, panic in her lungs. And the box, she wanted to know. Where did it come from? And if Rudy's collar was in Abby's pocket—why did no one find it?

"Grandpa Pete gave you the box when you were at the hospital. He'd put peppermints in it and some cookies from the tin canister at Nonna's."

"And Rudy's collar? They never checked my pockets?"

"No, they never did."

"I never saw the box before. I didn't know I had it."

"You saw it. You just don't remember."

"But we looked for Rudy. We never found him."

"We found him," Seda said.

"I don't understand."

"Dad buried him at the burn site."

"How do you know this?"

"He had a shovel in his truck the day after the fire. I didn't think anything of it until I went back to the woods and Rudy wasn't there. There was dirt on the shovel. The burn site is the only place where the ground wasn't frozen."

Abby's eyes blurred, a painful constriction at the back of her throat, the roof of her mouth. "Why didn't Dad tell me?"

Seda shrugged. "He wanted to give you something. That was the only thing he had—letting you believe Rudy might still be alive."

"It's not right," Abby said. "He's still lying to me."

"A lot of things aren't right."

"You're still angry at him. Why?"

"He wasn't there."

"He was working."

"No, he was at the bar."

Abby's fingers trembled. She picked up the matchbook.

"It was lying on the table in Nonna's kitchen," Seda said. "People were talking. Nonna was crying. There were neighbors and strangers coming in the house. I reached for the matches and slipped them in my pocket with Rudy's collar. No one saw."

"There were four matches missing."

"That's right."

"You said I struck two matches when I found Rudy. What about the other two?"

Seda shook her head. "I don't know. That's for you to remember."

Tears ran like streams. Abby's chest lifted and fell. "I can't. I can't remember anything."

39

ABBY MADE COFFEE THE NEXT morning and climbed up to the rooftop. The sky was still dark. She'd slept little through the night.

"Seda, are you there?" Abby said.

"I'm here."

"You're being quiet."

It was then that Seda said what Abby knew was coming. "Abby, it's time for you to go."

That was the last thing Seda said to Abby—just those words—it was time and Abby needed to go. There was nothing else Seda could give her. The rest Abby would have to figure out on her own.

Abby packed her belongings and left that morning, the sun still not over the horizon. The boat rocked from side to side as she climbed in. She started the motor. She pulled out of the cove. It would take time getting used to this, she knew, as if she were entering a life she'd not actually lived and thoughts she'd not had. She tried talking to Seda on the boat ride back. The hull rose and fell, slapping hard on the water; the engine whined from the propeller. Seda didn't answer.

Abby returned to Bear Slide, dropped her backpack on the floor, poured more coffee. Uncle Dennis was at the table.

"You're back early."

"Wanted to get a start on my day."

"You okay?"

"Yeah."

Uncle Dennis had made scrambled eggs. Did Abby want some? No, she wasn't hungry. She needed to tell him something, she said.

He set his fork down. He wiped his mouth. He was looking at Abby.

"It has to do with the trailer," she told him. "The police were right. The paint was mine. I'm the one responsible. I don't think I ever said I'm sorry. But I am."

"I know you are," Uncle Dennis said. "We've all done stupid things."

"But I didn't break into the camps," Abby said. "I didn't steal anything."

"I know that too. I spoke to Travis. He told me about the boys from Schoolcraft County."

"Anyway, I just wanted to clear the air."

"Consider it cleared."

"Thanks," Abby said.

Then Uncle Dennis said, "You should eat. We got a big day ahead of us."

• • • • • • • • •

Uncle Dennis kept them busy in the days ahead. Less than two weeks remained. He was feeling the pressure of things wrapping up. Abby was glad for her assignments—familiar tasks that kept her occupied and gave her the freedom to be alone, to walk the destinations. Thoughts drifted in, like horses in a pasture. Head down, she was praying. She still needed to know if she started the fire.

It was on one of those days when she stopped to pick the wild raisins from the hobblebushes that grew like saplings that she came upon an outcropping of rock—a ledge emerging from a hill. The ledge was steep, and Abby didn't remember noticing it on any of the maps. She climbed to the top, where she had a view of the treetops descending to the shoreline. To her right, yes, she was sure of it, there was the cove where she would bring the *Little Daline* and where Seda and she swam.

Abby thought she saw someone moving on the beach. She removed the binoculars from her pack and brought them into focus, certain a woman was looking right at her. But Abby was in the shadow of the evergreens, and her clothing—denim overalls and a green field shirt—wasn't conspicuous.

Then the woman walked along the shore until she came to the trail, the footpath that led to the Falcon's Nest. Abby knew instinctively that the woman was Gale. She had to be Gale. She was wearing a red cap, like the one with the *Wings of the Wild* logo, and around her neck, Abby was sure of it, was a camera.

Abby was instantly taken back to the evening she and Seda went swimming, to the flash of red they'd seen in the trees, to the sound of footsteps moving away that Abby tried to convince herself were simply the sounds of a bird in the branches, or the wind, or a limb falling. Abby was reminded of sitting with Gale at her kitchen table while she told Abby stories of nights she'd gone owling, or on owl prowls, as she called these excursions. What if Gale saw Abby swimming and talking to Seda? What if Gale knew about the cabin? She would think Abby was crazy and tell Uncle Dennis. And Abby wondered—*was* she crazy? She found herself turning up the radio dial when WUPX, an alternative station out of Marquette, played Ani DiFranco singing "Buildings and Bridges." Random thoughts came to her—images like memories, though unfamiliar—a clothing rack at a Salvation Army, the layout of Piper's apartment, the metal folding chairs at his kitchen table, the salt and pepper shakers—a ceramic apple and pear, next to his stove.

Abby continued to look through the binoculars, to glass the cove. Just as quickly as Gale had disappeared down the path, she returned to the shore, and, facing away from Abby, began taking pictures of something in one of the trees. "She's just birding," Abby told herself. "She never saw the cabin."

Abby scooted back against one of the cedar trees that grew out of the ledge, to make sure she remained hidden. It was a peaceful spot, the ledge dappled with yellow and orange lichens and rounded clumps of moss that looked like the dome-shaped tops of mushrooms. Little flowers sprouted here and there, including the sleepy catchfly with its upright pink bud growing at the tip of a long, thin stem. Abby rubbed her fingers over the sticky bands beneath the pale pink bloom where insects could be caught, and imagined the flower devouring insects for its sustenance.

The air was cool beneath the trees, and the rock ledge was cool beneath Abby's palms. She looked out across the treetops at the horizon. The color of the lake had changed over the summer—from a deep blue to more of a teal.

Then, in that exact moment, an awareness struck Abby. This was the ledge Charlotte had captured in the painting that hung above the mantel at the cabin. Charlotte was here, Abby thought to herself.

Abby's first instinct was to tell Seda, to scramble down from the ledge and call out for her until she answered. "Seda," Abby wanted to say. "She was right here. All those years ago, she saw the sky as I'm seeing it now—the color of a jay's feathers—the crisp blue that comes with the end of summer. She saw the deep blue-green of the lake."

Abby sat against the cedar tree a little longer. Gale was no longer in sight, having disappeared around the far bank of the cove. Abby wondered where her access point had been. No doubt she knew these woods better than Uncle Dennis and Abby combined, but in different ways, Abby was sure. Gale would have memorized the treetops, the best perching branches. She would know the ideal nesting spots and understand the birds' migratory patterns.

Abby climbed down from the ledge and moved through the woods toward the water. She wasn't worried about running into Gale, who'd already sighted whichever bird she'd been looking for. She'd taken her pictures. She'd moved on.

On the other side of the trees was the cobble shore where Abby found the caribou sacrum. The water sparkled, the stones shone brightly in the late afternoon light—speckled browns like the eggs of a crow, glistening amber like tree sap, dark gray like shiny metal, others white and green and pale buff, and some burnt-orange red. Abby thought of the color of the red teakettle on the stove, the color of her favorite pair of pajamas she wore as a child, the color of the berries on the bearberry shrubs that reminded Abby of Christmas.

She turned up the trail and walked the hundred yards or so toward the clearing. Beyond the columbines that had bloomed earlier that summer, and the wild roses and purple-tailed spearmint—was the cabin. The straw hat still hung by the door—difficult to make out from where Abby stood, but it was there, and Abby wondered how long it would remain hanging where she left it, before getting tossed aside by the wind. Behind the rooftop upon which Abby climbed so many mornings, was a silhouette of the black-green crowns of the pine trees, with their upswept branches gently rising and falling with the stirring of the breeze.

Abby didn't go back to the cabin. Instead, she turned and retreated into the woods, pausing only briefly to determine her path to the truck, then moved in a northeastward direction.

40

IT WAS THE WEEKEND BEFORE Abby's last week on the peninsula. She sat around a campfire by the lake in front of Nonna's house and next to Uncle Buckley's cabins. All of the family was there—Nonna and Aunt Jo-Jo and the girls, Aunt Reese and Uncle Ronnie and Brew, Uncle Dennis, who'd brought Gale and introduced her to everyone, and Abby's great-uncle Buckley. They'd just finished eating fried perch and whitefish, sweet corn that Abby purchased from Geri, green beans from Uncle Buckley's garden, and wild blueberry pie.

There were threads of conversation—Gale talked about Thunder. She was almost at her peak weight and would be released sometime the following week. She talked about the mercury levels. Uncle Buckley said the same thing happened with DDT back in the seventies. "That's when the eagles made the endangered list." Then Uncle Dennis said that the eagles had stopped reproducing because their eggshells were too thin. "But they're making a rebound," he said. And it was true; just the year before they'd been moved from endangered to threatened.

Abby wanted to talk to Gale more about the birds. She wanted to visit the Whitefish observatory. Maybe she'd become a raptor counter—one of the scientists who spent months at a time on the dunes at Whitefish Bay. It wasn't just the eagles that had become endangered and then threatened, but the peregrine falcons also, Gale said.

The conversation moved on to other things—the Packers preseason game against the Ravens—the picture of Travis and the Palmer girl in the paper—would Uncle Dennis be back for the wedding?—What was the latest word Aunt Jo-Jo had from Brian?

Brew was sitting beside Abby on a picnic bench they'd pulled up to the fire ring. Aunt Jo-Jo was on another bench beside them. She'd brought her guitar and was plucking each string and adjusting the tuning pegs. She'd talked to Brian, she said. He might be coming home in the fall. Gracie was walking around with an open bag of marshmallows. Catherine was poking the fire with a long stick.

As Abby watched her family around the fire, she became aware of something much bigger than herself. She wasn't the only one who'd experienced loss. Uncle Dennis had lost his best friend. He and Aunt Reese and Aunt Jo-Jo had lost a sister. Nonna had lost a daughter. Abby's father had lost his wife. Abby saw her family differently—as if seeing them—really seeing them for the first time. Her family's loss was cumulative and inclusive. So was their love. Love and melancholy and loss and these simple pleasures—a summer night and music and sticky marshmallows and conversation—all of it a synthesis, rooted in this place, rooted in each other.

Brew asked Abby if she wanted to go for a walk. They left the fire and the pieces of conversation and Aunt Jo-Jo's guitar strumming. They walked along the water's edge, past the cabins and the fish house and on to the graveyard. There was the gillnetter, their names still scratched into the side, and they hoisted themselves aboard.

Brew said he'd found something when he was packing for college. He reached into the front pocket of his shirt and brought out a photograph.

"It's of your mom. I found it with some of Reese's things," he said.

He and Abby were leaning against the gunnel on the starboard side of the boat, facing the water. Abby held the photograph in front of her. Her mom looked to be about Abby's age. She was standing next to J.P. They were at a carnival, and what Abby recognized in the photo was the purple stuffed hippopotamus her mom was holding, with its tiny ears and short tail and enormous snout, like something a person might win at a ring-toss. Abby's mom was wearing a pair of flare-bottom jeans and a pink, sleeveless shirt. Her eyes were almost closed because she was laughing, and there was J.P., his head turned toward her, as if he had just said something.

"She looks so young and happy," Abby said.

"Might have been at the carnival over in Escanaba," Brew said.

"That's what I was thinking. She was really pretty."

"So are you."

Abby pushed into him with her shoulder. She was wearing the red hooded sweatshirt and slipped the photo into the pocket.

"You okay?" Brew asked.

"I'm okay," Abby said.

"Just okay?"

"I've been remembering things," Abby said. "I remember that stuffed animal. I used to sleep with it. I had it with me the night of the fire."

Brew's arm was now around Abby, his hand just above her hip. He pulled her closer. "Do you think remembering things is such a good idea?"

"Yeah, I do."

Abby felt Seda with her, pressing her on. Mice didn't start the fire. Brew couldn't go on protecting Abby.

"Has anything else come back to you?" Brew asked.

"I know there was a snowstorm that day. My dad was out plowing."

Then Brew said, "Do you remember the snowstorm?"

Did Abby remember it?—enough accumulation for the plows to be out.

"I'm not sure."

"Do you remember the saucers we used to have? The red and blue ones? We'd take them down the bank on your parents' property."

"The hill at the side of the house. I remember that. Did we take the saucers out that day?"

"Yeah, I think we did."

"We never talked about this before."

Images came back to Abby—she and Brew in snow pants and snow boots and heavy coats, pulling their saucers up the hill, then bumping into each other on their way down, saucers spinning, the two of them toppling over at the bottom of the hill, Abby's fingers cold in her mittens, Brew's cheeks red, his knit hat plastered white.

"I asked my dad what we had for dinner that night," Abby said. "He couldn't remember."

"I remember."

"Wait, you had dinner with us?" Abby pivoted so that she was facing Brew.

"Yeah. We'd come in from playing in the snow. Your mom was in the kitchen. She had a box of macaroni by the stove and was slicing sausage. She asked if I wanted to stay for dinner."

"Why didn't we talk about this before? Seriously, Brew. We never talked about this."

Brew was uneasy. Abby knew it.

"It was when we were at the cave," he told her. "You said four matches were missing. I remember showing you that trick."

"At Uncle Dennis's birthday."

"Yeah."

"Brew, I know you. What aren't you telling me?"

With both hands he pushed his hair back from his face. He pivoted away from Abby. He turned and faced her again. "I'm not sure this is a good idea."

"Talk to me, Brew. I have to know."

They'd come in from playing outside, Brew said. Abby's mom was busy in the kitchen. They took off their hats and boots by the door. They brought a puzzle to the front room of the house—a living room the family never used, with a brick fireplace that ran up the side of the house to the second floor and along the wall of her parents' bedroom. They laid the puzzle pieces on the floor. Abby was cold and still wearing her coat. Her hands were still red.

"We should build a fire," Brew had said.

There wasn't any wood in the fireplace, or a log holder, or a screen. They rolled up school paper from Abby's bookbag, twisted the paper and set it in the fireplace. There was kindling in a brass holder on the hearth, for decoration. They laid kindling over the paper. Abby brought out the matches from her coat pocket.

At this mention, emotion lunged in Abby. "You said I didn't start the fire. You lied to me!" Brew held on to Abby's shoulders, his face like Abby had never seen it. A pressure was building in his voice—"You didn't start the fire, Abby. I did. I took the matchbook from you. I struck the matches. I lit the paper in the fireplace."

The color went out of his face. He dropped his hands from Abby's shoulders.

She stared back at him, all her emotion escaping her.

"No, Brew. We both did."

41

IT WAS THE MIDDLE OF Abby's last week. She'd just finished another day of work and was on her way back to the camp. She was feeling many things—agitated and sad and overwhelmed, and maybe just tired out from everything, from the guilt she and Brew carried—two children, seven years old—that was all they'd been—two little kids, and all these years later, trying to get on with their lives, trying to make decisions—and now this decision—whom should they tell? This was the question that followed them after their conversation that night on the boat at the graveyard.

The day was unusually warm for this time in August, and perhaps that contributed to Abby's mood—everything feeling like a pressure oven. The pavement was broken and potholed, and soon the blacktop ended and Abby was driving along the gravel-and-dirt road. She'd passed this way more times than she could remember—fields and woods, tractor trails and barbed-wire fences with rustic cedar posts at precarious angles, farms set back from the road, a few poplar trees here and there as if their sole purpose was to offer shade to the grazing cattle.

And there was this—a memory Abby had of her mom sitting in a lawn chair next to a campfire. Abby was standing between her mom's knees, both of them facing the fire. Aunt Jo-Jo was playing the guitar and singing. Abby's mom held up Abby's hands with hers as the two of them clapped in time with the music.

Abby slowed the truck and turned onto the tractor trail on her right. She drove until the trail gullied out, then parked and walked the rest of the way. The trail, which used to be a driveway, was uneven and rocky, and all around were weeds. Abby wondered when the last time was that the field had been mowed and the grass cured and baled into hay, or when the clover and alfalfa had stopped growing.

Off to Abby's right was a gray-weathered barn, the roof collapsing in on itself. Beyond the barn was the hill where she and Brew used to bring their saucers. When they were tired out, they'd bring the saucers into the barn and lean them in a stall. Sometimes they climbed on top of the hay bales, stacked three and four bundles high, and tried to stand, balancing themselves, their weight rocking back and forth.

Abby turned from the barn and looked past an old metal swing set, mostly the color of rust now, to where the house had once stood—the two-story farmhouse, painted white. Some of the paint on the siding had been peeling. Abby would stand outside the house and slide her fingernails beneath the paint edges. She'd see how long of a strip she could peel away.

Abby walked across the driveway. The foundation of the house was still there. Broken glass and beer bottles lay inside what used to be the cellar, and between the crevices grew thistles and dandelions. She continued around the perimeter to the far side, where the front room had been, with the fireplace the family never used, and its brick chimney that ran up the exterior wall and alongside her parents' bedroom.

Abby picked up a brick, soot-stained and charred—hot from the sun. She felt the heat against her palm. She brought the brick to her face, laid her cheek against it. The brick hearth, the brass container filled with kindling—small pieces of blond, splintered wood. A bookbag filled with old papers. The bookbag was green and made of vinyl.

Abby looked around her. There were other bricks strewn about. She gathered them and built a cairn. She pulled up weeds around the cairn, her back bent over, her fingers digging into the dirt. She tossed the weeds aside.

She and Brew had twisted paper—old math quizzes, a spelling test marked with red ink. They set the paper in the fireplace. They laid kindling over the paper. Then Abby brought out the matchbook from her coat pocket.

"Here, let me do it," Brew said.

He flipped over the matchbook cover. He struck the match, just like he'd shown Abby on Uncle Dennis's birthday. He lit the paper. He struck another match. Abby held her hands over the flame. They heard her mother calling for them. "Quick," Brew said. He scrambled to his feet. They left the room. Her mom wanted them to help with supper.

There was a paper bag of groceries on the counter in the kitchen. Abby took the groceries out of the bag—a can of coffee, a box of cereal, a box of saltines. Abby opened the saltines and set them on the table next to the butter dish. She and her mom liked to spread butter on the crackers and eat them one after another.

Her mom had left her purse on the table, along with her keys. Abby picked up the keys and dropped them into the leather purse with the wide opening, where there were other things—a wallet, a paperback book, a package of gum, some coupons from a magazine, a purple lighter. Abby set the purse on the stairs while Brew laid napkins and silverware on the table, and Rudy ate kibble from a bowl on the floor, and her mom stood at the stove dishing macaroni made with sausage and tomato sauce and cheese onto a plate.

And just this—this moment, barely a few seconds, when Abby paused and reached into the purse and picked up the book to see what it was. On the cover was a picture of a woman walking through a field and a title in blue, cursive letters—words Abby could no longer recall. Then there were the seconds that followed, when Abby returned the book, and at the bottom of the purse, next to ballpoint pens and a piece of mail, she saw an open pack of cigarettes.

"Abby, come bring the plates to the table," her mom said.

Abby walked over to the counter, and one by one, carried the plates to the table, while her mom took down glasses from a cabinet and Brew ran the faucet and filled Rudy's water bowl.

Her mom didn't smoke—not since she'd met Jack, when Abby was two years old, and her mom and Jack decided to get married. The cigarettes might not have been hers, except there was something else—a few days before, when her mom picked Abby up at the bus drop-off, and the ashtray in the truck was open. Inside were ashes and a white cigarette butt, and though the day was cold, the truck windows were cracked open. Her mom saw Abby looking at the ashtray and pushed it shut, then glanced at Abby—a quick glance, before staring at the road. "Don't tell your dad."

• • • • • • • • •

Abby wrapped her arms across herself. Sweat trickled down her neckline. She stared at the cairn of bricks.

She remembered Uncle Ronnie coming by to pick up Brew. "Don't finish the puzzle," Brew said. "Wait for me."

Abby had a bath that night. She remembered the smell of the bubbles, something sweet. Her mom came in to check on her. She drained the water from the tub and dried Abby off with a blue-striped towel.

They were watching TV, the two of them propped up with pillows on her mom's bed, Rudy lying next to them. He started scratching his collar, making a lot of noise, and Abby and her mom told him to be quiet. Abby was wearing her red pajamas. Her mom wrapped her arm around Abby and ran her fingers through Abby's hair. She was drinking a glass of ice water with her other hand. The dish Abby made her mom out of clay and painted yellow with pink flowers was sitting on the nightstand. Next to the dish was the purple lighter.

A movie was playing, or a television show. A girl was sitting on a wall over a body of water. She was sitting too close to the edge. But then a man appeared, wearing some type of flying device, and swept the girl up in his arms.

Abby was getting tired. Her mom said it was time for Abby to turn in. Rudy followed Abby to her room and jumped onto the foot of the bed. Her mom pulled the covers up to Abby's chin and handed her the purple hippopotamus. Then she bent over and kissed Abby on the forehead. Her brown hair swept across Abby's cheek.

Abby awoke, smelling smoke—from the house, from her own hair and the fabric of her clothes. At the end of the hall, she saw her mother's bed covered in flames. She heard cello music playing from the TV, and then a loud bursting sound as the TV screen shattered.

Standing in front of the cairn of bricks now, arms still wrapped around herself, Abby remembered the woods and the cold night, and that horrible, grating noise as Rudy struggled to breathe. Long pauses followed—another gasp for air—another pause until everything was quiet. "No!" she'd cried, and clutched Rudy tighter, buried her face into his fur—his sweet musk mixed with the smell of smoke and the taste of damp snow, his body still warm. She continued to hold him. She continued to cry, till her bare feet felt numb in her boots, and her hands were stiff with cold. She kissed Rudy's head. She reached for the buckle of his collar, the clasp painful against her fingers as she unfastened it, the matchbook still in her left hand. She slipped the collar in her right pocket. She promised Rudy she'd be back. She promised she'd come for him.

She made it through the woods and onto a road, banks of snow piled high on the shoulders. A car approached. A woman in the passenger seat got out. She knew who Abby was. She helped Abby into the backseat and handed her a handkerchief. A man was driving. He said they were the Pelletiers. They knew Abby's grandparents. A hockey game was playing over the radio. The man looked over the backrest of his seat. His eyes were blue. "We'll take you to their house," he said.

• • • • • • • • • •

Abby sank to the ground. She crossed her ankles and pulled her knees up to her chest. She rocked in this position, back and forth, back and forth. The sun was hot. The breeze didn't stir. The tears ran down her face. She remembered everything.

42

ABBY DROVE TO BREW'S HOUSE—STILL in her work clothes, grass-stained and dirt-stained and bog-stained from the summer. She knocked a couple of times on the door and let herself in. Aunt Reese was in the kitchen preparing dinner. A pot roast was in the oven. "He's in his room packing," she said.

Abby walked down the carpeted hallway. Brew's door was open. His back was to Abby. He was standing next to his bed, going through a stack of CDs. Abby slipped into the room quietly and slid her arms around his waist. He started to turn around.

"Abby—"

She held him tighter and pressed her face against the back of his green T-shirt.

"We didn't start the fire," she said.

Again, he tried to turn around. Again, she held on to him.

"Shh. Brew, listen to me. We didn't start it."

He let out his breath—heavy and deep. What had she found out? he asked.

"It's what I remember," she told him.

She couldn't hold him any closer than she was. His body relaxed.

He crossed his arms and laid his hands over hers, his chest rising and falling in even breaths.

"I remember we had homework that night. Your dad had already come to pick you up. I went into the front room to get my book bag. The fire was out. I got down on my hands and knees to look at the puzzle pieces. The box was on the floor next to me, with a picture of a red barn and horses. I looked at the picture, then fit two pieces together. There weren't any crackling sounds coming from the chimney. The room didn't smell of smoke. If anything, the room smelled of the pasta and sausage we had for dinner."

Abby went on to tell Brew about the cigarettes, the lighter, the window her mom kept cracked open by the bed. "I don't know why she started smoking again. I don't know how she thought my dad wouldn't know. But I know she was tired. She was always tired, between work and school and taking care of me. Each night there would be books on her bed and the TV would be on. There was a textbook on her bed the night of the fire. I'm sure she was smoking that night. She must have fallen asleep while she was studying."

Brew brought Abby's arms down from around his waist. He turned to look at her, cupped her face in his hands, fingers reaching into her hair. At some point, Abby had started crying, tears down her face, down her throat. All this time—all the guilt they'd both carried. Brew kissed Abby deeply. She knotted her fists in his shirt, pulled him closer against her still, this love that they had, always there, so true, so real, so certain, ever stronger.

They stayed together a long time that night, even after supper—sitting on the floor in Brew's room, going over everything—Abby chasing Rudy through the woods, her dad burying him at the burn site.

"How do you know all of this?" Brew asked.

"I had some help," Abby said.

But when he tried to press her further, she deflected to things

Nonna had told her, and Uncle Dennis, and even Brew. Maybe they'd talked enough, she said. It was late.

• • • • • • • • •

The next morning Uncle Dennis left to have breakfast with Gale. It was just Abby at the camp. She set her duffel bag on the bottom bunk and began packing her clothes. She then began gathering some of her other belongings from around the camp and setting them on the mattress.

When Abby picked up the anthology of poems that her father had given her for her birthday, she found a note tucked two-thirds of the way into the book, at a poem about chrysalises and butterflies and metamorphoses. Abby recognized Seda's handwriting from when she'd copied the cicada haiku into Abby's field journal.

CARIBOU GIRL, IT WAS YOU. IT'S ALWAYS BEEN YOU.

Abby sank onto the bed—the caribou bone, the sacrum houses. "They draw energy from the earth," Uncle Dennis said. The caribou had come to teach Abby and to give its energy back to her. More than ever, Abby felt Seda's presence as part of herself—stronger, braver than Abby had ever been before. She felt bigger. She felt *more*.

Abby would need to turn the sacrum over to a museum, Uncle Dennis said. And she would, she told him, but she wanted to hold on to it a little longer, and he was all right with that.

Abby finished packing. The cap Brew had given her hung on one of the posts of the bed. She reached up to the top bunk to grab it, but then it was as if she were seeing the hat for the first time.

Whenever Brew and Uncle Ronnie made a delivery to Chicago, they'd stay over and catch a game if the Cubs were playing at home. The cap Brew gave Abby was a Cubs hat—royal blue, with a bright-red letter *C*, trimmed with reflective silver thread. Just the letter *C*, catching the evening light with its silver thread—a flash of red, no bigger than the head of a pileated woodpecker or the body of a male cardinal or a tanager.

Abby knew then that Brew had been to the cabin the night she and Seda went swimming. He no doubt heard her voice coming from the cove and followed the trail down to the water.

Brew, who when they were young, protected Abby from the remains of a dog that had washed up onto the beach, because she'd recently lost Rudy. Who'd carried his own memories and guilt from the night of the fire because he wanted to protect Abby from blaming herself. Brew, who knew Abby better than anyone, had known Seda too. Abby thought of all the times he wanted Abby to talk to him—all the opportunities he gave her.

What Abby understood was just how much Brew cared for her unconditionally. To be known, truly known, and to be loved, that was the greatest gift of all.

43

ABBY WRAPPED UP HER WORK early on Friday, turning in the rest of her notes. Brew would be leaving the next day to move into the dorms. Abby would be leaving to drive back to Eagle River. They'd only be a two-hour drive apart from one another, and yet Abby knew things wouldn't be the same—they wouldn't always have a summer like this one—Brew's words to her at The Bluff when he gave her the pendant.

Abby invited Brew to attend the book event with her—the one about the loons.

They dressed up for the evening, Abby in the one dress she'd brought with her, and Brew wearing a blue, button-down shirt with his jeans. Before the event, they shared a pizza at a restaurant that served dinner on the sidewalk.

With plates now cleared away, Abby gave Brew the book she bought him for his graduation—at last, she thought. And on the inside cover she'd written: *For Brew, Don't forget the loons. Congratulations! Love, Abby*—words inscribed almost three months earlier.

"I'll never forget the loons," Brew said. "I'll never forget you. I love you, Abby. My love's not going anywhere."

Everything Abby ever felt for Brew was there—yearning, understanding, resonance, empathy, and compassion—and this—a mutuality—each wanting to make his and her own life exemplary in a world so full of paradox. Didn't Uncle Dennis have that same dream? And her mom—studying to become a nurse, taking care of Abby, helping to run the farm.

"Brew, there's something I need to tell you," Abby said.

Brew continued to look at her.

"It has to do with the girl I met the night of the party. I met someone that night, remember?"

"I remember you telling me that," he said. "The friend in Fairport. The one Uncle Dennis said you were staying with."

"This is going to be hard for me to talk about."

"Abby, you can tell me anything."

Her head dipped in a nod, "Yeah, I know I can."

She took a deep breath.

"Her name was Seda."

44

ABBY TOLD BREW ABOUT THIS other part of herself—this very real persona, with whom Abby co-existed over the summer, and who had taken the lead at different times throughout Abby's life, who had gotten Abby out of the house the night of the fire. She told him the things Seda shared with her—the memories she held—the tragedy she witnessed. Seda—beautiful and brave—daring the world—daring Abby.

"You're all of those things," Brew said.

"You don't think I'm crazy?"

"What you told me doesn't make you crazy. You're crazy in other ways—you're crazy in all the ways I love about you."

And then he was quiet, and Abby said, "I know you went to the cabin before you left to see your mom. I know it was you when Seda and I were swimming. And yet you didn't tell anyone. You kept it to yourself. You've known all along," Abby said.

"I knew something. I didn't know all of it."

For a little while it was Brew and Abby at this table, at this restaurant. He put his hand over hers and clasped it. His head was down. Then he looked up, tears along the edges of his lashes. What could be said when there were no words—a touch, a glance. The power of all that had happened, and the greater power still of Abby having lived with what happened. Pain couldn't be explained. It could only be carried. Pain too deep to bear, but she'd kept on bearing it. She was the strongest person he would ever know, he told her. He loved the very miracle of her.

Their fingers tightened. They were committing to something—Abby knew it then—a life they couldn't fully imagine, the enormous, absurd, magnificent open space of it.

• • • • • • • • •

The two authors of the book, a husband and wife, covered many topics at the library that night—the different loon species, how loons communicate with one another, how they breed and raise their young, the independence of their loonlets. They told the audience that loon-like birds dated as far back as seventy million years. Upon this last comment Brew raised his eyebrows and looked at Abby. For a fleeting moment she saw him as the archaeologist he might one day become—or a paleontology scholar.

One of the authors then said the loons were poor colonizers. "They don't move far from where they've hatched or from their breeding territories." What he expressed was the relationship the loons had to their territorial region, that it remained a part of them. Abby thought of the connection she and Brew had to one another through their relationship with the bay and the graveyard and the *Little Daline*—The Bluff and Spiderman Cave—the birch trees and cedar and jack pine, the sandpipers and seagulls and loons—to the way the sun slanted over the water, and the way the wind blew from the north and the west in the winter, and the south and the west in the summer—to the farmhouse where they played in the barn and rode down the bank on saucers, where they worked puzzles and math problems and wrestled on the floor with Rudy, and drove snowmobiles across the winter fields. And not just the connection she had with Brew, but with everything and everyone she loved, including the Falcon's Nest and her mom and Uncle Dennis and all her family.

She remembered the sensation she'd had in the bog upon seeing her mother's and J.P.'s names carved into the bench, as if the trees and ferns, the mosses and lichens held everything Abby could never know. They'd been witness to Abby's mom in those woods. They connected Abby to her, as did the cobblestone shore in front of Nonna's house and the waves of Lake Michigan and the great blue heron and the dog-day cicadas that came and went at the end of every July.

Abby's thoughts flashed to J.P.'s death, and to her mom standing on the Abbaye Peninsula only two weeks after. She saw her mom in such awesome light—strong, and brave, and daring, carrying her grief into a future she made beautiful. Images came to mind, photos of her mom in album sleeves and in frames. There was one picture in particular, of her mom and her aunts standing together. Her mom was wearing some ridiculous sweater and was bent over laughing. She was older in this picture. J.P. would have already been gone. Another photo came to mind—her mom holding a chicken in her arms, and her eyes looking at the chicken as a mother might look upon a child. There was that smile, sweet and gentle and kind, never knowing her own life would be cut short.

Her parents' deaths were horrible and random and preventable, and the depth of that knowledge was scary. Yet, more than fear, Abby felt compassion—an acute love magnified in everything. She had rediscovered her own biology, and family, and community, and place, a sharpness of the senses. How wonderfully it all fit together.

She thought of her afternoon on Big Summer Island. There was a moment when Seda had knelt and made a handprint in the sand beside one of Thunder's footprints. This is what happened to Abby over the summer. This is what changed—sister to the birds and other animals, daughter and cousin and niece and friend. She found strength, she found hope.

Abby remained transfixed. Brew leaned toward her ear. "Are you okay?"

She smiled and met his eyes and nodded, then took his hand—really held it, wanting him to know everything she was feeling, wanting him to understand.

45

THE PLAN WAS THAT ABBY would meet Uncle Dennis and Gale at Peterson's for Thunder's release, before making the drive back to Eagle River. Abby stopped by Geri's one last time. She picked up sweet corn and squash to bring back to her dad, and a couple pints of blueberries.

When she pulled up to the jetty, Uncle Dennis and Gale were already there. Tanner and Ellis were there as well.

"So this is the big day," Tanner said.

"This is it," Gale said. "Time to get Thunder back where she belongs."

"I feel like there should be a drumroll," Uncle Dennis said.

Abby felt the same thing.

Gale opened the back window of her camper shell and then lowered the tailgate. She brought the crate out of her truck, with Thunder inside, making a racket.

They walked as a group down the jetty and to the end of the wooden dock, the sun at their backs, a slight breeze eddying around them.

"Shall we do this?" Gale said.

"We're ready," Ellis said.

Gale set the crate down and unfastened the door. Thunder emerged, her plumage looking shiny and full with a striking blue cast in the light. She took a couple of steps forward and then lifted off the dock, flapping her wings in magnificent, sweeping motions.

"And she's off," Uncle Dennis said. And there was Abby's own, quick drawn breath.

"You know, they really are beautiful creatures," Ellis said.

Abby felt the surge of life all around them. There was no greater peace.

Acknowledgments

"If I could have, to hold forever, one brief place and time of beauty, I think I might choose . . . ," wrote Marjorie Kinnan Rawlings in *Cross Creek*. For me, I would choose my grandmother's home on the Garden Peninsula of Michigan, set on a hill, overlooking Garden Bay. This place, this time, the beautiful, ordinary life of it, and my deep desire to experience it all again, inspired me to write this novel, to give honor to my family and to offer my enormous love and gratitude for a little peninsula on the southern shores of the Upper Peninsula of Michigan.

The undertaking of writing a novel is never a straight line, and always there are challenges. In the middle of writing Abby's story, I underwent brain surgery to repair five brain aneurysms. Without the brilliant mind and skill and compassionate care of my surgeon, Dr. Rafael Tamargo, this book and my life would not be possible. I will forever be indebted to him and his team at Johns Hopkins Medical Center, including Stephanie Garfinkle, Tracey Strzegowski, Dr. Fernando Gonzales, Dr. Risheng Xu, and all the caring nurses, physicians, and staff.

I am also indebted to my church family at St. Andrew's Episcopal Church, for meals and prayer and love and friendship. You have walked closely beside me over these four years, and I love you.

I am grateful to my father, who said to me during one of our afternoon phone conversations, "I think you should write a book that takes place on the UP." And in another conversation, "Maybe your next book could take place on the UP." Anyone who knows my dad knows how persistent he can be. Throughout the writing of this book, his encouragement and support never faltered.

About eight months after those conversations, the beginnings of the story took hold. I called my friend and author John Philpin to see what he thought. For the next couple of years, he was the only one who knew what the novel was about, reading and rereading page after page and deliberating with me for hours on the phone, with keen insight and discernment. I am just so grateful for John's friendship and all the support he has given me.

My love and gratitude are so immense for my mom, Sandra Kyne, and friend and writer Alison Taylor-Brown. They became almost daily contacts and readers, and when I was running low on confidence and steam, they kept me inspired, including a stretch of time when I texted Alison my word count at the end of each day. In fact, it was Alison who agreed to finish the novel for me should my surgery prevent me from doing so, and my mom who continued to line edit and initiate grammar discussions.

I am grateful for my stepbrother Jamie Kyne, who put me in contact with his colleague Christina Oliver, and for her time and expertise and the resources she provided.

Thank you to my cousins Jim "Moe" Hermes and Mike Hermes, who own and operate Big Bay de Noc Fisheries, and my cousin Kitty Lovell, and to my uncle Dale VanRemortel and my late uncle Bill Hermes for their time and patience answering my questions about commercial fishing and boats and lake conditions, and for their fish house banter and all things Yooper related.

Others who contributed to my research and to whom I extend thanks include Bob Burnham, unit manager for the Michigan Department of Natural Resources' Shingleton office; the Friends of Portage Bay and Fayette State Park; the Village Artisans of Garden; the Garden Peninsula Historical Society; the rangers at Fayette Historic State Park; former fire chief Dan Andrus; Trevor Harvey for taking me out on his boat; Paul at Portage Bay—I would not have made it to Point Detour without your encouragement; Amy at Michigan's Department of Natural Resources customer service center in Baraga; my sister-in-law Melissa Boesch; my daughter-in-law Julia Boesch; my daughter-in-law Marianne Boesch; my son Jake Boesch; my cousin Susie VanRemortel; my aunt, Barb VanRemortel; my web designer and friend, Nikki Terry; Grandpa's Barn, a seasonal book store in Copper Harbor, referred to fictiously in the novel; Peterson Brothers Fairport Fishery; the Dock restaurant, which I have referred to fictitiously, as it did not open until 2015; and the Ninga Aki Pathway, which I have also used fictitiously, as it did not yet exist when the novel takes place.

I am grateful for the following published resources: *The Loon Feather*, by Iola Fuller; *Northern Flights: Tracking the Birds and Birders of Michigan's Upper Peninsula*, by Sheryl De Vore; *Michigan Wildflowers in Color*, by Harry C. Lund; Barry Lopez's entire body of published works; and *The Prehistory of the Burnt Bluff Area*, edited by James E. Fitting. (I was unable to visit the caves while working on the novel and was only able to view them from the water. Though the caves are on parkland, they are landlocked and closed to the public, and trespassing is not permitted.)

Other works that are referenced in the novel include *Call of the Loon*, by David C. Evers and Kate M. Taylor; *The Red Book: Wildlife in Danger*, by James Fisher; the movie *A Simple Twist of Fate*, directed by Gillies MacKinnon; Johann Sebastian Bach's Cello Suite No. 1 in G Major, the Prelude; "God's World," by Edna St. Vincent Millay; "Sic

Transit Gloria Mundi," by Emily Dickinson; "The Cry of the Cicada," by Matsuo Bashō; and *Animal Dreams*, by Barbara Kingsolver. The epigraph is from "Within Birds' Hearing," the introductory essay in Barry Lopez's 1994 collection of essays, *Field Notes*.

Thank you, Ed Fairfield, who advised me on how to turn my writing shed into a tiny cabin, for letting me borrow tools, for shop talk, and Intervale breakfasts, and friendship.

Dave Eilenberger, I will never be able to keep up with your intelligent mind and energy. Thank you for thawing pipes and plowing snow, for all the music and book talks and inspiration, and for fixing so many things that needed fixing.

To Glade Hadden and Susan Jeansonne-Hadden for letting me camp on your land, for porch talks and wolf talk—you guys are just so generous and kind and good. And thank you for extending your kindness to my son Seth. Never before had we seen a petroglyph of a crane in the desert!

For your guidance and wisdom and walking this journey with me, thank you, Reed Loy, Anne and John McCausland, Cate Regan and Jim Garrett, Polly and Byron Burrus, Polly Ingraham and Rob Hirschfield, Karen Butt, Judy Eskelson, Chris Gately, Mike Costello, Michael Herrmann and Gibson's Bookstore, Joe Figureo, Lisa Allen, my Al-Anon group, Vicki and Rick Kardos, and each of my women friends in S.T.O.R.M. There are so many people who have contributed to both author and story that I could never name you all without leaving someone out. You are loved, and I am grateful.

Thank you to the book's early readers and for their feedback: my dad, Jack Jacques; my brother Rick Jacques, who came up with the title; my stepdad, Pete Kyne; my sons Seth Boesch and Nate Boesch; my husband, Gregg Mazzola; friend and mentor Bob Begiebing; gifted author and wise teacher Ann Hood; and my fearless agent Michelle Brower, who brought me back to my center.

I owe so much to my editor and champion, Olivia Taylor Smith, who never forgot this story. Her sure insight and gentle touch enriched both writer and novel. She is a dream to work with, as is assistant editor Brittany Adames. Many thanks to my entire team at Simon & Schuster: publisher Sean Manning, who made all of this possible, and associate publisher Irene Kheradi; my marketing manager, Emily Farebrother; publicist Hannah Bishop; Math Monahan for the gorgeous cover design; artist Jim Musil, for his beautiful painting on the cover; production editor Michael Trudeau; interior designer Milly McKinnish; and copyeditor Patty Romanowski. And to every single person at Simon & Schuster who has worked and is working so tirelessly for this book—thank you!

My family is a blessing every single day—always. My deepest appreciation for each of you—especially my husband, my parents, my brothers, my children and grandchildren—I love you. And I would be remiss not to mention this woman's best friend, Izzy, my faithful canine companion through it all.

Thank you, God, thank you, Jesus, for the extraordinary natural wonders you have given us, for your love. May we be kinder to your creation. May we be kinder to each other.

About the Author

Diane Les Becquets is the author of *Breaking Wild* and *The Last Woman in the Forest*. *Breaking Wild*, an Indie Next Pick and a national bestseller, received starred reviews from *Publishers Weekly*, *Kirkus Reviews*, and *Booklist* and was featured on NPR's *Morning Edition*. It was the recipient of the Colorado Book Award in Fiction and the New Hampshire Outstanding Work of Fiction and was shortlisted for the Reading the West Book Award in Fiction.